MAC'S LAW

REG QUIST

Mac's Law
by Reg Quist

Paperback Edition

CKN Christian Publishing
An Imprint of Wolfpack Publishing

6032 Wheat Penny Avenue
Las Vegas, NV 89122

Paperback ISBN: 978-1-64119-640-6
Ebook ISBN: 978-1-64119-639-0

MAC'S LAW

1

Fremont County

IT WASN'T THE RIFLE SHOTS THAT WOKE Casey Bechtel and drove him from his bed. The first shot didn't come till a bit later. What woke him was the flickering light on the bedroom window. At two AM on a cloud-dark windy night, there was no natural or good explanation for such as that.

Throwing back the covers, and waking his wife in the process, he leaped from the bed and took the two steps to the window. Startled, and still half-asleep, it took him a moment or two to accept the truth of what he saw. The haystacks. The haystacks, and the barn close by. Both were on fire. The yard was not large, so the building was not far from the house. The smaller buildings—chicken coop, tool shed, and smokehouse—were weird, shimmering outlines as the flames danced in the breeze.

Now he could hear the squealing and screaming of the terrified animals trapped inside the burning structure: three saddle horses, the work team, the milk cow and her calf, a sow and her litter. The tinder-dry board-and-batten barn was going up in an unstoppable fury of flames.

Casey's wife Florence jumped from the bed and scrambled across the dark room to pick up two-year-old Albert. Holding him tight, she turned to look out the window. Neither she nor Casey considered that their images would be lighted by the flames. Stunned into immobility, the young couple stood just long enough for the first rifle shot to shatter the window, blasting bits of sharp glass onto both of their faces. The bullet passed between them and slammed harmlessly into the back wall of the bedroom, embedding itself in a pine log.

Florence screamed and fell backward, striking her head on the wooden frame of the home-built bed. She wrapped the baby more securely in her arms and huddled on the floor.

Casey took a moment to pull on the pants and shirt that were hanging on the chair beside the bed, then bent to see that Florence was not badly hurt before he rushed into the other room. If they were burning the barn, they wouldn't stop there. The house would be next. He had to get his family out. The house and all their meager possessions were going to be lost. He had no doubt about that.

Safety. Safety was the only thing that mattered now. Perhaps they could hide in the dark of the bush surrounding the house. But could they somehow get there?

The combination kitchen and sitting room offered the only door in the small structure. Plucking his carbine off the pegs above the door, he squatted behind the log wall. He knew they had to get out of the house, and having no other escape path, he reached out with one hand and lifted the bar from the closed door. If they could scramble for the cover of the bush, it might be possible to escape.

He didn't know who was attacking his little ranch, but he knew who was behind the ugly deed. He'd often wondered what lengths his adversary would go to, but he'd never once suspected burning and murder.

He pulled the door inward just a crack. Easing his head around the doorpost, he squinted one-eyed at the yard and the surrounding wooded hillsides. Despite the light from the burning of his winter's supply of hay, and the barn his uncle had built with his own hands, he saw nothing. He pushed the door farther open, hoping for an escape path, or at least a good shooting position. He got neither. A flurry of shots hammered through the newly opened door, pinning him in position. The shots struck the stove, the back wall, and the cupboard holding Florence's carefully stacked dishes, and ricocheted off the wooden table.

Quickly pulling his head back, he was unable to shoot at, or even see his attackers.

The volley of shots and the thudding of many hoofs told Casey there was more than just the one shooter. The hoofbeats came closer, rattling out the rhythm of at least three galloping horses. He couldn't make sense of the running horses until, with Rebel yells and the sounds of breaking glass, flaring torches were flung through the windows, and one through the door. There were probably torches on the roof, too. He couldn't see, and it didn't really matter. The others would complete their destructive work. The cabin was doomed, so the roof no longer mattered.

One torch landed on the bed, igniting the bedding and terrifying Florence anew. She crawled toward the bedroom door, screaming and clutching the baby. There she rose to her feet, and in an unreasoning, mind-numbing panic, charged into the little kitchen.

Casey, intent on the activity in the yard, didn't hear her bare feet approaching.

She might have been trying to escape through the door, or she might have meant to hunker down beside her husband behind the safety of the thick log walls. Casey would never know.

In her mad rush, she unseeingly crashed into the table. Her progress toward whatever destination she had in mind was stopped long enough for two rifle slugs to find her. The first shot struck her chest, and the second passed through the baby before continuing on to complete whatever damage the first shot had inflicted in Florence. Dead on her feet, she was battered backward by a third slug. She flopped onto the big cast iron stove and rolled sideways. From there, she glanced off the wood box and settled onto the floor. Her dead baby fell from her arms onto the plank floor, beside his dead mother. Casey hollered a pain-wracked *"Nooooo!"*

Whether he lived another minute or a hundred years, Casey would never forget the dreadful sounds of lead slugs smashing into his beautiful Florence and their baby. Three shots, thuds something like rocks thrown forcefully into deep mud, only with more violence and infinitely greater consequences. The continuing rifle shots were drowned out by those horrifying sounds.

With anger and despair such as he had never experienced in his twenty-five years, he leaned into the open doorway, pumping off shot after shot at the circling figures in the flame-lit ranch yard. Two horses plunged to the ground, throwing their riders aside. Another rider fell to Casey's carbine, lifted right out of the saddle to flop off the horse's rump. He hit the ground and didn't move. The two downed riders sought cover behind their dead animals.

In the momentary pause, Casey got a clear look at the leader of the attack. Sitting his horse at the edge of the yard, partially protected by the big corral posts and guarding his own skin, was his close neighbor Herb Clover.

The Clover spread was one of the larger ranches in this mountainous district, although none of the ranches would be considered big by open-range standards. The mountains and the forests pushed the ranchers into a series of mountain valleys strung together into a single spread.

Clover was known as a man full of self-centered ambition and conceit, and his greed for land knew no bounds. He ignored the fact that he was a decade or more too late for the might-makes-right days. Days when the big ranchers ruled and gunslingers were in ready supply, many of them footloose and desperate following their time in the big war.

Most of the gunmen didn't live long enough to

get old, but there were still some around. Clearly, Clover had found a few, and now he was going forward with his murderous intent.

Casey doubted the attackers would be regular Clover cowhands. Clover kept a small crew. In this mountain-and-forest country, the terrain acted as fences. There was no need for the big crews of the open range country. Clover had only four riders, as far as Casey knew, and he believed those men would tie their bedrolls behind their saddles and ride out before they had anything to do with murder and burning. They might run off a head or two for beer money if opportunity provided, but it took a special breed of hardened men to take on a task like this night's dreadful business.

Clover had been pushing Casey to sell ever since he rode into the territory with the deed to the B-Bar in his pocket, barely three months ago. Casey's uncle, Randolph Bechtel, had died childless, leaving all his worldly possessions, including the B-Bar and its cattle, to his only nephew.

Casey's single debt was a verbal guarantee to his uncle that he would keep the B-Bar going, and care for the land and cattle.

Over the past few years, the senior Bechtel had refused multiple offers from Herb Clover. Even when those offers came thinly veiled with threats, he'd held fast.

Herb Clover was not a man to accept defeat gracefully. There were cut fences, a burned hay field, rustled cattle that were driven out of the county before they were missed, and several shot-out windows in the dark of night. That was all followed by more verbal threats.

Herb Clover saw himself as one of the big men in the territory. He was big in size all right, tall and thick in the shoulders and chest. His broad face was set off by a solid jaw, constantly blackened by heavy whisker growth that he had to shave daily.

A married man with three growing kids, two sons and a daughter, it appeared that he carefully sheltered his family from the aggressively violent side of his ranch management.

There wasn't much room to grow in this mountainous territory, where the ranches were made up of irregularly shaped patches of grass wrapped around the hills and forests that dotted the countryside. Clover wanted the B-Bar land and its abundant water, ignoring the fact that the water had come only after Randolph Bechtel had spent money, sweat, and effort drilling wells and digging storage tanks on the little streams that flowed from the snowmelt in the upper levels of the surrounding hills.

Several of the other ranchers knew Clover for

what he was, but none felt it was their responsibility to call him on his actions or rein in the terror he was forcing on the B-Bar. The belief of the time was that a man hunted his own wolves and stood up to his own challenges. It was doubtful any of those good men believed Clover's actions would come to outright murder and burning out the young family.

After the initial few moments of angry despair at the shooting of his little family, Casey thought about his own survival. He had to live. Live, not to fulfill his promise to keep the B-Bar operating—that time had passed, shot to ribbons by the raiders—but to take revenge on Clover. Live to put a stop to him and those who were supporting him.

Could a man even continue calling himself a man if he allowed the murderers of his wife and child to go free? Would hunting Clover down be revenge, or would it be justice? There were few laws in these new territories. Men were expected to take care of themselves.

Although he didn't think about it until later, he was sure there were a lot of safe city dwellers who wouldn't understand. He might be open to criticism, but he would brush it off.

Even a man of faith had the right to protect himself. Didn't the people of Israel rebuild the wall with swords in their hands? Or was he trying to justify actions he had already decided to take?

His first move was to hunker down beside the thick log walls again, but first, he reached up to the shelf above the door and pulled down a box of 44-40 cal. shells for his carbine. Squatting safely behind the wall, he reloaded, then pushed the remaining shells into his pockets.

His safety would hold for no more than a few minutes. The roaring flames in the bedroom, fed by the blankets and the clothing hanging from pegs inserted into the wall, were now finding their way into the kitchen. The second bedroom, a lean-to attached to the back of the kitchen, was now aflame. The torch that had been flung through the open door had landed near the wood box, and Florence lay in the center of that spreading fire.

He would be trapped between the murderous raiders and the killing flames in no time at all.

Still squatting, Casey leaned into the door opening to find his target. There had been no shots from the yard for the better part of a minute. With his left elbow planted on the top of his bent knee and his hand firmly gripping the carbine, he sent a shot toward Clover. He saw the man jerk and drop his weapon. Clutching his arm, he kneed his horse into the darkness of the outer yard as a second shot from Casey hurried him along.

Casey's shots seemed to awaken the two riders who had taken refuge behind their horses. Foolishly, one rider rose, lifting his carbine toward the doorway. Casey's weapon was already pointed in the right direction after shooting Clover. He had only to lower the barrel to sight on the attacker. His shot glanced off the ribcage of the horse before crookedly slamming into the rider's face. The man's head literally blew apart. His gun slid down the horse's side as he sank from sight.

Another gun spoke from beside the garden fence, off to Casey's right. The shot was low, sparing Casey's life, but it took him in his left thigh. Entering behind the inside of his knee, the shot traveled slant-wise toward the thickness of his thigh, coming close to but missing the big bone on the way through. It exited near the hip on the outside edge of the thigh.

Before Casey had a chance to react to the first shot, another found its way to the fold of his right arm, which held the carbine. The slug grazed the skin on his arm, then tore a strip of skin and muscle from his ribcage.

The pain and the fear of death hit him at about the same time. But he couldn't die. He had a man to hunt down and this matter to set to rights. Yes, that was revenge. An ugly word, and an ugly concept—one that, as often as not, turns against the hunter.

Never in his peaceful life had Casey ever dreamed of hunting a man down, but now it was all he had left to live for. His wife and child were dead, gone forever. The flames were already licking at their flimsy nightclothes. He could do nothing for them, not even drag them out of the fire. His only wish now was to exact revenge, and to do that, he had to live.

He staggered to his feet behind the shelter of the logs and turned to seek an escape, but there would be none through the door. The men behind the rifles made that impossible. The bedroom was in flames so he couldn't get out through there either. The back bedroom held little promise, but it was all he had. The bedroom doorway and the back window, now holding with jagged remnants of glass, were well lined up to allow a straight run from one to the other.

Perhaps there was a small chance. The wall of flames was terrifying, but if he ran and covered his face... Run? He could barely stand, but he had it to do. Run or die; those were his choices. He might die anyway, but he wasn't ready to die. He would have to run, as small as that chance was.

If a rider had been stationed at the back of the house, he was as good as dead already. But he pushed one bare foot forward, ready to make his move.

After a quick glance out the door, Casey breathed a short prayer, took a firm grip on the carbine and considered those six or so steps to the back window. He had to move right now. He couldn't avoid the flames, and delaying would only make it worse. He had already swallowed more smoke than was good for the human body.

Gritting his teeth at the pain, he ran, or rather, hobbled and hopped would be more accurate. His bleeding leg threatened to collapse under him, but he steeled himself. Within the first two staggering steps, his hair was singed and his shirt was afire, but he couldn't stop.

With fierce determination he took the next few steps, his feet landing on shards of broken glass, adding pain to pain. Without stopping, he bent from the knees and launched himself through the window.

His head-on leap would put him in the questionable safety of the backyard. From there, a fifty-foot scramble would see him into the woods Uncle Randolph carefully preserved, just because he liked the trees and the shelter they provided. The woods backed onto a rocky outcropping that signaled the entrance to the higher hills beyond.

2

Fremont County

LANDING AND TUMBLING ON THE SHORT grass of the yard hurt more than anything Casey could have imagined. The pain spiked in his head, and for a moment, he was disoriented. With panic pushing him, he forced himself forward. Rolling over twice reduced his flaming shirt to a smoldering ruin, and somewhere he had lost the carbine. Momentarily, he fought for consciousness. Crawling rather than trying to walk or hobble, expecting a bullet every second, he pulled himself forward with his elbows and his good leg. The other had become a dead weight. Miraculously, he made it to the fringe of the forest without being challenged.

Through bleary, smoke-reddened eyes, he spotted the butt of the carbine lying under a small bush and grabbed it, then pushed forward. Although tempted to stop and give it all up, he fought back, finding determination. Continuing his wiggle-scramble, he went farther into the bush. He knew the spot he was longing to reach.

In the pitch-dark of the cloudy night, he might never have found the one large tree that towered over the landscape, except for the reflected light of the fire that was destroying all he ever loved or cared for. At the foot of the big tree was a large log; a tree that had died and fallen years before. He had noted it on one of his exploring walks. Spotting the outline of the large spruce, shadowed against the cloudy sky, he adjusted the direction of his crawl and was soon able to roll over the log.

He pulled off the remnants of his mostly-burned shirt and tied it as tightly as he could over the exit wound on his leg. He could do no more. He hoped that if he laid still, the bleeding and the pain might both settle down. The wound under his arm and along his rib cage was sore and stinging with sweat, but it wasn't serious. Not deadly serious, anyway.

He wiggled into the long grass and undergrowth, pulling as much debris as he could reach over his legs and body. He knew the shelter wouldn't hide him in the light of morning, but he hoped the raiders would be long gone by then. Now as concealed as the situation allowed, he just let go. "That's all I can do, Lord." Whether he spoke out loud or just in his head, he couldn't be sure. Whispering the names of his wife and son, he tried to let the tension drain out of him. Within moments, he was mercifully unconscious.

3

Fremont County

CASEY WOKE TO DRIZZLING RAIN. HE
had no idea what the time was, nor did it matter.
Under the shelter of the big spruce, he remained
relatively dry. He was cold and desperate for water, but he was more desperate to remain alive.
Without moving more than one arm, he pulled a
handful of grass. Licking the collected moisture
felt good, but it did little more than wet his lips.
He repeated the action several times, which finally gave the inside of his mouth and throat some
relief, although it left a lot to be desired.

He coughed up smoke, each heave of his chest
reminding him of the bullet wound across his rib
cage.

Casey asked himself what Clover might be
doing. A rational man would have paid off his

warriors and sent them on their way. A rational man would have breakfasted with his wife and gone about his daily tasks as if nothing at all had happened, but Clover wasn't a rational man. A rational man would not have mounted a murderous attack on a neighbor in the first place. Also, Casey didn't know how serious the wound he had inflicted on Clover was. Perhaps he lay abed with his wife nursing him, spinning some nonsense story to explain the damage.

Perhaps the rancher had posted a guard, or maybe he was acting as his own guard. But then, why would he? The fire had surely done its deadly job. Not totally convinced, Casey lay still. He was as comfortable as the situation allowed, and he had nothing else to do, so he would wait. He would watch. He kept the carbine close to hand, the hammer pulled back and ready, as he dozed and watched and then dozed again. At one point in his delirium, he thought he heard hoofbeats, or perhaps he just imagined them. So went the morning.

Only a slight brightening of the cloud-covered sky barely visible through the branches above him suggested it might be nearing noon. There had been no sounds during the long, slow morning hours except the hoofbeats, which he wasn't sure he had really heard. Still exercising caution,

Casey spent another hour alternating between dozing and making plans. Thoughts of his little family were never far from his mind.

He hurt, and every move he made caused more pain. His anger was near the breaking point, but that would have to wait. At all costs, he must remain alive.

Finally, carefully and as quietly as he could, Casey pushed back the grass and debris he had buried himself in. By wiggling, and lifting with his arms, he managed to sit on the downed log, stretching out the injured leg. The blood clot seemed to be holding. He didn't dare remove the bandage for fear of starting the bleeding again.

As slowly as he had ever done anything in his life, he stood and started making his way from tree to tree. Pausing often to watch and listen, it took him nearly a half hour to make his way to the edge of the forest. By this time his leg was throbbing with pain, and a trickle of blood was showing.

He got his first clear look at the ranch house. Most of the logs were still standing, but the roof was gone. Through the back window, he could see a jumble of half-burned timbers. The stove lay on its side; the floor must have burned away under it. The small collection of hand-built furniture was gone. Mercifully, he could see nothing of his wife or child.

Smoke rose from several spots under the debris. He suspected the overnight drizzle had cut the fire short, leaving the remainder of the roof and interior as charred remnants.

He still heard nothing.

A clear look at the dreary day without the overhanging branches told him the morning was not as far advanced as he had thought.

Slowly making his way to the log wall, he cautiously stuck his head around the corner, far enough to get a look at the yard. The barn was a pile of smoking char. He hoped the attackers had taken pity on the stalled animals and turned them out. Much of the split-rail corral was burned or lying on the ground. Still, he saw no one and heard nothing.

He eased his way along the side wall and looked around the ranch yard. He was alone unless someone was squatting back in the trees, past the barn.

The wellhead hadn't burned, and the pully and rope were still intact, so he slowly made his way to it. Resting his good hip on the rim of the well, he lifted the lid and slid the bucket off the peg it hung from, then slowly let the coiled rope slide through his fingers almost soundlessly. He soon had a half-bucket of well water in his hands and he took a sip, rinsed out his mouth, spat out the accumulated smoke and char, and then drank.

He dumped the remainder of the water over his head. Not knowing how badly his head had been scorched, he came near to screaming in pain when the cold water hit the raw, open wounds, but he steeled himself and gritted his teeth.

Gripping the edge of the well, he rested while the pain subsided. After pulling himself together again, he drew more water and drank his fill.

The chicken house hadn't burned. The chickens were all clustered around the gate, waiting to be released. He poured another bucket of water into the trough beside the well where the chickens regularly came for water.

Casey needed food. He had heard about people eating raw eggs, but his stomach roiled at the thought. Still, if others could do it… He hobbled to the chicken yard and opened the gate. The chickens scrambled and fluttered over each other getting out. Placing his carbine against the fence and taking up a shovel leaning there to use as a crutch, he hobbled across the pen to the coop door.

Leaning in far enough to access the nests, he reached under a hen and pulled out an egg. With serious doubts but fierce determination, he cracked the shell on the shovel handle. Holding the egg over his tipped back mouth, he pulled the shell apart. The yellow slime ran over his lips and into his mouth, and some dribbled down his chin onto his bare chest. He gagged and spewed the mess out, but then, feeling foolish, he reached for another egg and repeated the process. This time he swallowed. He held onto the door frame and shuddered in revulsion before reaching for another egg.

After swallowing four eggs, he shuffled back to the well for more water. He needed a drink.

4

Fremont County

CASEY FOUGHT DOWN THE TEMPTATION to scramble through the darkened pile of debris inside the charred log walls to search for Florence and the baby. Instead, he looked longingly at the door to the kitchen and then the bedroom window, remembering their brief but happy time on the ranch.

Finally clearing his head, he turned away from the burned-out house and wondered how he would put the morning's plan into place. Lying under the big spruce tree all those hours had given him time to think and plan.

He had to find a way to get to town. He couldn't crawl or hobble the eight miles using the shovel as a crutch. His feet were in dreadful condition, with glass cuts that had scabbed over during the night but were now bleeding again. If he could make it to the road, eventually someone would come along with a wagon.

The problem with going to town was that the sheriff and Clover were the best of friends. Casey had no proof of his claim that Clover had been involved in the murders and burning. Clearly, something had happened, but laying it at the feet of Herb Clover was accusation only. Without evidence, the sheriff would do nothing.

Then there was the issue of revenge. Having serious doubts about justice ever being done, Casey was determined to see to it himself. That was a totally new thought. Never, until those flames had torn up his future, could he have imagined something like that, but now he felt the want. No, it was more than a want—it was a need, a demand, a scream from his very soul for justice. Justice for Florence, for the baby, and for himself. And for Uncle Randolph, whose years of hard work lay in blackened ruin.

Letting everyone believe he had died in the fire would simplify his actions and his future.

Zeb Stringfellow. That was who he needed to see. Zeb Stringfellow had proven himself to be a good neighbor and a willing helper in times of need. The Stringfellows' K-K ranch was in a series of small high-country valleys above and behind the ridges forming the western boundary of the B-Bar. Although the K-K had wagon-trail access to the town road, there were also several other horse trails through the high country adjacent to the holdings.

One of those steep, crooked trails wound its way from the B-Bar to the K-K, looping its way through a series of hills and ridges for three miles before finally leveling out at the entrance to the K-K Ranch headquarters.

Stringfellow wasn't a loner or a recluse. He and his family simply valued their privacy. Being mostly self-sufficient, they seldom went to town. They showed up at church perhaps once a month, which was where Casey and Florence had become acquainted with them.

The Stringfellow family included three nearly-grown sons and two daughters spaced between the boys. Raised to be expert hunters and serious cattlemen, the boys were capable of either running the K-K or of pulling out and starting their own brands.

No matter where the two girls settled, they would be considered the most attractive young ladies in any company. Looking at the mother and mentally subtracting twenty-five years would demonstrate to anyone that the family line ran true.

Zeb Stringfellow was a tall, slim man, all lanky muscle and smiles. An easy-moving man, as at home in the bush as he was on horseback, and seldom seen without his Henry rifle, he welcomed visitors right up until there was a sign of trouble. At that point, the inner nature of the old man fought its way forward. No one was about to burn the Stringfellow Ranch to the ground.

Casey was sure that if he could just make it to the K-K, one of the Stringfellows would patch him up, and perhaps allow him to lie low there while he healed up a bit. He was sure Stringfellow would hold his secret as if it were his own.

The only way to get that crooked trail behind him was to put one foot in front of the other and keep going. In Casey's circumstance, it was one foot in front of the shovel and hop. It was slow going.

At the back of the burned-out house, Casey heard something rustling in the forest. He stopped and raised the carbine in one hand, holding to the shovel for balance. At first, he saw nothing, but the rustling continued. He almost laughed out loud when the month-old calf stepped into view, followed quickly by the milk cow.

The gentle old cow was as glad to see Casey as he was to see her. He took her by one short, crooked horn after scratching her forehead and between her ears to comfort her and gently led her back to the well, where he filled the bucket with water. He held the bucket while the cow drank and then did it again. The calf was more interested in milk than water.

Casey drew fresh water and rinsed out the bucket. Easing the old cow against the wellhead to keep her from sidestepping, he managed to draw a quart of milk. He almost screamed when he bent his knee to reach the cow's udder, but he finally got it done, then tipped the bucket up and slowly drank the milk. Again, he rinsed the bucket before hanging it back on its wooden peg and closing the well's lid.

While he was caring for the cow, he started wondering—would that gentle old animal tolerate his weight on her back?

There was only one way to find out. Gradually, so as not to startle her, Casey leaned far over the cow's back, slowly lifting his feet from the ground. The cow turned her head to see what this strange activity was and spread her front legs to take the weight. Since she gave him no real problem, Casey eased back to the ground and took a better grip on the animal's neck. Pushing with his one good leg and pulling with his arms, all the time conscious of his damaged ribcage, he hoisted himself far over the cow's back. Keeping his balance as best he could while protecting his injuries, he swung his good leg over. A push on the cow's shoulders and a couple of wiggles along her spine, and he was sitting upright, ready to ride.

Neither cow nor rider moved for a moment as they both tried to figure this out. Finally, taking a firmer grip on the short horns, Casey gently kicked the cow into movement. Expecting disaster from this experimental situation, the rider kept a firm grip on the horns as the cow took a few hesitant steps. It took perhaps fifteen minutes and several frustrating side trips to ease the cow to the back of the property and onto the trail to the K-K.

Three hours later, after Casey had slid off twice to allow the animal some rest, the weary cow and its hurting passenger pulled up before the barn on the K-K. Casey was lying almost prone on the animal's back. Suffering from loss of blood, his strength was completely depleted. The cow had covered the last mile with no directions from Casey.

Julia, the eldest Stringfellow daughter, came running but stopped a few steps away, holding her hand to her mouth.

Casey raised his head. Most of his hair had burned off, leaving just a small tuft above each ear. His eyebrows were gone, and all his exposed skin was scorched, some spots worse than others. His face, over the scorch marks, was blackened with soot. His bare back and chest were equally black, as well as scratched from struggling through the forest. His pants were torn and charred, and his bare feet were damaged almost beyond repair, starting with the shards of broken glass embedded in them and followed by the variety of thorns and twigs picked up in his hobbling around. There was no need to wonder why the young lady was staring in horror.

"Mr. Bechtel, is that really you? Oh, my. We thought y'all were dead and burned up. It looks like...well, it looks like you came close."

The young lady clearly didn't know what to do next, and she hesitated for the best part of a minute. Casey slumped back down on the cow's back. Finally, Julia made a decision. She stepped forward and gave a little tug on the cow's horn and started to lead it to the house, hollering, "Ma. Ma. Come. It's Mr. Bechtel, and he's hurt bad."

Mrs. Stringfellow and Daisy, the younger daughter, stepped onto the porch, stared across the ranch yard, and then came running. Mrs. Stringfellow placed her hand on Casey's back to hold him steady.

"Lead the cow up to the steps and we'll get Mr.

Bechtel inside. My, oh my. He does look like he's been through it. I don't know what all we can do, but let's at least get him off this cow and lying down."

After a few more slow steps from the weary animal, Mrs. Stringfellow said, "Daisy, you run ahead and clear off that couch in the back room. Put a clean sheet on it, and a pillow."

As Daisy started to run, her mother hollered, "And put on a couple of pots of water to heat."

With considerable difficulty, the three women got their injured neighbor off the steady old cow and into the house. When he was lying on the couch, Mrs. Stringfellow said, "Daisy, you take that poor cow and put her in a stall with her calf. Take her to water first, then give her a good load of hay and some of that ground grain your father feeds our milk cows. Check her over for injuries. The calf, too."

Daisy was reluctant to leave, but a no-nonsense look from her mother had her seeing to the cow. She moved as fast as the weary animal would let her and was soon back in the house, staring at Casey as her mother and Julia attempted to wash off the blood and soot and grit and grime. Her mother said, "Daisy, get the washbowl off the back porch and fill it with warm water, then take one of those rags and see what you can do with his feet."

Daisy was delighted to be included in the nursing duties.

Julia helped Casey lift his head enough to take a few sips of water, then laid his head back down and, as gently as she could, started soaking the soot and dirt off his face and head. The scorching made the area tender to even the lightest touch, but the women had made the decision that the young man had to be cleaned up to prevent infection if nothing else.

Casey was somewhere between conscious and unconscious. He cried out a few times when someone touched a particularly tender spot.

When Julia had his head cleaned as well as she could, she said, "There's no injury here, just the scorching from the fire. My, I can't imagine how that all hurts. It's a mercy he's asleep."

The mother said, "Well, the same can't be said for his chest or this arm. These are bullet wounds, or I miss my guess. And they bled on that ride up the hill. I've got them clean now. You get that salve from the kitchen shelf, and we'll plaster some on here. And bring those clean cloths piled up over there. A tight bandage might hold back the bleeding."

With Casey's feet and chest cleaned, the women rolled him over and began again, cleaning his back. Daisy had managed to get his feet in reasonable condition, then did the lower half of his legs.

Mrs. Stringfellow looked at Casey's feet. "Good job, Daisy. There's a lot of healing needed, but you've done what can be done."

"Not totally, Mother. I can see bits of broken glass in some of those cuts. We'll have to get those out somehow."

Mrs. Stringfellow bent and looked at the cuts. "You're right, Daisy, but we'll do that later. I think Mr. Bechtel needs to rest before we do any more digging around."

There was now nothing left to do but attend to the wounded leg, and there was only one way to do that.

With Casey again lying on his back, Mrs. Stringfellow said, "Girls, you're done here. You did good, but I'll take it from here. You go clean yourselves up and see to dinner. The men will be hungry when they return."

With a good deal of trepidation, Mrs. Stringfellow cut off the only garment Casey was wearing and proceeded to deal with the filth and the blood and the bullet wound. It bled some more as she worked, but a double layer of clean cloth seemed to put an end to that. A further half-hour of washing and bandaging completed the task the ladies had undertaken.

Mrs. Stringfellow wrapped Casey in a clean sheet, covered him with a blanket and went to have a wash herself, and put on clean clothes.

5

Fremont County

ZEB STRINGFELLOW AND THE BOYS RODE into the yard at sundown, dealing with their riding animals before making their way to the house. Zeb was within fifty feet of the house when he saw Casey sitting on one of the porch rockers. He was dressed in a clean pair of Zeb's pants and a shirt of his eldest son Noah's. Both pants and shirt were big and loose on the injured man. He wanted nothing tight around his burns or injuries. His feet were bandaged but bare.

Zeb smiled and stepped onto the porch. "We'd given you up, and here you sit. While that's good news, I'm guessing the news ain't so good for Florence and the baby, else they'd be here with you."

"Not good at all," was all Casey could say.

"I'm sorrier than I can say about the family, but it's good to see you alive and sittin' here. Looks as if you had a close brush with that fire, what with your hair mostly gone and the burnt skin. I'll want to hear all about it, but Maudie will be settin' table about now. We'd best not keep her waitin'.'"

After washing up, the men took their places around the table. Casey joined them, although he had taken on a feeding soon after awakening. There was a pause while Zeb offered thanks for the meal.

As was typical of ranching families, they ate in silence.

The dinner completed, and the dishes cleared, Zeb got up and brought the coffee pot to the table. He refilled their cups and sat back down. "Now, Casey, I know there's little but hurt in the telling, but we'd best hear it."

Casey hesitated and stumbled here and there, nearly coming to tears before the telling was completed, but he finally got it out.

The family sat in stunned silence. Every eye was on their neighbor, and each mind was struggling with the story they had just heard. No one knew what to say next.

Zeb finally put his coffee mug on the table and leaned his chair back on two legs. Idly, Casey wondered how he managed that without falling over backward.

"Casey, there's something you need to know. It wasn't the time before, but now it is. You already know we were gone for the day. We was rounding up your animals, and we brought them up to the ranch yard. We're going back tomorrow to make a final sweep; find those we might have missed."

Every eye was on Zeb as he paused, collecting his thoughts and choosing his words.

"What you don't know is that your uncle Randolph feared something like this. He came close to changing his will, fearing for your life if you were to follow in his footsteps. He finally decided that you were a pretty handy guy, able to take care of yourself and your family. What he didn't figure on was out-and-out murder."

Zeb dropped his chair back to the floor, placed his elbows on the table, and leaned forward, indicating that what he had to say needed to be heard.

"Randolph wrote up a document that he left with me, all signed and witnessed. Legal. He made it out, fearing for his own death. He wasn't thinking of murder at the time. He was more afraid of an accident. Ranching in these high mountain valleys offers a lot of ways for a man to come to the end of his days.

"He changed his will to include you after he

did up that document. Maybe he forgot about it, or maybe he decided to just let 'er ride. In any case, I kept the document, and it's still legal."

Casey asked, "What is it?"

"It asks me to do certain things should Randolph die or be killed. That's what the boys and I were working on today. We seen the flames reflected over the treetops and rode down in a hurry last night, or as much of a hurry as that pitch-dark trail allowed. It was pretty much all over, time we got there. The flames were dying down, and there was no sign of life anywhere. Course, it was dark. Couldn't see anything on the ground to tell us what happened. Saw more this morning. Lots of blood on the dirt. Saw drag marks where horses were pulled from the yard. Expect we could follow and find the carcasses but couldn't see the point.

"This is the hard part, Casey. The stench of burned flesh hung over barn and cabin both. Left no doubt in our minds. What we didn't know was that you weren't under the rubble too."

Casey lifted his eyes from the table. "I know. I nearly gagged on the smell this morning, knowing the cause."

He studied Zeb for a moment and then looked around the table, taking in the hard-working sons and the women who had helped him that day. "It's hard to believe I slept that soundly lying in the forest. I didn't hear you last night or this morning, either one. Not clearly, I didn't. Once, when I woke up, I thought I'd heard hoofbeats earlier on. Made up my mind it was just a dream. Maybe it was, and maybe it wasn't. In any case, I went back to sleep and didn't do anything about it.

"But I need to thank you for your work and your caring. I'm glad you didn't find that milk cow. I don't think I could have ever made it up here without I had her to sit on."

Everyone was silent. The Stringfellows weren't a talking bunch anyway, but he knew their silence was an invitation for him to say more. All he said was, "So tell me about this document."

Zeb sat up straight and spoke directly to Casey. "Randolph left instructions, along with his will, with his lawyer in Santa Fe on his last trip down that way. He said he had a visit with you on that trip but chose to not tell you about the will or the document. The document instructs me to gather up his cattle as soon as his death was known for sure. He feared Clover would grab them, and he was right.

"This morning, as soon as we'd made up our minds you were gone, we figured it was the same as if Randolph had been struck down. We started right in gathering the cattle. Randolph put up a bit of fencing between him and Clover, but it was cut in several places. We were pretty sure to find some B-Bar stuff on Clover, so we rode on through and ran into some Clover riders almost first thing. They were pushing maybe fifty head of your stock. Not sure where they had in mind to take them to. They said they were bringing them back to your grass, just getting them off the Clover. Following orders. They didn't look like they really expected us to believe their story. We explained how uncomfortable life could become if they didn't ride for home, leaving the animals behind.

"We were on Clover land, but they seemed to feel it might be better to let us get on with our task. It might not have worked out that easily if Clover had been among them. You say you hit him with one shot? I'd sure like to know if he's hurt or dying, or maybe up to some other scheme. Not like him to not be with his men.

"According to your uncle, we were to gather the animals and find a buyer for them, taking them down to the flat land if necessary. He left instructions on payment of wages for the work. He also left instructions on the sale of the land. All the money was to be sent to that lawyer. He holds instructions on where the money is to go from there.

"Most of your B-Bar stock was together, and we gathered them without too much trouble after we cleared out the Clover graze. We have nearly five hundred head in your upper pasture, and ten horses. We'll finish up come first light."

Casey lifted his eyes and looked around the table again. "I can't thank you enough for all you've done. You and the ladies, too. If you'll let me rest the night here, I'll try to figure out my next move. Perhaps we could discuss it in the morning."

6

The K-K Ranch

CASEY WAS STILL HURTING IN THE morning, but after a good night's sleep, he felt ready to move. The Stringfellow women were not so sure, but he insisted.

"If you'll let me have the loan of these clothes and give me something to ride so's I can get down the hill with you, I'll take one of my own horses from your gather and move along out of here.

"I've thought it over from every angle I can figure. Although I made a promise to Uncle Randolph to keep the B-Bar going, neither of us foresaw anything like this. I'll not be ranching here again.

"If you'd find a market for the cattle and horses and let it be known that the land can be bought, and follow through on that written agreement,

I'd be forever grateful. I'll want you to cover your wages from the sale of the animals, and top that up a good bit for your neighborliness and concern. And see that Clover don't get his grubby, murdering hands on the land or cattle.

"I'll visit the lawyer in Santa Fe and square things with him. I'm convinced it would be best if everyone thought I died in the fire with Florence and the baby."

Casey could see that Zeb had something to say, so he waited.

Finally, the father and head of the clan cleared his throat. "Casey, we've sat up a good part of the night discussing what to do. You can easily see that our family is about growed. Noah there, he's the oldest, and he's been courting a young lady from up north a ways. Wants to have his own place and make his own way in the world. Start a family too, if'n I don't miss my guess. That's all well and good. It's the natural order of things. He was thinking to have to go farther afield to find available land, but if it suited your needs, he could make you a deal on the B-Bar. Land and cattle both."

It was the first time Casey had smiled since the fire. "Why, I can't think of anything better, except to wish that none of this had ever happened. If you can come up with somewhere around market value, I'd be delighted. I think to make it all legal you'd have to take a ride down to Santa Fe. See that lawyer whose name I gave you. He has all the papers, title and such, and a power of attorney, given to him in the will Uncle Randolph insisted I have written. Take you a couple of weeks to make the ride, but I don't see any way to do it without making the effort. I'll make a slow ride south. Give you time to get there and back, then go see the lawyer myself."

After a bit more discussion Casey said, "I wish you the best of success on the ranch, Noah. I'm hoping that with you being in possession, Clover will back off—for a while, at least. Could be that something will happen to eliminate his threat."

The Stringfellow family looked at each other at that statement, wondering what Casey had in mind.

"When things settle down, maybe I'll ride back up this way to thank you proper for all you've done."

Mrs. Stringfellow said, "You getting well is all the thanks any of us needs, Casey. And to set your mind at ease on another thing, lay your concerns to rest. We'll care for Florence and the baby. Do right by them, for our part, anyway."

Having said that, Zeb shook hands with Casey and went to ready the horses.

Mrs. Stringfellow pushed aside all objections and laid out a good set of clothing for Casey to ride away in. She didn't have boots to spare, but the winter moccasins she offered were better for his damaged feet anyway. Casey waited while she cut out a pattern of lamb's wool and pushed one into each moccasin. The soft padding would provide his badly injured feet some comfort.

As Casey slipped the moccasins on, Julia asked, "Are you sure you're up to this? Wouldn't it be better if you rested up a while?"

Casey looked at the beautiful young lady who had cleaned and bandaged his head so tenderly. "I appreciate everyone's concerns, but I have miles to make. I'm figuring I can heal up sitting on the back of a slow-walking horse as well as I can sitting in a chair on your veranda, as much as I enjoyed that last evening."

Zeb saddled an animal for Casey to ride down the hill on. "You switch that saddle over to your own horse and keep it as long as needful. You're not going to get far riding bareback. I put a few dollars in the saddlebag, along with a few trail fixings. Not much, but it'll buy you a few meals along the way."

"That's thoughtful of you, but I may not need it. I hid a little extra at the ranch. If no one's found it, I'll be all right."

Before they rode out of the yard, the sun barely showing itself over the hilltops, Casey turned to the ladies again. "I don't hardly know how to show my thanks for all you've done. I'll be praying for God's blessings on y'all."

He let the horse take a few steps, then turned in the saddle. "Keep the milk cow. She's a good old girl." After a couple more steps, he stopped again. "And go gather up those chickens." He tried to join in when the ladies laughed, but somehow, he couldn't get it out.

The three-mile ride to the B-Bar hurt Casey more than he was willing to admit. His leg started bleeding again, and the sweat was stinging his arm and rib cage. He kept his mouth shut and concentrated on riding.

At the ranch, he stepped down and walked to the root cellar. The soft, padded moccasins cushioned his feet to where he was able to walk more or less normally, although the bullet hole in his thigh caused a bit of a limp. After a quick glance at the burned-out cabin where his wife and child lay, he lifted the root cellar door and let it flop open. Cautiously stepping down the four wobbly stairs, he knelt in front of a set of shelves, pulled the bottom one out, and dug into the soft dirt beneath it. Within a couple of minutes, he had a sealed coffee can in his hands, and he pried off the lid. His stash of emergency money was still there. He retrieved the money and carefully pushed it into his pockets, bills in one, coins in another.

By the time sunset was upon the land, Casey was twenty miles down the valley, sleeping in a loft. The rancher's wife had fed him, and with the promise that he wasn't a smoker and wouldn't light the hay on fire, the rancher showed him to the loft ladder.

Two days later he swung east and crossed a high, rock-strewn north-south ridge, before swinging back south. That evening, after a longer day than he had planned on, he rode into a Mexican sheep camp. The Bar-M brand on the vaquero's horses meant nothing to him. A tough looking rider came forward and asked his business.

"A meal and a corner to sleep in, my friend. And perhaps some feed for the horse, if it pleases you." He spoke in fluent Spanish.

"You speak the language well, *mi amigo*. Put the horse up." He pointed at the corral. "We will have food soon. For now, coffee. I am Manuel."

Casey offered his hand, and Manuel responded with a firm grip. "And I am called Casey. Thank you for your kind offer. It would be better for me if you could forget my name or that I was here."

Manuel nodded knowingly. "I too have wished

the same in past times. Now we live here in peace, but sometimes…" Manuel looked off into the distance with a wistful expression on his face.

With a bit of warm water and a clean cloth supplied by Manuel's wife Imelda, Casey cleaned and rebandaged his wounds. Imelda said nothing as she helped him tie the split ends of the cloth. She had seen many bullet wounds before this time, and she was content to leave this stranger to his own path and his own secrets.

Before the sun was fully up the next morning, Casey was saddling his horse. Imelda called softly from the kitchen tent, "Come, food and coffee are ready."

After a good breakfast of tortillas and goat cheese washed down with strong black coffee, Casey said his goodbyes to Manuel and Imelda.

"You are very kind to a traveling stranger. Thank you. *Vaya Con Dios.* God bless you."

With a crooked grin, Manuel responded, "I don't know what you talk about. There has been no stranger here for many weeks."

Casey returned the grin, waved his thanks again, and rode south, heading for Santa Fe.

7

Bar-M Ranch

WHEN THE THREE RIDERS ESCORTED the top buggy into the yard of the Bar-M, the first to notice it were Adam and Jerry, the ten-year-old twins. They rode over and escorted the wagon the last hundred yards, leading them to the tie rack in front of the cookhouse.

Adam spoke right up, looking at the distinguished looking man in the buggy and ignoring the three riders. "You're on the Bar-M, mister. Who've you come to see?"

One of the riders said, "Keep a civil tongue in your mouth, kid, else I'll be teaching you a lesson in manners."

Adam sat back down in his saddle with a startled look on his face.

A man just stepping out of the cookhouse

said, "This young man belongs here. You don't. If there's any lessons to be learnt, I guess no one on the Bar-M will need any help from the likes of you. Now, the lad asked you a fair question, and he asked it politely. If any of you can keep a civil tongue, now would be a good time to answer the question."

The tension in the air lasted only a brief moment before the duded-up man in the buggy gave a brief hand signal to the outspoken rider. He then turned to the cowboy on the cookhouse porch. "I'm Federal Deputy Marshal Mordecai Granger, and these are my district deputies. Galen Pickard, Blaze Randolph, and Buzz Dover. Who might I be speaking to, please?"

The cowboy smiled a bit at the attempt at formality, seeing the fancy talk more like what a strutting rooster might say if it was given the gift of speech.

"I'm Taz Johansen, the Bar-M foreman."

He let that information settle for a moment, then said, "Now, back to the lad's question. Who do you wish to see?"

"I've come to see Mr. Walker Samuel McTavish. I believe he is commonly known as Mac. Would he be available?"

Taz was impressed by few things in this world, and the deputy marshal and his three tag-a-long riders weren't about to be added to that short list.

"Lawman, is it? Could've used the likes of you fellas some time back. As to Mac, whether he wants to see you or not is up to him. Right now, he's down at the feed yard. Kinda busy sorting out a situation. I expect he'll be back here by 'n by when his work is done. Could be a while."

The belligerent deputy, who turned out to be Galen Pickard, said, "Mayhap you could ride down and get him. Tell him he's needed now. We didn't ride all this way to waste time."

Taz smiled openly this time. "No, I don't believe I *could* do that. I have never once seen Mac turn from an unfinished task. I believe the governor hisself could be sittin' here, and Mac would tell him to wait till the work was done.

"Why don't you fellers take your horses over to the corral and care for them? There's coffee in the cookhouse you can help yourself to. These chairs behind me are about as good as we have to offer, and you're welcome to them. Why don't you just sit here in the shade a while? Mac will turn up presently."

Deputy Pickard looked down at his boss in the buggy. "I believe we should ride on, sir. I don't see these to be the kind of people you're looking for. Probably on the dodge themselves, some of them, anyway. Surely don't seem to be cooperative."

Before the chief deputy could speak, Taz

stepped down from the porch in front of the cookhouse and said, "Mister, you just called me a thief or worse. You take off that pretty badge and step down here, and we'll discuss the matter."

The deputy was just about to swing his leg off the horse when a strident female voice said, "What's going on here?"

Pointing her finger at the deputy, she said, "You get back on that horse until I invite you to dismount. I heard most of what your foul mouth has to offer. You threatened my son, and then our foreman. You should be thankful Mac isn't here. He'd have your hide.

"Now you turn that horse around, and you ride out to the road gate and wait there. If Mac wants to see you, he'll call you in. Take your two partners with you."

Ignoring the riders as they turned around and headed to the gate, Margo spoke to the man in the buggy. "You and your men seem to have gotten off to a hard start on the Bar-M. First, you speak harshly to my son, then our foreman."

Before the deputy could speak, Margo held up her hand to silence him. She spoke to Taz. "Thanks, Taz. I'll handle this. You can go about your work."

Turning back to the buggy, Margo said, "Mister, your man doesn't know it, but I just saved him a whipping. I don't know if there's a man alive who can match Taz in a stand-up confrontation.

"It usually doesn't pay to invite yourself onto another's property and start throwing your weight around. If Mac had been here, you would have already been started back down the town road. Mac will brook no foolishness.

"Now, if you care to tell me, I'll listen to your reason for being here."

Deputy Marshal Granger had already removed his hat and laid it on the buggy seat beside him. "Mrs. McTavish, I sincerely apologize for my men. Deputy Pickard can be a bit abrupt at times, but I've never known him to be belligerent or to speak roughly to a child. I promise I will deal with him privately."

Margo said nothing, but she indicated with her attention that the man should continue.

"My business is with Mac McTavish, but it is neither confidential nor intended to be secret. All the same, I would prefer to speak to you privately. Could the children be excused for a while? What we have to discuss falls better on adult ears."

Margo told the twins, "You two ride out and see how long your father's going to be."

She turned back to the deputy marshal. "Step down. We'll sit here in the shade, and I'll have some coffee brought out for you and your men."

Going into the cookhouse, Margo made the request of the cook and was soon back and seated beside the marshal. Just as that man was about to speak, the cook arrived with four mugs and a steaming pot. He poured a mug for the marshal and walked across the yard to the three men squatting beside the gate. Margo waited while the marshal stirred sugar into his mug.

After a satisfying sip of the sweetened drink, the man cleared his throat. "What I wish to talk about, Mrs. McTavish, is the need for law enforcement across the several counties that make up this portion of southern Colorado."

Margo had somewhat tempered her personality over the years, but there was still a fair bit of fire in her. "You didn't show much concern for law enforcement when the Bar-M was in need a few short months ago. Men were hurt, and others died. I'm sure some deaths could have been prevented if you or a couple of your maverick deputies had been here."

Her words were biting, and the marshal flinched. "I take the blame for that. Colorado is a big state, and I'm afraid it sometimes overwhelms me with the resources allotted. You are right to lay the blame for the recent unfortunate incidents on me and my office. I freely apologize to you, and will do so to Mr. McTavish when we meet. I know that doesn't repair any damage, but I can do no more."

Before the marshal finished his coffee, the twins ran their horses across the yard and pulled them to a dust-raising stop in front of the cookhouse.

The marshal smiled at Margo. "Don't know as I've ever seen better riders for their ages. I suspect they're twins. I'm guessing perhaps twelve years old?"

Margo replied with a single word. "Ten."

With no more than a look, Margo signaled to the kids that they should speak.

"Pa's got that mess about straightened out. He says he'll be here shortly."

Both the marshal and Margo understood that on a ranch of this size, "shortly" could be fifteen minutes or it could be half a day. The situation eased when the cook arrived again with the coffee pot and a pot of tea balanced on a tray. In his other hand, he held a plate of oatmeal cookies, the ranch favorite. He poured a refill for the marshal. No one mentioned the three riders at the gate.

The marshal thanked the cook for the refill before saying to Margo, "I see you're a tea drinker. My wife is, as well. I take a cup now and then just to put on a more genteel image."

"But you'd prefer not to if you're like the men on the Bar-M."

"Truth be told, Mrs. McTavish," he said with a small smile, "I'd rather drink three-day-old coffee warmed up over a cow-patty fire."

"I'll remind the cook to make sure he has coffee on hand, although I don't ever remember a time when it wasn't. We go through a fearful quantity of coffee beans on the Bar-M."

8

Bar-M ranch

MAC RODE INTO THE YARD BESIDE A young cowboy driving a team and wagon. The wagon was clearly a work vehicle, with a few fence posts stacked along one side of the box, held back by a couple rolls of barb wire. The wagon bed was covered with tools of every sort; shovels, a pick, post hole diggers, wire pullers, and several neat coils of rope and chain.

Margo was still sitting with the marshal, and the three deputies were sitting on the grass outside the Bar-M gate. Margo couldn't see clearly, but she suspected there were grim looks on their faces.

"That's Mac and our son Jerrod. They'll be along just as soon as the horses are cared for and the harness cleaned and hung up." She said it as if it should be understood that the care of the animals came first.

The wagon was backed under a shed to ward off any rain that might bless the dry land. Mac stepped down and helped the young man lead the animals to the water trough and then into the barn. It was a while before the men emerged, closing the big door behind them.

Margo could see Mac's weariness in the way he walked.

"Marshal Granger, please remember that Mac has been working since well before daylight."

"I'll be sure to respect that, Mrs. McTavish."

Mac and his son walked slowly toward the cookhouse, the older man limping a bit. Jerrod looked exhausted and Mac looked indomitable, but Margo knew better. Her husband was one of the strongest and most determined men she had ever known, but he had his limits, even if he hid them well.

The marshal stood as Mac approached, but Mac ignored him.

Margo, still sitting, made a slight flip with her hand. "That leg need some attention?"

Mac answered, "Later. It's nothing."

Jerrod, who seldom let his father out of his sight, grinned at his mother. "Mule kicked him. It was a small mule, though, so I expect it can wait."

Mac still ignored the marshal. "Who are those men sitting at the gate?"

Margo started to give a brief explanation.

Before she was finished, Mac said, "Jerrod, whistle up Pepe."

With no more than a curl of his lip, Jerrod responded to the order with a shrill whistle that could be heard all over the ranch yard.

Pepe, the Bar-M wrangler, came on the run.

Mac waited the few seconds it took for Pepe to sprint across the yard. Nodding toward the gate, he said, "Pepe, I'd like it if you would go tell those three men to hang their gun belts on their saddle horns and walk up here. You take their horses and care for them."

Pepe asked no questions, simply turned and trotted to the gate. Margo could see a long discussion taking place between Pepe and the three deputies. They were, no doubt, reluctant to give up their weapons. She also knew that Pepe could not be moved away from one of Mac's orders.

Mac turned his attention to the marshal but said nothing.

The marshal finally held out his hand. "Deputy US Marshal Mordecai Granger, Mr. McTavish. I'm pleased to meet you."

Mac ignored the outstretched hand and asked, "What can I do for you?" There was no warmth in the question.

The marshal pulled his hand back but continued to stand. Mac had his back turned to the gate, but the marshal and Margo could see Pepe leading three horses toward the horse corral with a gun belt draped from each saddle horn. The three district deputies were making their slow way to the cookhouse.

Mac noted Margo's nod as if it were a silent signal. "Marshal, I'll have no man say he was ill-treated on the Bar-M. Tell your men there's coffee in the cookhouse, then they can find some shade to wait in. They're to have no contact with any Bar-M rider or my family."

The Bar-M owner spoke as if he expected no argument.

While the men were walking up from the gate, Mac and Jerrod went to the cookhouse for their own coffees. Even the owner wasn't served on the Bar-M.

The single exception was Margo. There was nothing the cook wouldn't do for the lady of the Bar-M. Margo in turn was careful not to abuse this respect.

In the case of the marshal, he had been served only because he was with Margo. The men at the gate had had coffee taken to them at Margo's request.

The marshal gave the orders to his three deputies. Going for coffee refills, they wisely stood aside, allowing space for Mac and Jerrod to leave the cookhouse.

Mac stepped off the porch to stand beside Jerrod on the dry sand of the ranch yard, and wordlessly confronted the marshal.

Knowing it was now or never, the marshal said, "May we talk for a few minutes, Mr. McTavish? The explanation for my presence here might take a while."

"I have work to do. You have until I finish this cup of coffee."

The startled marshal saw that Mac was not joking, so he started right in.

"Well, the truth of the matter, Mr. McTavish, is that there are more reports of crime in these southern counties than I ever expected. When your father came to see me on your behalf a few months ago, I was busy with a minor crime wave in the north of the state. I should have taken his request more seriously. I have apologized to Mrs. McTavish already, and now I am offering you that same apology. I am truly sorry I didn't take your message much more seriously. Unfortunately, I can't fix that past lapse in judgment.

"But it's the present situation that brings me here. In cattle country, there is always someone trotting off with one or two head for beef, or even a small bunch to sell for drinking money. But now the reports of outright rustling are becoming worrisome. You've probably heard those reports yourself."

The marshal paused to allow Mac to respond, but the rancher remained silent.

"There was a shooting south of here, but no one was killed. By the time I heard about it, both men had left the territory.

"The normal bunkhouse quarrels and fistfights and other minor situations have always been left to the ranchers to handle."

Nervously clearing his throat, the marshal continued, "My deputies will attend to the rustling and perhaps a few other minor matters in the southern counties. They have just been to Denver with a report, and for some downtime. Now they will return south, hoping to put an end to the matter of lost cattle, even if that end is temporary.

"But now we've had a burning and a murder. Multiple murders, actually, not too many miles from the Bar-M. Just west and north a ways. Up in the hills of Fremont County.

"Perhaps that news has reached you already. I'm afraid it took far too long to reach my ears. This is a big place, and news travels slowly.

"The truth of the situation is this, Mr. McTavish. I need a senior deputy down this way. Someone highly respected in the community. A man who has proven his character over time. A man who has shown wisdom in his dealings. A man who has earned the trust of the other ranchers. I need that man to take responsibility for the district deputies and bring some order and fear of the law to the area. And I need that burning and murder solved.

"In short, Mr. McTavish, I, and your country, need you. I've made discrete inquiries among the ranchers, and every finger pointed back at you. I have a deputy badge I'd like to pin on your shirt. Whether for a few weeks while that murder is solved or for a longer period, I don't know. That's a question for the future."

The silence dragged on for an uncomfortable length of time before Mac took a final sip of coffee and flipped the dregs onto the ground. With the mug hanging at his side, he studied first the marshal and then Margo. He turned sideways a bit to study Jerrod, then he looked back at the marshal. That nervous man was shuffling his feet as he stood on the porch. Even though he was two steps above Mac, he felt small in the presence of the McTavish family. The twins had ridden their horses up close again and sat silently watching the interplay before them.

Mac finally spoke. "You can stay here the night if you find the hayloft to your comfort. Eat in the cookhouse. Or you can move on to Pueblo if that suits you better. I'll give you my decision in the morning."

With that, he passed his empty mug to Margo and limped off in the direction of the big corral.

After the evening family meal, Mac and Margo made the slow climb up the small rise behind the house. When the ranch was first established, Mac set this hill aside as a special place. There were to be no horses ridden up here, and no children shouting. There was a small pool of water, and a cluster of willows and small bushes. Mac built a bench beneath the shade of the willows many years before. It was a quiet place. A place to be alone. A place to think. A place to pray.

Mac and Margo often sat there in the evening to discuss family or ranch matters, or just to be quiet as the sun sank behind the Sangre de Christos.

Mac started every day in the darkness of the hilltop. Rain or shine, he trudged alone up the short trail to sit on the bench or stroll around the little pool. In the quiet of the morning, he worshipped and prayed. He brought ranch and family matters before the Lord, and quietly waited for wisdom. Only after that did he go to the cookhouse for his breakfast and start his work day. Even then, he was usually the first one at the breakfast table.

Mac and Margo sat silently for some time. Margo knew he was waiting to hear her thoughts.

She wasn't afraid of guns or what sometimes had to be done. She had lived all her life in a land of self-administered law, but she longed for an end to the violence. She truly wished that the battle over fencing that had taken place so recently would have been the end of hostilities in the territory.

Jerrod, her oldest child, carried a saddle gun but did not belt on a revolver, and she hoped he would never have to. Still, for now, the law was thin on the ground. Someone had to step up to the task, but did it have to be Mac? Mac, nearing the age of forty, was no longer young, yet he waited for her words. What should she advise?

Taking Mac's work-hardened hand in hers, she said, "Mac, there's two things I could wish for. One is that there was no need for anyone to enforce the law on the community because everyone would just naturally do what is right. But since that is not the case and probably never will be, the other thing I would wish for is that there was someone else to take on this trouble. But the marshal is correct. You carry the honor reluctantly, but there is no more respected man in many a mile than my husband. If you agree to take this on, I'm hoping that respect will go a long way toward mellowing any difficult situations you run into."

After a further pause, she continued. "It would be wrong to let a murder and a ranch burning go uninvestigated or unpunished."

She said no more.

Mac got up and paced in front of Margo a couple of times. The darkness had almost swallowed the day.

Without looking at his wife, Mac said, "The boys should be home soon. Their letter said they left Los Angeles three weeks ago, but those brothers of mine have been known to take an interest in a side trip or two on their travels. Bobby has a wife riding along, so that might hold them to the direct trail. They might have boarded a train for part of the way, too.

"Bobby and Jeremiah have carried badges for some years. I think they like the freedom and travel the job offers."

Mac paused for half a minute before he continued, "You're certainly right about one thing. We can't let murder slip past without someone doing something. That's not the question."

He paused long enough for Margo to say, "The question is, does it have to be you?"

Mac found no reason to answer.

When Mac finally spoke again, he said, "There's three things I'd insist on if I take this job. The first is that Jerrod has no part in it. He'll want to ride with me, but I'll not have it. He stays on the ranch. The second is that the boys get home and agree to sign on. The third is that the badge is only mine until the murder and the current rash of rustling are dealt with."

There seemed to be as much silence between the two as there was talking. Finally, Margo said, "I'm all right with that, as long as you agree that I can remind you to be careful every time you saddle up."

Margo couldn't see Mac's grin in the darkness. "I think I could tolerate that."

After thinking it all through again on the hilltop in the darkness of the early morning, Mac talked to the sleepy marshal. The man looked as if he hadn't slept in a loft for many a year, if ever. After laying it all out, Mac said, "Does that get done what you're looking for?"

The marshal grinned and reached in his pocket for a badge, which he passed to Mac. "Thank you, Mr. McTavish. The job is yours as of now, even if I'm a bit surprised you didn't ask about the pay. You pin on the badge when it suits you. And although messages are slow arriving, you send me a note from time to time. Or send me a wire if you find yourself near the rails. And thank you."

Mac turned to the three deputies standing close by. "You three go see if you can catch some thieves. I'll be down that way by and by, me or another deputy. You find anyone stealing cattle, I'd rather *you* arrest them. I prefer that no one gets shot. You shoot anyone, you better have a good story to tell me. You need any trail fixings, you can find them at Adkins just a few miles to the west."

Mac gave the three the look that had stilled more than one angry cowhand over the years. "Understand me clear. Almost everyone in these southern counties is known to me. Some are family, and some are close friends. Ad Adkins in my father-in-law. There's a Mexican sheep camp over west that's part of the Bar-M. Those folks work for me, and they are also my trusted friends. I hope you understand what I'm telling you."

He turned his back on the marshal and walked to the corral to saddle his horse for the morning's work.

The marshal watched as Mac walked away and correctly assumed that the conversation was finished.

9

TWO WEEKS OF CASUAL RIDING PUT Casey in Santa Fe. The short days and slow riding gave his wounds a chance to heal. He traded with Manuel for a large sheepskin that he used as padding between his wounded leg and the saddle skirt, and riding was much easier after that.

He arrived in the city feeling healed and strong—in body, at least, except for his badly torn-up feet. He wasn't sure they would ever heal.

His heart and soul might never be right again. The loss of Florence and his son would forever be an open wound.

That thought drove Casey's need for vengeance, which was growing stronger each day.

He had purchased a piece of lambskin at Rancho Garcia on the way through. The Garcia family watched in fascination as he fashioned new insoles for the moccasins.

The hospitable Garcia family was anxious for news. He exchanged a bit of news for his noon meal and then, aware of the poverty on the small sheep ranch, slipped a coin under the dinner plate.

A few days after leaving the Garcias' small ranch, he arrived in Santa Fe. The purchase of new clothing, two nights in a Santa Fe hotel, a leisurely bath, and several good feedings had Casey ready for the next step in what he believed was a well-thought-out plan.

To confirm that he was healing, Casey visited a doctor. The doctor, familiar with the ways of the frontier, asked no awkward questions. He looked at Casey's badly scarred head and said, "You're going to have to get used to being bald, young fella. Think of all the money you'll save not having to visit the barber shop."

Casey had wrapped a large bandanna around his head and fitted his newly purchased hat over it to hide the scarring. He wanted no questions from anyone, although he couldn't deny the reality that his eyebrows were not growing back in. He had let his beard grow. A careful trim at the barbershop left him with a somewhat distinguished appearance.

During the years he lived in Santa Fe, he'd learned a good bit of the Mexican language, adopted a love of heavily-spiced food, and made friends with a Pueblo Indian from the Santa Clara Reservation.

Pueblo Johnny, as the man called himself, traded crafts and Pueblo-made items for groceries and other things his people didn't have or couldn't produce themselves. He seemed to come and go with the wind, never announcing himself and never saying goodbye. He wasn't there and then he was, silent and cautious.

One day when Pueblo Johnny and Casey found themselves sharing the trail, Casey nudged his horse close and said, "Good day for a ride."

The answer was quietly spoken, "To be alive and riding is always good."

"You speak good English."

"The missionaries. They came, and they taught."

"May I ride with you? I would like to know you."

"The way is open. The trail is wide enough for two."

From that simple beginning, a friendship was born and grew. Johnny had another name, of course, but he preferred to keep it to himself. It was one of the last things he had that was wholly Pueblo. He found it easier to answer to Johnny, a name he knew was common in the towns and villages of the whites.

When Casey asked about his name on one of their visits, he replied, "The Mexicans and the white men have taken much that was the Pueblos', but the name is mine. A Pueblo name. A good name, not to be taken by any man."

Casey inquired at the trading post. He was told that Johnny hadn't been in for some time, but he was expected. Rather than leave a message that might draw unwanted attention to himself, Casey found a comfortable chair in front of the livery. There he could sit in the shade, visit off and on with the livery owner, and watch the trading post a short block away. He waited only three days, then watched until Johnny completed his trading. When the Pueblo mounted and turned his horse to the trail for the return trip, Casey saddled his own animal.

An hour of slowly following the Pueblo trader put the men far from the town in a place where they could be alone. Johnny looked back only once, but Casey knew he had been seen. At a wide clearing beside the trail, a place where some trees offered a bit of shade, Johnny pulled off and dismounted, tying his horse to a low branch.

As Casey rode into the clearing, Johnny reached for his reins. Casey dismounted while Johnny tied the horse beside his own.

"It is a good day for a ride," was Johnny's greeting.

"To be alive and riding is always good," answered Casey.

The two men smiled at each other. Closing the short distance between them, they exchanged a firm handshake.

Johnny indicated the grove of trees. "Come, we will rest in the shade."

After the two men were settled, Casey said, "It is good to see you. It has been a while."

"I have been here."

Casey laughed out loud. "Yes, I'm sure you have been. It is I who has wandered."

Johnny studied his friend for several moments, seeming to look right through Casey. "Do you wish to tell your story?"

Casey was slow in answering. "I don't really want to, for there is much hurt in it, but I will share it with my Pueblo friend because I trust you. I do not want the story told to others. That is because the Casey you knew is dead. It is best that he remains dead, for there is something he must do. The doing will be much easier if he remains dead. The sheriffs will not be hunting for a dead man."

Johnny wrote in the sand with a twig for a long time before speaking. Casey had learned to wait out these silences with patience.

"To speak with the dead is a serious matter in

my culture. I will hear your story, and then we will decide if we should speak further."

Casey slowly said, "I understand. That 'Casey' is no more is a small thing. That a new man, a man named Raleigh, is here, is a better thing."

Casey told the story in as few words as he could. At one point, he had to stop and take firm control of himself to hold back the tears.

When the story was completed, he said, "I come to my Pueblo friend to ask for a favor. I wish to learn the bow and arrow. I have a need for a silent weapon, and for someone to teach me."

Johnny studied this white man he had be-friended. "You seek vengeance. You wish to put the killer of your wife and son in his own grave."

Casey knew there was no need for a response.

There was another long pause. "Before the missionaries came, I would have taught you, and then ridden with you to do this thing. A warrior must seek vengeance or leave the village. It would have brought me great honor to ride beside a warrior. Many of my people still believe this way."

Casey, perhaps too quickly, asked, "And now?"

Johnny was working the twig in the sand again. "There is much of the old ways still in my heart. I weep for your loss, and I know the urge to kill in revenge. But the new way..."

Casey almost blurted a question into the

lengthy silence, but he fought down the urge until Johnny said, "I will teach you the bow, and I will ask you to think much on what you plan to do."

10

The Texas Trail

WHEN JESSIE MCTAVISH FIRST SET HER eyes on Tyler Hobson, who was known as Ty, her future was fixed. It took many months and much conniving by Jessie before Ty figured out his part in her future.

Rounding up ornery longhorns in South Texas kept the large group of family and friends who gathered around Mac busier than they had ever been. But the many months of hard work ended with sold herds and prosperity for all of them. It wasn't until the group was leaving Fort Dodge, Kansas that Jessie finally brought Ty in on her plans.

After being married by the military chaplain, the bewildered Ty was led off into the darkened prairie by his smiling wife, there to spend their one-night honeymoon in a tent Jessie had purchased many weeks before in preparation for this night.

Liking Colorado well enough but missing his Texas home, Ty loaded up a wagon with their accumulated goods, bid farewell to Mac and the rest of the family, and took his wife back to South Texas. Mac and the rest would stay and settle on the south Colorado grass, but for Ty, home meant Texas.

Now, fifteen years later, Jessie sat on the seat of a tarpaulin-covered wagon holding the reins of a team of matched grays and watched as her fourteen-year-old son Mosby, called Moss by the family, stepped down from his gelding and opened the wire gate. His twelve-year-old sister Judith, mounted on a beautiful black gelding, held his reins while Moss was working on the gate. On the gatepost was a hand-painted sign announcing that the traveler was entering the land of the Bar-M. "The sign says Bar-M, Ma. This must be Uncle Mac's ranch."

"Must be," agreed his weary mother.

Jessie had prepared well for the trip. Not bothering with a traditional covered wagon with its hoops and white canvas top, she had purchased a heavy new work wagon with an extra-wide bed and high sides. In the wagon, she stored only what they needed for the trip. Anything else she wished for could be handmade or purchased after they arrived at their destination. Most of the proceeds from the sale of the ranch had been deposited in the local bank with instructions to forward it to a large Denver bank her sister's husband worked at. She carried only enough funds for the trip, and most of that was secreted in a built-in metal box beneath the seat.

Aware of the hazards of frontier travel, Jessie rigged a shelf on the wagon's dashboard. There she stored a supply of ammunition for the several weapons the family carried. The bulk of her ammunition was carefully hidden in the wagon.

The shelf had been rigged with three leather-lined gun holders. These were arranged to sheath a double barrel shotgun and a .44 Henry repeating rifle, both in the upright position where they were easy to see and quick to hand. To keep dust and rain out of the barrels, Jessie put a small leather patch over the muzzles. She could shoot right through the patch if the need should arise.

The third leather pouch held her .44 revolver.

From her early youth, Jessie had seldom been known to miss a shot.

Jessie drove the wagon through the opened gate and kept going at the plodding pace that suited the team, knowing the kids would catch up soon enough. Judith would push the cavvy of spare horses through, and Moss would close the gate.

On the seat beside Jessie was ten-year-old Michael, who was called Mike by everyone but his mother. Mike's well-disciplined gelding trotted along beside the wagon, ignoring the cavvy. No lead was necessary as long as Mike was within sight.

Moss rode up beside the wagon with a weary grin on his face. They had been on the trail for weeks.

"Will we soon be there, Ma?" asked Judith.

"I expect." was all Jessie had to say in answer.

An hour after riding onto the Bar-M, Jessie drove her wagon toward a large herd of white-faced cattle, and the animals casually parted to let her through. The kids held the cavvy behind the wagon to keep them from scattering the cattle. Jessie, looking at the contented herd and comparing them to South Texas longhorns, figured these short-legged beasts had no intention of running very far.

Two cowboys rode alongside Jessie's wagon. She didn't bother stopping but acknowledged the men with a nod and a lift of her rein-filled hand. Her other arm was draped around the shoulders of the sleeping Michael. Moss was keeping a close eye on the two strange men.

"Howdy, Ma'am. You know you're on the Bar-M, do you?"

"I know it."

"The Bar-M doesn't mind folks crossing as long as they don't tarry along the way. Did you close the gate behind you?"

"Gates closed, and we'll not tarry."

"Mind if I ask your business, ma'am, and where you're going?"

Jessie was fatigued almost beyond telling after the weeks on the trail. The miserable weather had alternated between scorching-hot, driving winds and wind-slanted rains, sometimes both in the same day. She had slept on the ground under the wagon, watching, and alert every minute for threats to herself or her family. The perpetual dust. It all worked together to make the end of the journey appear like the morning star in its promise.

Being this close made it difficult to remain strong and determined. Every muscle in her body wanted to just lie down and give up.

On the long trip west, she had protected her privacy as well as her family. It went against her nature to answer questions, but the cowboy asked nothing that shouldn't be expected.

"My name is Jessie. I'm Mac's sister, and these are my children. My very tired children. We'd like to know the shortest route to the ranch and how long it will take.

The cowboy lifted his hat a touch and said, "Well, I'll be dogged. We all know Mac has a couple of sisters. He'll be pleased to see you. Margo, too. Mac talks about you from time to time."

He seemed to then remember his manners. "I'm Buck Travers, ma'am. This here is Chuck Mason." Jessie nodded to one and then the other.

Buck picked up the conversation again. "As to the distance, ma'am, you'll not make it today without you drive well into the night. Be best if you was to follow us to the line shack about an hour ahead. You can rest the horses, and we'll give them a bit of corn. Rest yourselves, too. We've lots of grub on hand, and you and the kids can have the bunks for tonight. Chuck and I can throw our bedrolls under the trees. That way you'll get a good rest and a fresh start in the morning. You'll be there by dinnertime tomorrow night."

"Thank you. Please show me the way."

11

Las Animas County

CASEY WAS BARELY TEN MILES NORTH OF the New Mexico state line when he was accosted by a rancher and three cowboys. Riding out of the cover of some brush, the rancher shouted, "Hold up there, fella."

Given that the carbines of all four men carbines were pointed in his direction, he didn't hesitate or argue. Keeping his hands well away from the Colt mounted over his left hip, the butt arranged for a right-hand cross-draw, he said, "What's up, men?"

A short man with a belligerent manner, almost comically sitting his saddle on a horse that had to be no less than sixteen hands, said, "Rustlers, that's what's up. Explain yourself. Who are you, and where are you going?"

In keeping with being dead, Casey had spoken only his new name since leaving Santa Fe. "Raleigh's the name. Raleigh Cater. Just came out of Santa Fe. Heading north to the goldfields. Figure to find work. Hoping to make more than the cowhand wages I've been starving on."

"You know you're on the G-H? This is private range. We don't appreciate strangers making theirselves ta home."

Casey could do little but remain calm and hope this angry rancher didn't do anything foolish. He certainly couldn't fight four men holding guns on him.

"Well, I'm sorry to hear about the rustling, but I'm sure you can see I'm not pushing any cattle before me. Fact is, I haven't seen any cattle for miles past. As to being on your land, I'm just passing through. Never heard of a rancher who ever worried much about that. A body has to travel somewhere. I was following a trail for a while, but it faded out a few miles back."

The rancher appeared to be thinking this all over.

One of the cowboys spoke up. "Doubt as how this here is one of the rustlers, boss. He's not geared up for it. Hasn't even got a rope."

The rancher studied the cowboy and turned to take a long look at Casey. "You ride on. Get off the G-H as fast as you can."

Casey tipped his hat. "Thank you, sir, I'll do that. May I ask your name, sir?"

"Handle. Grady Handle."

"Any law on this range, Mr. Handle?"

"There's been talk of federal deputies looking into the rustling, but we've seen no signs of such."

Casey thought that over a moment and then asked, "None of my business Mr. Handle, but how many head do you run?"

"You're right, that's none of your business. Why do you ask?"

Casey slumped in the saddle and tipped his hat back. "Worked for a man back in Texas. Big rancher by some accounts. We was driving a small bunch to market when a storm one night brought the critters to their feet and lightning got them running. That rancher wouldn't have even missed that little bunch if he never saw them again. Should have left them till morning, but we didn't. In the rush and tear of the chase, we lost two men. One cowboy ground into the mud under running hooves, and one gored by a maddened steer. The cowboy was my riding partner, and the gored man was the owner. That owner, he don't own anything anymore. Gave me something to ponder on, that did.

"Don't know as how I'd risk my life over something I could really do without."

Every man there sat silently for a few moments.

Casey finally lifted his hat again. "Better move along if I'm going to find supper and a loft to sleep in at some ranch along the way. Ride well, men."

As he rode away, Casey asked himself, "Now, where in the world did a nonsense story like that come from?"

A bit farther along, after thinking the meeting through, his mind mostly on his need for secrecy, he pictured the big cowboy who had been sitting the gray gelding a few yards to his left. The man said nothing, but Casey was sure he took note of the bow tucked under the fender and the quiver of arrows tied behind the cantle, along with the saddlebags and his bedroll. Thankfully, the man asked no questions.

After three more nights on the trail, two bunked down on welcoming ranches and one huddled under some bushes, Casey rode back onto the Bar-M sheep ranch. Manuel was nowhere in sight; he would show up after his work was done. But Imelda saw him and called him to the kitchen.

After a goat-stew dinner, Manuel looked over his coffee mug at Casey. "Some things have changed here, my friend. The ranch owner, Mac—Mr. McTavish—he is now the federal deputy for these south counties. He waits for his two brothers to return, then they are to seek rustlers. He is also to seek those who burned a ranch and did much killing north of here."

The two men sat silently, both studying the ground in front of them. No more words were spoken on that subject, but when Casey rode out the next morning, Manuel shook his hand and said, "It is one thing to wish to not be known. It is another to make that come true. Ride carefully, my friend. I will pray that you will ride with God."

12

Bar-M Ranch

THE WAGON WAS BARELY IN SIGHT OF the ranch when the twins came bolting across the prairie grass, their ponies running full out with them standing in the stirrups. A short way behind, Jerrod rode out at a more leisurely pace. Their mother had called them for the evening meal, but as they were heading for the corral, they spotted the wagon.

Moss and Judith immediately closed in and bunched the cavvy, watching every move the twins made. The ten-year-old riders made a big loop, one on each side of the wagon, and pulled up with a slight tug on the reins of their well-trained horses.

"Welcome to the Bar-M," said Adam.

"Who you lookin' to see?" asked Jerry.

The questions were received better than they had been by the federal deputies.

By that time, Jerrod was close, and Jessie had pulled the wagon to a halt. She smiled and said, "My, what a reception. I'm hoping this is the Bar-M and that Mac—that is, Mr. McTavish—is available. Either him or Margo."

Jerrod stopped a respectful distance away and touched his hat. "Sorry for those fool kids raising dust and startling y'all, ma'am. Mother's at the house, and Pa will be along shortly. You go right along in. I'll help get your animals into a corral. Can the twins tell the folks who to expect?"

Jessie was pleased by Jerrod's manners but privately delighted by the antics of the twins.

She turned to Adam and Jerry. "You go tell your pa that his sister, Jessie by name, has come visiting."

The twins kicked their horses into a gallop with what was either a Rebel yell or a Ute war cry. They changed their story from time to time.

Mac, walking from the barn to the house, waved them over. Excitedly, the kids tried to outshout one another. "Lady in the wagon says she's your sister, Pa. Come ta visit."

Mac turned to look, but the wagon was still too far away to be sure. Without turning his head, he said, "Go call your Ma."

Jessie urged the team into a casual trot. Judith was on the wagon seat beside her mother. Mike, who was now mounted on his pony, rode alongside the wagon while Jerrod and Moss ushered the cavvy toward the corrals. After an ear-piercing whistle from Jerrod, Pepe stuck his head out of the barn door and, with a quick look at the cavvy, trotted to an empty corral and swung the gate wide. The horses were soon inside, with the two boys and Pepe seeing to their needs.

Walking away from the corral, Jerrod looked at Moss. "That right? Your ma is Pa's sister Jessie?"

"That's what she claims."

After a moment of thinking, Jerrod said, "That would make you and me cousins, I suppose."

"I suppose."

"Well, welcome to the Bar-M."

Jessie pulled the team to a halt and tied the reins off, then slumped against the back of the seat and tipped her hat up a bit. Mac set his eyes on his sister for the first time in nearly fifteen years. Margo came running from the house, flying across the yard as if a bear were chasing her.

Jessie looked at her with a big grin. "Careful there, old girl. You're too aged to be running like that."

Margo said, "Get down from that wagon so's I can give you a hug. My, what a sight for sore eyes you are. Welcome, welcome."

Jessie climbed down and stepped into Margo's welcoming embrace, then turned to Mac and gave him a hug. Mac was happy to see her but was clearly uncomfortable with the hug.

Mac, always one to get business behind him first, said, "I see three kids, but I don't see Ty."

Jessie answered, "Let us get our breath, and I'll tell you all about it."

Jessie and Margo introduced their families and explained that the kids were cousins.

Adam said, "We've got cousins up Denver way, but we haven't seen them for a time."

Pepe started leading the wagon away. Jessie could retrieve the overnight necessaries from it later.

Margo soon had Jessie and the kids sitting around the big kitchen table. The kids studied each other through squinting eyes as Mac gave thanks.

They ate in silence until Margo laid out the apple pie and coffee. She had tea, but Jessie accepted the coffee.

Mac pushed back his chair, ignoring the pie. He looked at Jessie and said, "We're sure happy to have you here, but I'm anxious to know what's happened."

Jessie, gathering her words carefully, slowly ate her pie before speaking. "We had a good life.

We'd finally gotten the borders of the ranch sorted out between us and a couple of neighbors. We were doing well. The money from those original drives put us in a good position for improving the stock. We lost a baby not long after Mosby was born, but otherwise, we had it good. We shared the ranch with Ty's sister and her family.

She paused and took a sip of coffee, almost as if she were hesitant to continue with the story. "You might remember that Ty was never afraid of work. He could handle just about anything that came along, and on a South Texas ranch, living that close to the border, just about anything was apt to come along. Ty took care of it all, but he couldn't handle pneumonia.

"He was pulling a stubborn steer out of the Nueces mud during a January cold spell. Ended up getting soaked, but he saved a ten-dollar animal. That was all that seemed to matter to him."

Mac didn't notice Margo giving him a look of comparison and understanding.

"I pleaded with him to come to the house for a change of clothes, but he begged off. Said he was fine."

There was a long pause as Jessie looked down at her empty pie plate.

"He wasn't fine. Halfway through that night, he started shivering. By morning, he couldn't get out of bed, and by noon, he was delirious. By the time the doctor made the long ride from town, all he could do was shake his head. Said it was in God's hands now. I guess God needed another rancher, or He thought I didn't. Two days later I was a widow, and the kids were without a father."

Jessie fought back tears as Mac and Margo and the kids sat silently. Judith started sniffling, and Jessie wrapped her in her arms.

Jessie finally finished the story. "Money was never a problem, so I was free to do what I wished. Ty's sister and her husband bought my half of the ranch. I found myself longing for family, to see you and the folks again, so I bought the sturdiest wagon I could find. We packed lightly, chose two good teams and spare saddle horses, and headed west. It's a long way. We've been almost two months on the trail."

The ever-practical Mac said, "A lot of risk for a woman alone with just the kids. Any trouble along the way?"

Michael spoke for the first time. "Mom killed a man. Shot him."

Judith put in, "Moss shot one too, only that man didn't die. At least we don't think he did, but he was sure spurring his horse away from there."

Jessie looked around the table at the startled eyes. "It didn't really amount to much, just two range riders thinking they saw easy pickings."

Everyone wanted more information, but Jessie made it clear that wasn't going to happen.

After everyone settled down a bit, Margo said, "I think the kids could be excused. You guys see to your evening chores and then show your cousins around a bit."

When the adults were alone, Mac said, "It's good to have you back. The folks talk about you all the time. What are your plans? Or do you have any?"

Jessie answered, "My plans are pretty vague. I'd like to stay here tonight and drive up to see the folks in the morning. We'll stay there until they get tired of us, looking at our options along the way. The only thing I know for sure is that I don't want to ranch."

Margo got everyone sorted out and settled in for the night, and after breakfast the next morning, Pepe harnessed the team while Jerrod and Moss saddled the riding animals.

Mac called Taz over and introduced him to Jessie. "Taz, I'd like it if you'd escort Jessie and the kids to the folks' place."

As ranch foreman, Taz would usually assign this duty to a working cowboy, but this was Mac's sister. Clearly, he wanted to be sure nothing happened to her or the kids.

When Mac made the request, he simply said, "I'll get my horse."

Jessie shook her head at Mac. "Always the big brother. Don't you ever stop? Me and the kids crossed most of Texas, a big part of New Mexico, and half of Colorado. I think we can get to the folks' place just fine."

Taz rode up a minute later. The kids had gathered around and were ready to go. Mac spoke to Taz. "Just see them safely there and then ride back. The twins will ride along with you. They'll want to stay but bring them home with you. Jessie can be a tad difficult at times. Might be good to ride out of rock-chucking distance."

Jessie gave her brother an exasperated look.

Mac's expression was as close as he ever came to a grin.

A mile down the trail, with the kids riding well ahead. Taz pulled his horse close to the wagon. "Sorry about all this, ma'am. Never knew a time Mac didn't have the other person's needs in mind when he gives an order. I generally find it best to follow them. Usually works out in the end. I'll just ride along, ma'am. Won't trouble you none a'tall."

Jessie showed a small smile. "Taz, is it? Interesting name. Don't think I ever heard it before. You just keep on following those orders, Taz. I know my brother pretty well. He ain't changed much since we was all kids together. He means well, but he's not real good at listening. And sometimes he gets to thinking that he's the only one who ever growed up."

Jessie was silent for a moment, as if she was thinking of times past when the family was all younger and home on the Missouri farm.

She looked up at Taz and grinned. "As to chucking rocks, I ain't thrown one in some time now, but you keep on calling me 'ma'am,' and I may take up the practice again. Jessie. My name is Jessie. Best you remember it."

"Yes, ma'am.

Jessie tried her best to hide her small smile.

13

Fremont County

CASEY, NOW RALEIGH, PUT THE SHEEP camp behind him and headed north and a bit west, up into the hills where he could pick concealed trails. Or make his own. The going was slow, but Casey was in no particular hurry. He had a stronger need for concealment than for haste.

One week after leaving the sheep camp and an hour before sunrise, he was hunkered down beneath some scrub brush above and behind the Clover ranch barn. He had scouted the position well before making his final choice.

One thing about hill-country ranching on the edge of the mountains: there was always a rock or a bush or a rise in the land that could be used to advantage. Casey was high enough above the ranch to give him concealment and a good firing position.

The big haystacks put up against the winter snows to come were easily within bow range. The house was farther away but no challenge for the Sharps rifle he had purchased in Santa Fe.

His plan was simple: build a tiny fire in the hollow he had already scratched out behind some stacked rocks. Lay out the four arrows he had wrapped with kerosene-soaked rags. Point his Sharps rifle in the general direction of the house and wait for daylight. He would hold his position until Herb Clover stepped from the house, then would come his satisfaction. His revenge.

His plan was the product of many hours of riding and thinking and plotting. Sitting a slow-moving horse didn't require much effort, so it left an abundance of time for thinking. First, put down the murdering Clover, then fire the hay. He had practiced enough with the Sharps that he was confident in his marksmanship, even in the dull gloom of early morning. He just needed a chance. He wouldn't miss.

Casey didn't want any animals hurt. Hopefully, the crew would clear the barn out before the fire leveled it. He wouldn't know, though. He would be miles away, following other hidden trails leading off in a different direction from his approach.

He had been thinking about the nonsense story he'd made up for the rancher down south. Why not the gold fields? No, he had no hankering to seek out the yellow treasure. However, working in a mill or clerking in a store away from the rains of summer and the bitter snows of winter might be a good way to put in a few months while whatever search was stirred up after he killed Herb Clover had a chance to quiet down.

Sitting in the chill of early morning, the time seemed to drag. Finally, there was a noise from the ranch—a door slammed at the bunkhouse. A few moments later, another door creaked open and slammed shut as the cook made his way into the cookhouse. The cookhouse windows took on reflected light as a lamp was lit. There must have been embers still in the stove because it was no time at all before smoke was blurring the sky above the roof, drifting off to the east as the gentle west wind pushed it along.

Another slam of the bunkhouse door, and the wrangler stepped out and made his way toward the barn. He lifted down the lit lantern that was always left burning over the barn door, then swung the big doors and blocked them open with something he kicked into place. Casey couldn't see what it was. Soon the lantern light was showing from the barn windows.

Casey had trouble holding back his excitement. Now was the time. His opportunity would be upon him at any moment. He would account for all the things that had brought him to this hidden hillside. The terrible pain of loss. The dull thuds that had taken his wife and child from him—those dreadful sounds that he couldn't shut off in the night. The sight of Florence staggering and falling against the stove and the baby dropping to the floor. The fire finding their nightclothes. Those sights and sounds brought him screaming into full wakefulness too many nights.

On those nights, he remembered his painful stagger through the fire to launch himself through the window. The burns. The injuries. The loss. The hopelessness.

He was going to account for it all any moment now. Wait. Be patient. Don't miss. One shot, and it's done. Just one shot to account for all the heartache. One shot and he would be able to sleep nights again. He would have leveled the playing field, even if it was a horrible leveling.

Then the fire-arrows, and the job would be completed. The stacks and the barn would be enough burning.

Clover had a family. Casey's argument was with him, not his family. He held no desire to risk the kids by burning the house.

After all the waiting, he had trouble believing his eyes. A light shone in the house; he guessed it was in the kitchen. Close to the back door, in any case.

He lifted the Sharps and rested his hand on the rock he'd rolled there for the purpose. Any time now. There. The inside door opened, letting a bit of light shine through the outer screen door. He heard heavy thumps as Clover stomped into his boots. A squeak, and the outer door opened. A slow movement inside. A shadow. Now. Stepping slowly into the early morning dullness was Herb Clover.

As all that was taking place, it was as if Casey were talking to himself. In a flash of memory, he went through the drill. *Level the rifle. Steady, now. Take careful aim. You know how to do this. Steady, steady, but quickly. There's not much time. Put pressure on the trigger. Just a little more pressure. Get control of yourself. Stop your hands from shaking. Blink away that moisture in your eyes. Quickly, it's almost too late.*

But his trembling hand shook the Sharps to where everything he saw in the sight was a blur. *Clear your eyes. Stop shaking.*

But Clover was now stepping down the three stairs into the ranch yard and was in almost total darkness. It was too late; Casey had missed his chance. The man he hated with all his strength was walking away alive.

The tremble in his hands told him he couldn't do it. He had failed after all the planning. All the preparation. All the many miles ridden.

'I was going to do it for you, Florence. For you and our son. But I couldn't. He's a murderer and deserves to die, but I didn't get it done.'

Murderer. What a dreadful word. So decisive. Nothing left out. Easy to understand. Clear cut. Nothing left to chance. Murderer. Clover was a murderer.

In the clear light of the sunrise, the thought of having that title placed on him overwhelmed Casey, no matter how much his old neighbor deserved the punishment.

He knew he had pushed the thought into the darkness of some hidden place in his mind, never to be considered. He had held the accusation comfortably at arm's length through all the weeks of planning and preparation. Pueblo Johnny had tried to get him to face it, and Manuel at the sheep camp had tried to warn him.

He hadn't been prepared to think of himself as a murderer until that very moment. That it was justified revenge put another face on it, but stripped down to the naked truth, what he had planned was murder.

Even if he escaped into a new world with his new name, he would know that Casey Bechtel was a murderer.

The ranch came to life below him, and men started moving around. Clover shouted orders for the day and the cook clanged out the breakfast call on the triangle hung beside the door. As Casey faced his failure in the solitude of his little alcove, he laid his head down on the Sharps and wept.

He had to get out of there. Casey was in little danger of discovery, but with the sun almost fully up, he had to move. There would be no reason for a cowhand to climb this rocky hillside. He could probably leave the kerosene-soaked arrows lying where they were. It could be years before anyone came this way. He chose instead to unwrap the soaked cloth and drop the pieces into the fire, where they flared up and were gone in mere moments. He buried the fire and the little hole under a few inches of dirt, then slid the arrows back into the quiver. He lowered the hammer on the Sharps and checked around his hideaway to assure himself that he was leaving nothing behind.

His horse was back in the brush about a quarter of a mile. He had a clear run to the animal once he crested the rise behind his hidey-hole. From where he sat, he would crawl to the top of the rise, staying behind the brush and trying not to move any branches or make noise. After ten careful minutes, he was in the clear, and he would be astride his gelding in fifteen more minutes. He would ride until he found a place to rest. To rest and consider.

14

Pueblo

BOYS AND GIRLS ALIKE CAME RUNNING at the blast of the big steam whistle. Horses plunged into their collars or fought the bit. Dogs barked. An unfortunate cowboy was tossed into the air by his normally placid mount. Men and women waved, and the engineer waved back. Great clouds of oily black coal smoke hovered over the train and the town. The column of hot steam forced wide-eyed admirers away from the tracks as the big locomotive ground to a stop.

The railway was still a new phenomenon in Pueblo.

The conductor climbed down and placed the stool below the passenger car stairs. A mystified cowboy stepped down and then turned to look in wonder at the big contraption he had ridden up from Santa Fe. A well-dressed lady with three children hovering around her came next, then a man who could have been a banker or a politician stepped to the platform. Finally, as if they didn't want the journey to end, the McTavish brothers, Bobby and Jeremiah, put their feet back on Colorado soil, or rather on the station platform that was anchored to Colorado soil.

Bobby turned and held out his hand, and a beautiful young lady took a firm grip, lifted her voluminous skirt with her other hand, and cautiously stepped down. Momentarily, she reveled in the feeling of having something under her feet that wasn't moving.

Jeremiah then moved back toward the stairs and repeated the gesture for another young lady. There was no show of affection between these two as there had been between Bobby and his lady. There may have even been a bit of tension, but it was difficult to tell from a distance.

The four travelers moved to the edge of the platform and looked at the gathered crowd, with all the wagons, buggies, and saddle horses.

"There's no sign of anyone from the Bar-M," reported Jeremiah.

Bobby had already figured that out. "I'll go check. Wait here a bit."

He stepped into the small station and was back

within a minute. "There's been no one in to pick up our wire. It's still lying in the pick-up box. I figure the only way to get that brother of ours to pay attention to a town or a telegraph wire would be to have it moo."

The men excused themselves from the ladies and walked along the train until they came to the single slatted livestock car, where they helped the train crew slide a loading ramp into place. In only a few minutes, they were leading four saddled horses to the tie rail beside the small station.

A couple of hours later, they had been to the hotel dining room for lunch, rented a room for the ladies to change into riding clothes in, arranged for the depot man to hold the single trunk and the three smaller bags that had been unloaded from the baggage car, and were set to make the four-hour ride to the Bar-M.

As they arrived at the end of the single street, they pulled up to allow a team and wagon to gain the trail ahead of them. Bobby looked, turned away, and then looked again. The woman handling the team sure looked familiar. Could it be? It didn't seem likely. Another, longer study of the wagon and its single passenger confirmed his first thought. He was sure now.

He spoke loudly, so his voice could be heard over the crunching of the steel-rimmed wagon wheels. "Jeremiah, if'n my old eyes ain't playin' nasty tricks on me, I'd say that just might be our little sister a-settin' on that there wagon. Long ways from Texas, but there she sits. What do y'all make of that?"

Jessie pulled the team to a halt and looked at the riding group. It took a moment for her eyes to adjust to the changes the passing years had wrought. Finally, satisfied with what she saw, she wrapped the reins on the brake handle and climbed down. Bobby and Jeremiah were already walking toward her and they met in a three-person hug, no one saying anything for a moment.

Bobby was the first to step back and speak. "You're a long way from Texas, Jessie. I'm guessing there's a story to tell."

"Let's get off this road so others can pass and I'll tell you all about it. Won't take but a few minutes."

After the boys introduced their lady friends and Jessie had shown her surprise that Bobby was married to Matilda, the girl their old friend Jerrod had been engaged to before his death on the trail west, she told her story in a few concise sentences. When she was done, she said, "You heading to the ranch or to the folks' place? The folks sure would like to see y'all again."

Jeremiah answered, "We'll be going to the

ranch, but I'm thinking we should ride along with you to see the folks first. The ranch can wait another day or two. But how would you like to swing that wagon back to the depot? We've some baggage that might fit behind that load of goods you've got there."

The boys received a grand welcome, with great excitement about Bobby and Matilda being married. An unspoken question left hanging in the air after Ma glanced at the other girl caused Jeremiah to clear his throat before explaining, "No, Ma, Greta and I ain't hitched. It's not for the lack of me asking, but so far, she somehow hasn't taken notice of my manly charms. I expect she will any day now, and I'll find her falling into my arms. Don't rightly see how she's resisted all this time."

His boyish smile was always able to take the tension out of a situation.

Greta, feeling a bit of explanation was in order, said, "I'm a city girl. I enjoyed my time on the Bar-M last year, but the thought of a lifetime with no theater, no arts, and no lighted streets, has me more than a bit concerned. I may head back East, or I may go back out to California. I sure enjoyed the weather out there, and the ocean."

No one in the large ranching family really understood her feelings, but they all let it pass.

Following an afternoon and evening of visiting, and a night with the folks, Jessie talked to her brothers. "Y'all better get down to the ranch. Mac's taken on a job for y'all, and he's been waiting for you."

Bobby grinned at her. "Don't really know as how I'm looking for a job. Thought I might extend our honeymoon a bit. You know, kind of laze around a little, enjoy the sunshine, watch my woman clean up around and mend my socks. That kind of thing."

Jessie and Matilda just looked at each other. There was not one sensible thing to say in response.

The brothers and their ladies were warmly greeted on the Bar-M, but it took Mac only a minute to get down to business. "Boys, we need to have a talk." With that, he headed for the coffeepot in the cookhouse. He naturally assumed his two brothers would follow.

Fortified with coffee and with their chairs pulled into a small circle, Mac explained the situation.

He finished with, "I told the deputy I'd only take on this lawman thing if I had you two with me. I know next to nothing about enforcing the law, but you two seem to have found your niche there. So, are you with me or do I send the badge back to the deputy in Denver?"

Before committing himself, Bobby discussed the matter with Matilda. With her agreement, the deal was made.

Mac gave his two brothers the badges Marshal Granger had left for them, and they put them in their pockets. Bobby said, "Don't want that shiny bit of metal to be the first thing a man sees when I'm riding."

Mac already had his badge hidden away in a pocket, with no intention at all of ever wearing it.

15

Fremont County

After retreating from the Clover Ranch, the site of his failed plan for vengeance, Casey rode into the hills and put together a simple camp. He needed to think and pray. He had nothing else planned for his life except going to the mining camps, and that had been just a spur-of-the-moment thought. It could wait.

Three days later, he brought down a nice buck with the bow and arrow. 'How about that, Johnny? That buck is a lot smaller than a haystack. You taught me better than you thought you did.'

He finally tired of sitting and napping all day. He broke camp, tying his simple pack behind the saddle and loading up what was left of the venison, then ambled on foot along a dim trail, leading his horse behind him. He'd tied the reins together and laid them on the horse's neck, then tied a lead rope to the bridle. The longer rope gave both the walker and the animal more freedom on the crooked path they were following.

His plan was to make a quick visit to the Stringfellow ranch and then move on north to the mines.

Unthinkingly, the face of Julia Stringfellow flashed across his mind. He recalled the gentle touch of her caring hands as she cleaned his head and face after the fire, and the way she had applied the salve might have been as healing as the salve itself. He shocked himself with these thoughts. With the grim and still-fresh memory of the fire and murder taking up most of his waking moments, it was no time to be thinking about another woman.

He didn't mind the walk. It made it easier for the horse on these steep, rocky hillsides. It also made it easier for him to pick his way down toward his old ranch. Where he walked was close to, but isolated from the old ranch by a steep hillside and the rocky terrain. There was very little grass among the rocks so no cattleman would trouble himself with the area.

It was on that chosen path, about a half mile from the ranch that his nostrils were assailed by the putrid stench of decaying flesh. The horse pulled back on the lead, balking at going closer.

The stench was different from the smell of burned flesh, but it made him remember—and it caused him to think. Was this where the dead horses had been dragged to?

He led the horse a short distance away from the worst of the smell. Firmly tying the animal to a sturdy branch, he slowly and reluctantly made his way back to what had to be the two horses he had shot during the fight.

When he found the animals, the story was clear. Someone had dragged the carcasses to the lip of a small wash and tumbled them over. They were perhaps twenty feet down the steep bank, one atop the other, and badly deteriorated by both time and scavengers. Folding his scarf into a thick pad, he held it over his mouth and nose while he scrambled down the rocky slope. He was hoping to find a ranch brand.

Using every ounce of his fortitude, he swatted away a cloud of the swarming flies. He grasped a rear leg bone and pulled it away from the pile. A large piece of flesh came with the bone. Thousands of maggots wriggled frantically, hating the sunlight. Pulling the leg bone and hair-covered hide away also exposed the hip of the bottom animal. The brands were clear: Clover. There was no doubt about it. These were the remains of the Clover horses. He managed a rushed scramble out of the wash and, pulling the padded scarf from his mouth, he walked quickly to his horse. He mounted and headed directly to where he knew a small run of water tumbled down the hillside behind his old ranch. He let the horse drink its fill while he took off his shirt and washed as thoroughly as possible from the waist up.

Desperate for relief from the sour taste in his mouth, he brushed his wet finger in a bit of sand and rubbed his teeth, then slurped up some water, swished it around his mouth, spat it out, and repeated the process, until the sand and most of the foul taste was gone. After as much cleansing as the circumstances allowed, he re-tied the horse and stretched out in some shade. He wasn't tired, he just needed to get his head around what he'd found, and what it might all mean. He had to figure out his next move.

Tired or not, he was close to drifting off when he was startled into a sitting position. The two men. He had shot two men. Where were they buried? The raiders had simply pushed the horses over a bank, but it was doubtful that the dead men would have received the same crass treatment. They must have been buried. Hurriedly, no doubt, but still buried.

The question was where. Logic said that with dawn approaching after a night of killing and burning, the raiders would want to get out of the vicinity. But they had to get free of incriminating evidence. Clover was wounded and had undoubtedly run for home and help, but the shooters were on their own, and they didn't know the country. It was dark, although the dull light of dawn might have been glowing on the eastern ridges.

What did all of that mean? Casey was willing to bet it meant that somewhere close by there were two graves, or one grave holding two bodies. Casey had only to figure out where.

He left the horse tied where it could pull on a bit of grass growing among the bushes. He could get a better, clearer look at the land on his feet rather than seated high on the horse. He was looking for disturbed ground, or perhaps a small mound. Maybe a rock pile that was too symmetrical to be natural.

He walked and paused, looking all around. He slowly turned in ninety-degree increments and studied the terrain with infinite care. Nothing looked unnatural, so he climbed almost another hundred yards up the slope and repeated the process, following the edge of the wash. By this time, his newly healed leg was throbbing with pain.

Twice he went to the wash and studied its bottom. Perhaps there would be signs of an unnatural cave-in? Again, nothing.

Another hundred yards uphill took him to the beginnings of heavier brush growing randomly among the evergreens. Ahead was a growth of aspens; those wondrously attractive but simple trees whose leaves shimmered in the slightest breeze. He almost walked past the growth, knowing how thick an aspen grove could be, its trunks merely feet apart and sometimes almost touching. A dense aspen grove was almost impenetrable.

What caught Casey's eye was a bit of bark scraped from the outer edge of a small tree. The bruised inner bark had turned rusty red, which was the first unnatural thing he had seen on the search.

Making his way step by slow step through the grove, starting at the bruised tree, he found a small clearing about fifty feet in. This was strange, because aspens grew from the wandering roots of older trees. Nevertheless, there was a small patch with no trees. Even with this anomaly, he nearly missed the grave. The raiders had gathered up fallen aspen branches and a couple of short tree trunks and dropped them randomly across the clearing. Aspens naturally prune themselves, so fallen branches were a totally normal occurrence.

After he kicked the branches out of the way and studied the grave, he found himself wishing he could turn to someone and say, "Here, dig this up and tell me what you find."

Of course, no such thing was going to happen.

He dug through the pile of discarded branches and found one about the thickness of a pitchfork handle, then broke it over his knee until he had a manageable length and bent to the grave. On his knees, he started plowing through the dirt. When enough was loosened, he scooped it with his hands, piling it close by so he could cover the hole in when his miserable task was done. It seemed like hours, but it really took only a few minutes to hit something solid. He knew it was a body.

He kept digging and scooping, and soon the digging stick snagged on a checked shirt. He was looking for pockets, either shirt or pants. He had no desire to uncover a face. The odor released by the moving of the dirt was mild compared to the horses, but still, he couldn't stop gagging.

He worked quickly now that his goal was in sight.

The shirt was covered in dried blood, but the leather vest the raider wore was in better condition. Casey uncovered the entire vest and probed the pockets both inside and out. In one inside pocket, he found a cheap pocket watch, three letters, and a wad of bills, undoubtedly payment for the night's work that had cost the man his life. The shirt pocket held a sack of tobacco and nothing else.

Casey exposed the second man's shirt before he moved to the pants pockets. This man had no letters or other identity, but a matching wad of money was tucked into the bottom of his outside vest pocket. He too had a cheap pocket watch, but this one had a name engraved on the back. Casey hoped it was the man's name and not the name whoever he had stolen it from.

Working quickly now, Casey dug until he could get a hand in a pants pocket. He didn't want to do it. The pants had been filthy before the burial and they were rank now, with the blood and the rotting of the corpse. He did it, though. He did it for his wife and son, whom these men had killed. He dug his hand in, grasped the cloth of the pocket and turned it inside out. A pocket knife, a small waterproof tin of matches, and some coins dropped into the dirt.

He repeated the process until he had explored all the pockets he could find. There was nothing else to identify the men.

The dead men still wore their gun belts. Casey unbuckled them and stood, then, reaching down to grab the attached holster, he pulled and lifted. The corpse moved a bit under the remainder of the dirt, but soon he had both belts lying on the ground at his feet. There was a Colt .44 in each holster. Obviously, the men who did the burying wanted nothing that might point to the raid. It was better to bury it all, although he was surprised that they hadn't taken the money.

Casey studied the collection of evidence lying on the ground beside his feet. What now? First, of course, was to fill in the grave and cover it as best he could with the dead branches.

The gun belts were filthy, caked with dirt and blood. They might ruin his blankets, but he had to hide them. He could get new blankets.

He would stuff the rest of the trash into a saddlebag and ride far and fast. Forget the visit to the Stringfellow Ranch. There would be another time.

He had to find a safe place to go through the letters. He hoped to find a name, or perhaps two names, and he had to think. So much to think about. He could think on the back of the horse, but he wanted to be on the ground when he went through the letters. He would look for a place. Perhaps he would settle down for the night. An early night might be just what he needed.

16

Huerfano County

GALEN PICKARD, BLAZE RANDOLPH, AND Buzz Dover, the district deputies assigned to the southern portion of the territory by their boss, Federal Deputy Marshal Mordecai Granger, sat on weary horses, each of them rolling a smoke. They had been two weeks roaming across the southwest grasslands and up into the hills surrounding the area.

"Lot of country," said Pickard.

"Lot of cattle," responded Dover.

They sat silently, blowing smoke into the drifting breeze. Their horses were about done in and needed a few days of rest. They were about the same, tired and saddle-sore. Pickard turned, pointing with his chin at the low-lying hills a few miles to the west.

"That was a nice little park we saw up top of that ridge. Good flow of water. Lots of graze. What say we take shelter there for two or three days and let these animals recuperate a bit? We can sit and talk things over."

"Punch will be lookin' for us. We're runnin' a bit late here," replied Randolph.

Pickard drew in smoke, blew it out, and looked at Randolph. "Punch and his boys can wait. We'll get there by 'n by. It's some ways yet to the cabin and that there hidden meadow. Anyhow, this ain't no scheduled thing we're doin'. Not exactly, it ain't."

Seated around a small fire in the grassy park atop the low ridge, the men watched the pot come to a boil. The horses were staked out on long ropes to graze since the little stream kept the grass along its bed green.

Gazing back to the east and flicking his hand in that direction, Pickard spoke again. "Mostly open range, just a few fences here and there. More cattle than I kin count. It's a rustlers' paradise."

The men let that settle for a moment before Pickard picked up the conversation. "Gettin' the critters is easy enough. Long, hard drive to market, though."

Slowly, almost carelessly, Randolph chuckled. "That ain't no concern of ours. I expect ol' Punch will be there, ready to take possession of a few critters. Then it's his problem."

The men nodded in silence at these spoken facts.

On their trip across the grasslands, they had stopped at each ranch along the way, introducing themselves as federal deputies and showing their badges. This gave them the opportunity to study the ranch layouts, the number of working hands each outfit had on the payroll, and how diligently the rancher patrolled his claimed spread.

They had heard stories of losses. Most ranchers figured their animals had been driven immediately across the border into New Mexico, yet they never found any worn trails to give proof to that suspicion. The ranchers, familiar with the mountainous lands to the west, doubted that anyone would attempt to drive stolen animals that direction.

At the old Cox Ranch, which was now the S-T, owned by Shep Trimble but managed by a Texas cowboy named TJ Marpole, they recognized immediately that it was time to hold back and watch what they said. Even after they introduced themselves as deputies, this TJ was showing no deference to the three riders.

TJ had pushed his hat back and studied them with an insolent grin. "Y'all can put them shiny badges back inta yer pockets, boys. I've known a lawman er two here 'n there. No-account bunch, most of them. Too lazy to work.

"As far as rustling is concerned, the S-T carries no cattle except that old milk cow over there. This here is strictly horses. We're well-fenced, and my riders keep a close eye on the herd. Anyone foolish enough to catch up a bunch of our broodmares or touch a stallion would be opening hisself up fer a world of hurt.

"Wouldn't be calling on no deputies neither. The S-T can look out fer itself."

The three riders carefully turned their horses and rode away.

At a few ranches, the deputies heard complaints about the lack of law and order. They dragged out a standard answer.

"Big country, sir. The rustlers could be anyone at all. Could be one or two of your men, or any cowboy on any ranch. We're only hearing about small losses. Could just be someone putting together some drinking money."

With their assurance that the law was active and diligent, they encouraged the ranchers to leave the search for stolen stock to them. Not every rancher agreed, but a few did.

17

Bar-M Ranch

THERE WAS A LOT OF LAUGHTER, A FEW tears of joy, and much storytelling as the family gathered at Hiram's and Della's small farm. Fifteen years was a long time, so Jessie and her parents had some catching up to do.

Mac and Margo rode up with the kids for the big celebration. Bobby and Jeremiah, with their ladies, rode along.

Nancy and her family were the only ones not there. Jessie had wired from Pueblo, but their older sister hadn't wired back yet, or if she had, the wire was still waiting for someone to ride in to pick it up.

Sitting around the outdoor fire pit after dinner, Bobby led the family in a few tunes. Della, called Ma by the family or Granny by the little ones, relished their grown and growing family, as did Hiram. Jeremiah decided it was time for the story of Jessie's travels.

"So, little sister, here we are in a land criss-crossed by railways, offering the opportunity to sit on a comfortable cushion and watch the world go past your window, and you chose to drive a wagon from one end of the country to another. I'd sure like to hear your explanation of that."

His grin was infectious, and the gathered family all turned to look at Jessie.

Jessie sat silently, her chin lifted a little and a stubborn look on her face. In her mind, she didn't owe an explanation to anyone. Anyway, it was a story she wasn't anxious to repeat.

Jeremiah laughed and shook his head. "Would you look at her? That's the same look I remember from when we were kids, when she knew there were two ways to do something and she had chosen the harder of the two."

Jessie still didn't speak.

Finally, twelve-year-old Judith couldn't hold back. "Ma had a bit of a set-to with the station man. She pulled her pick on him and scared him almost into his grave."

Jessie shot a stern look at her daughter, but it was too late to stop the conversation.

Someone asked, "You still carry that big blade you found on the trail West?"

Moss said, "Ma's never without her pick. She got one for each of us before we set out to come West. She always says, "You just never know…"

There was more laughter, interrupted by Moss offering further explanation.

"That there station man," he said with a grin, "He suggested he could save Ma a site of expensive travel if'n she was lookin' for a new husband.

"He appeared to have more to say, but by that time he'd forgot all about it. Seemed he had eyes and thoughts only for that blade pressed against his throat. Everyone in the station kind of took notice and stood silent for a bit while Ma thought it through.

"Then Ma, she marched us all out of the station and over to the livery barn, where they had wagons and teams for sale. Took no time at all for Ma to pick out that big wagon and rig it out. She'd made up her mind to have nothing to do with the steam cars.

"We drove the wagon back past the ranch and picked up our riding animals and some spares, then loaded up a few more things for the trail, and here we are.

"We never once got to ride on the cushions. Ma, she put some padding on the wagon seat. Said that was cushion enough.

"Seen a lot of country. Got wet, got cold, and

got awful hot for a spell, but it was all kind of fun, too."

Hiram, who had been silent up to this point, cleared his throat. "Well, Jessie, you were always one who could make a decision. Take care of yourself, too. We're awfully glad to have you back, no matter how you got here.

"Your ma and I have taken up a lot of the Lord's time praying for y'all over the years. I expect He's had His eye on you the whole time; knew just where you were and what was best."

Jessie enjoyed a full week with the senior McTavishes before she sensed a restlessness in the kids.

"I think I'll take the kids down to the ranch and let them run around and play with their cousins for a bit. They're getting kind of rambunctious."

Two days later, everyone was settled down on the Bar-M. Every sleeping space was full to overflowing.

Margo and Jessie gathered the kids around the big kitchen table for school work in the mornings. After lunch, they ran their horses far and wide on the Bar-M.

Jessie stopped Taz one morning as he was walking toward the corral for his horse.

"Good, morning, Taz, or Mr. Johansen, if you prefer. You did such a good job of guiding me to my folks' place, I wonder if you could find time to show me around the Bar-M? There's no rush since I expect we'll be here for a spell. I've heard so much about the changes and improvements that I'd like to see them for myself."

Silently Taz wondered why Jessie didn't ask Mac to do the guided tour, but he said nothing.

"I'd be pleased, Jessie. I'll need to sort a few things out with the crew. See them to their work. But I'll probably be able to find time tomorrow morning after that's done."

"Thanks, Taz. I'll be ready. And if it doesn't work out, we'll do it another time." She smiled at the foreman, then headed back to the house.

Taz, watching her walk away, asked himself, "Now, what in the world?"

18

Fremont County

MAC, BOBBY, AND JEREMIAH RODE FROM
the Bar-M with their deputy badges well hidden.
They had dug into the ranch's store of weapons,
some of which hadn't been carried or used for
years.

Mac said, "We'll try to avoid trouble, and hope
for the best. But we'll be prepared in any case."

To keep their saddle mounts free for action,
they loaded their required gear onto a single pack
horse. They drove the horse ahead of them rather
than burden one rider with holding a lead rope.

They headed west along the Bar-M fence line.
Determined to look into the murder and burning situation first, Mac said, "All right, we have
miles to go and hours to talk. Tell me whatever
you think will be helpful for this lawman busi-

ness, and how we should approach this murder investigation. You're the ones with experience. A couple of months have gone by, so we can't hope to find a trail that will tell us much. How do we start?"

The conversation was interrupted by a visit to Ad's Trading Post and Smithy. Mac's in-laws always gave him a big welcome whenever the family dropped by. Coffee was soon boiled up, and lunch put together.

Clara and Shep joined the group for lunch. Clara, Margo's younger sister, and the last of Ad's family to live at the trading post, had married Shep Trimble the year before.

Shep raised horses for sale on his S-T ranch, south of the Bar-M holdings, and his friend TJ Marpole managed the ranch and the breeding program. The plan was to move the horses up from the S-T when they were ready for training and riding. Being less than a full year since its establishment, there were no young ones to work with yet, so Shep had bought a few colts from neighboring ranches. He would train them thoroughly and offer them back for ranch work.

As always whenever Bobby was present, there was much laughter and joking around. It made the lunch break pass all too quickly.

Mac, being the serious one, finally said, "We

appreciate the lunch, but we have to be on our way. I don't want to be gone from the ranch any longer than necessary."

A short five miles farther west, the trio of riders pulled up to greet a disheveled man riding east on an overloaded horse.

"Howdy," greeted Mac. "Don't know as I've ever seen you around here before. Not many folks come this way. I'm Mac McTavish, Bar-M." He pointed one finger at the land they rode beside and waited for a response.

The rider was cautious, as if he were nervous or perhaps hiding something. "Raleigh Cater. Heading to the mining country. Hoping to find a job."

"You're a long way from the mining country Mr. Cater. And a long way from most everywhere else too. Mind if I ask how you come to be in this neck of the woods?"

The rider slumped back in the saddle and turned to look behind him. Pointing back with his thumb, and thinking up a story as he spoke, he said, "Big country. I had no idea. Set out from Santa Fe. Was in no particular hurry. Thought I'd see a bit of the world along the way. Saw more than I ever knew existed. Beautiful, though. Nice country."

The speaker seemed to be searching for words.

Finally, "Hills and hunger come near to putting paid to what was left of me, but I finally brought down a nice buck. Might've saved me from starvation. I hope you're going to tell me I'm on the right trail to the mines. Wouldn't like to have any other unwelcome news."

His scruffy beard hid most of his facial expressions, while his hat shaded his troubled eyes and his burned scalp.

Mac studied the man with a critical look. He had no interest in the story about looking for work, true or not true.

Lifting the badge from his vest pocket, he said, "Mr. Cater, you need to understand that the three of us are sworn federal deputies. Now, we have no reason to not believe your story, but since you've been rambling around, you might have seen something or someone that you should tell us about. In particular, we're interested in a rustling problem south and west of here. That, and a murder and burning to the north a ways."

Mac studied the man in the pause that followed. He thought he saw a startled look in the man's shaded eyes, and perhaps a constricted swallow.

As if he had much to consider, Raleigh took an awkwardly long time answering. His first temptation was to step down from his horse, open his bedroll and show these deputies all he had found. What stopped him, he couldn't have really said.

Deciding to hold his findings secret for the time being, he finally spoke. "I've heard nothing about those matters. As far as that goes, except for a couple of ranchers down south who fed me and put me up for a night, I've seen very few people. Wish I could help you."

There was a suspicious silence among the four men, but finally, Jeremiah spoke. "Odd to see a white man carrying a bow strapped to his saddle. You got arrows to go with it?"

Raleigh seemed to brighten and sit up a bit straighter. "Sure as you know. Pueblo friend down Santa Fe way, he taught me the bow. I'll never be as good with it as he is, but I brought that buck down with a single arrow. It can't hold against a rifle in a stand-up quarrel, of course, but it's a great tool just the same."

The explanation brought no verbal response, but the three men studied him even more carefully.

Jeremiah, wishing to test the truthfulness of the tale, asked, "That Pueblo friend have a name?"

"Most everyone has. Why do you ask?"

Jeremiah tried to remain casual. "Spent some time down that way myself. Met a few Pueblos. I might know your friend."

In his mind, Raleigh reverted back from his fictitious name to Casey again. He tried to think if giving out Johnny's name could bring the man trouble. He finally decided that this conversation would be forgotten before any of them ever saw Santa Fe again.

"Pueblo Johnny, he calls himself. Rides in from time to time with carvings, trinkets, gemstones, and such. Trades at the post for things the folks on the reserve need. Good man, and a friend for a couple of years."

Jeremiah knew the truth of the claim and said no more.

Bobby said, "Mr. Cater, happen to be you know the name of the sheriff in Santa Fe?"

Raleigh looked suspiciously at Bobby. "Don't know why you would ask me that. I expect maybe you don't believe my story. Far as I know, the sheriff this past quite some time has been a lazy kind of feller. Never met him my own self. Name's something like McCabe, or maybe it was McCobe. The thing about that, the talk around the town, was that this McCabe didn't do much to earn his keep. Depended mostly on a couple of deputies. Brothers, they were, as the story went. I had no reason to know them, so I don't know the truth of all that. Don't know as I ever heard their names.

"Story was that one brother pretty much held down the sheriff's office, while the other entertained the mayor's daughter. But that might all be gossip."

Mac and Bobby were both holding back grins as they studied Jeremiah.

Mac said, "All right, Mr. Cater. You be on your way. Just keep on as you're going. You'll find Pueblo, and the railway soon enough. You can ride horseback or take to the rails from there. Good luck on your job search."

When they were well out of hearing range, Bobby burst out laughing. Mac didn't laugh out loud—he seldom did—but his grin was nearly splitting his face open. Jeremiah could do nothing but sit and take the ribbing. He finally said, with his own face grinning, "Well, she was actually quite a nice girl if you weren't hoping to hold a deep in-ti-lec-tual conversation." He strung out the pronunciation of intellectual.

This caused Bobby to double up on his laughter.

They camped that night on a little stream flowing down from the low hills that bordered the western edge of ranching country. After an early start the next morning, they were well along the way to the only settlement in the area.

Arriving in the little town of Clarence, they

looked for the locally-elected sheriff at the board-and-batten office anchoring one end of the town's only street.

"You'll find our useless sheriff acrost the street at Minnie's café. Spends more time there than he does earnin' his wage."

This helpful information came from a bewhiskered oldster holding down a battered kitchen chair leaned against the small ranch supply store next door.

"That so?" asked Jeremiah. "If I was to flip you a silver half-dollar, would you feel up to telling the sheriff he has three federal deputies wasting time on his doorstep? Be much appreciated if he could wiggle his posterior over this way just as soon as it's convenient."

The old man shot to his feet with his hand extended. "If'n you hadn't already offered the silver piece, I'd a done it fer the pleasure of seein' the look on his face when I tell him."

Jeremiah flipped the silver in a small loop through the air, and the old man grabbed it like a snake grabbing a mouse.

The sheriff's office door wasn't locked, so Mac and his brothers walked in and made themselves at home, with Mac taking the chair behind the desk. The two cells at the end of the short hallway were both empty, their doors half-open.

Within a couple of minutes, the sheriff came puffing in.

"Gentlemen, welcome to Clarence. Don't know as we've ever had the pleasure of a visit from the feds before, but I'm pleased to see you. How can I help?"

All the chairs were taken, so the sheriff stood on one foot and then the other, looking uncomfortable. Jeremiah and Bobby were enjoying his discomfort. Mac was indifferent.

Mac took the lead. "Understand you had a multiple murder and a ranch burning up this way recently. We'd like to know what you've done about it, and what you've found out."

The sheriff's discomfort was now complete. After stammering a bit, the worried man said, "No evidence. Just none at all. Professional hard cases, I'm thinking. Knew what they were doing."

"So, what did you do to find evidence?" asked Jeremiah.

"Why, why, I went right down there just as soon as I got word."

"And how long after the murders was that, Sheriff?"

"Well, it, let me think. Yes, it was two days after the fire, or so the neighbor told me. Fire was all out, time I got there. Coals were cold to the touch. Of, course, there had been a bit of rain, so that would account for all of that.

"Man named Stringfellow, he sent one of his kids to bring the news. Ranches higher up the mountain. Grazes a bunch of connected valleys. Big family of mostly growed kids. Eastern mountain folks. Never caused no trouble I know of, but no better than they need to be, I'm thinking. Growed son is ranching the old Bechtel place. That's where the fire was. Not altogether sure how he got to do that. Has some kind of paper. Says he rode all the way down to Santa Fe and closed 'er up with a lawyer down there. Paid out his money and came home with a title. I'm no lawyer so I couldn't argue the point. Could even be he was the one behind the fire."

The three deputies carefully followed each word of this short speech. Clearly, the sheriff was avoiding the major detail. His suspicion of the Stringfellows was also evident.

Jeremiah continued his questioning. "I'm wondering, Sheriff, why you keep mentioning the fire when there were three murders."

The sheriff looked around his little office as if another chair might have magically materialized. Then he looked back at Jeremiah.

"Well, there was a suggestion of murder all right, but all we know for sure is, the folks that were living there are gone. Could have up and rode away for all we can prove. No evidence at all to go by. Just that they're gone, and this Stringfellow boy is holding the ranch and the cattle that were on it."

Mac found it interesting that the sheriff was determined to implicate the Stringfellow family.

Jeremiah finished his questioning. "Did you sift through the fire debris looking for bones or evidence of burned bodies?"

"I did. Took an unburned shovel I found leaning on the fence and went all through the place. Not very big. Just a two-room log cabin. Bit of a lean-to on the back. Logs were all charred but were mostly still standing when I was there. Lean-to was pretty much burned to the ground. That's all there was. Hardly anything left. All the furniture, beds and all, were made of wood. All gone. Only the stove left. The stove and a rock chimney."

Mac asked a question. "I understand the barn and haystacks were also burned. Any animals burned up in the barn?"

"None that I could tell. The milk cow was running loose, and the horses were found grazing along with the cattle. Story was that Bechtel had a sow with a litter. She hasn't been seen, far as I know.

"I saw no large bones in the mess of leavings. No stink of burned flesh. Of course, the rain might've washed the stink.

"Onliest thing that seemed strange. Bechtel looked to be a neat kind of man, with everything in its place. But on the ground beside the burned barn was a set of unburned harness. If Bechtel was using his team the day before, why didn't he hang up the harness? I got no answer to that."

It was Jeremiah's turn again. "What motive do you see for this crime, Sheriff? Why would anyone want to murder a man and his wife and child and burn them out of their home and ranch? Why would anyone want to do that?"

The sheriff had his own suspicions to that very question, but a troublesome friendship kept him from looking directly at it.

"The onliest ones I can see that benefited from the whole thing is the Stringfellow bunch. Still, that's a heavy accusation to lay on a man. I've made no such suggestion to Stringfellow nor anyone else."

There was silence in the little room for a couple of minutes, each man studying the other.

Finally, the sheriff said, "Look, men, I know full well how this all looks. But you got to understand. I'm just a small-time sheriff in a mostly peaceful, nowhere village. I'm hired to keep the odd drunk under control and to keep the population of stray dogs down to manageable numbers. I look into a lost animal once in a while, wondering all the time if we're dealing with a strayed cow or a rustler. So far, they've all been strays.

"I didn't know what else to do. That's why I wrote to the marshal up to Denver."

Mac sat up straighter, surprised at this statement. The marshal had said nothing of that.

"You're telling us it was you who wrote to the marshal?"

"Telling you straight. Look, I don't know if there was murder done that night or no. Stringfellow said they buried some bones dug up under the kitchen leavings. Maybe they did, and maybe they didn't. What I do know is that there was a nice young family living there after Old Man Bechtel died. I'm hoping they just rode away for some reason, although I can't think why they would.

"What is for sure is that the cabin and barn were burned. I'll welcome whatever help you can offer.

"I'm sure old Windy out there told you I'm lazy and not much as a sheriff. Well, I own up to a part of that, but after too many wrecks on too many bad riding animals, I couldn't hold a ranch job anymore. This looked like a simple enough way to ease into old age, and it was, until that night."

Mac mellowed just a bit. "You want to tell us a name, Sheriff?"

"Most folks just call me 'Burns.' Full name is Dirk Burns. That's not a name my pa would recognize, but it'll do."

Mac stood up. "Sheriff Burns, I'd like it if you were to get your horse. We'll need you to show us the way."

The sheriff gave his first half-smile. "I'll gladly ride with you, but you don't need me. You rode right past the place on your way here, or at least the trail into the ranch. You just ride back about seven, eight miles and watch for a trail off to the right. There's only just the one. You follow along for another mile. Trail keeps going up into the hills. You take a short hook to your left, and you're there."

19

Fremont County

THE THREE MCTAVISH BROTHERS RODE into the old Bechtel ranch yard two hours later, with their deputy badges pinned in plain sight. There appeared to be no one there, and except for some random clucking from the chickens, there was no sound. They eased to the ground and tied their animals to the garden fence.

Stepping toward the remains of the log cabin, they were challenged by a voice coming from the woods at the edge of the yard. It was a female voice, hidden, but clearly heard.

Mac turned toward the sound and lifted his hat and, holding it in front of him so the woman could see his face, answered, "Federal deputies, ma'am."

There was silence for another half-minute.

When the woman spoke again, she said, "That's easy enough to say. I see no reason to trust you until I'm sure." She didn't sound nervous, just cautious.

"What proof would satisfy you, ma'am? You can see that we're all wearing deputy badges." He paused for just a moment. "Would your husband be around, ma'am?"

"One shot from this gun I'm holding, and he'll come a-runnin'. There's been some awful bad things happenin'. I don't know as what you might be the ones what done it."

Mac looked at his bothers. He was getting nowhere talking with the woman. He couldn't blame her either, but they had to get on with it.

"We'd like to talk to your husband. ma'am, so you go ahead and pull that trigger. Just make awful sure you're pointing it at the clouds when you do it."

Bobby and Jeremiah spread out a bit, Bobby stepping behind the henhouse and Jeremiah moving toward the burned-out cabin.

The shot reverberated through the little ranch yard, and then all was silence. Everyone waited. Within three minutes, a male voice called from behind some brush on the rocky hillside behind the garden, "All right, you men. I've got you all spotted. Stand still and tell me who you are and what you want. Make the wrong move, and you're going to see for yourselves what's beyond the Great Divide."

Mac held his hat in one hand and lifted the other hand well away from his body. The brothers made no questionable moves. Bobby was watching the hillside closely, while Jeremiah was casting his eyes all around the yard to see if anyone else was sneaking in.

Mac spoke firmly, without shouting. "We're looking for Mr. Stringfellow. Mac McTavish here. My brothers, Bobby and Jeremiah." He pointed at Bobby. Jeremiah was behind him.

"Federal deputies, Mr. Stringfellow. At least, I'll assume that's who you are. The sheriff in Clarence told us a feller named Stringfellow had taken up the place."

There was silence again as the man thought this through.

Mac spoke again. "I understand your nervousness, Mr. Stringfellow. Murder and burning are nothing to think small about. But you got to take a chance on folks sooner or later. You can't live in the forest the rest of your life."

Suddenly another voice chimed in over the rapid clopping of a horse's hooves from the town road. The sheriff hollered, "It's all right, Noah. These men are who they say they are. Come down from that there hillside so's we can all have us a talk."

Slowly, Noah Stringfellow made his way down the slope. He had to walk around to the east for a hundred yards, to a gentler slope, before he could safely make it to the ranch yard. He held his carbine at the ready the entire time. None of the McTavishes took their eyes off him or his gun for even a moment. The woman was still off to the side in the trees, but the shot she took   told the men she was holding a pistol. She was pretty much out of good pistol range, so they concentrated on her husband.

The sheriff showed his frustration. "Stringfellow, step it up and get down here. And quit acting so skittish. There's law business to deal with here, and we need you to help with it."

Noah Stringfellow finally lowered his carbine to hang alongside his right leg while he studied Mac and the other deputies.

"So, I heard your talk, and I see those tin badges, and I heard our useless sheriff. Now say something that will convince me you are who you say you are."

Mac was ready to take a switch to the man, but he swallowed his impatience. "Is it possible, Mr. Stringfellow, that you've heard of the Bar-M ranch? It's not so very far from here. South and east a bit."

"I've heard of it. Biggest in the whole country, they say. First on the ground after the buffs were shot out, they say. Best stock, best land, most water, toughest riders. That's what folks say. Rich as Solomon, they say. Yah, I've heard of the Bar-M."

Mac thought out his words carefully. "I won't bother commenting on all that. But know this: the M in the brand stands for McTavish. I've already told you that I'm Mac McTavish. These with me are my brothers Bobby and Jeremiah. We've left the ranch at the special request of the marshal. We've been deputized to try to sort out this murder and burning."

Mac gave the reluctant rancher only a moment to think through what he'd been told, then spoke in that practiced voice that had controlled those around him since his Santa Fe Trail days.

"Now, put down that rifle and come up here. Get that woman out of the trees, too. And I don't want to see a weapon in her hands."

His voice of authority impressed the sheriff and shocked the rancher.

"Do it now."

Noah Stringfellow walked past Bobby, who had stepped from behind the chicken coop, and met his wife, slowly coming from the shelter of the trees. A black and white dog walked ahead of the woman, looking for a greeting from Noah.

Noah ignored the animal, put his arm around his wife's shoulder, and faced the gathered men.

Everyone was silent until the sheriff decided to try to ease the situation.

"Never heard you was married, Noah. That's one of the Bright girls, if'n I'm not mistaken."

Noah answered the sheriff without taking his eyes off Mac.

"Lois and I were married two weeks ago after Pa and I got back from making the deal for this ranch in Santa Fe."

The sheriff wanted more information.

"Why don't you go ahead and tell us how that deal come to be?"

Noah saw no choice. He slowly told them as much as he thought he could without bringing Casey into the story. He could probably get into trouble by lying to these lawmen. Truthfully, he was more in awe of Mac as the owner of the Bar-M than he was of the law.

He figured holding back was different than lying. Anyway, his first loyalty was to Casey. He had no belief that the murders and burning would ever be solved or Clover punished, no matter how many lawmen they dragged down here.

When he finished the story, everyone stood silently for a long while. It was a little off the immediate topic, but the sheriff asked, "I don't see no new cabin. Where y'all livin', you and Lois?"

"We pitched us a tent back in the trees. It'll do 'til the fall weather drives us out. We hope to have a cabin put up by then. I was up the hillside cuttin' trees for a cabin when y'all rode in."

Mac asked, "Have you moved anything out of the burned cabin or barn?"

"No one's touched it since the sheriff poked all through it with a shovel. Pa and me, we pulled the big stove out before the sheriff got here. Set the stove up in the bush beside our tent. Took a sight of cleaning, but it's usable."

"The sheriff says you found some bones and buried them."

"I did. That was the first day after the fire. The rain cooled the coals down enough so's we could go through the mess, Pa and me. Didn't find much. I don't have any idea how much fire it takes to burn up a body or the bones, but all we found were trapped under the tipped-over stove. Protected a bit, I'd guess. That was only parts of bones. There was nothing looking like hide nor hair nor clothing. Couldn't tell if it was a man or a woman. The smallest were surely the boy, though."

That information sobered the group, and silence followed.

Jeremiah quietly asked, "What did you do with what you found?"

Noah turned to look at Jeremiah and then back at Mac.

"Dug a little hole back in the trees. Wasn't much to bury, so it didn't take much of a hole. Put a wood cross over the spot, made from a couple of tied-together aspen sticks. There wasn't no lumber around that hadn't been burned in the fire.

"Hardest thing I ever done was dig out and then bury them bones, me seein' Casey and Florence and the little boy in my imagination the whole time. Hope to never do anything like that ever again."

Allowing enough time for everyone to absorb this information, Mac held his silence. The investigation of murder was new to Mac. He hoped he wouldn't be a deputy long enough for it to get old.

20

Fremont County

BOBBY, ALWAYS ONE TO DIVE RIGHT IN, asked, "Do you have any suspicions you need to tell us about, Mr. Stringfellow?"

Noah hesitated, kicking his foot in the grass. He studied the sheriff and then looked back at Mac.

An idea he wasn't comfortable with bloomed in Mac's mind. He looked around the old ranch site, buying some time to think, and then glanced at the sheriff.

He finally turned to the sheriff and said, "Sheriff Burns, I believe we can take it from here. If we need anything more from you, we'll ride back into town. Thank you for coming out. Your arrival eased the situation some. I'm sure your services are needed back in town."

Mac turned his back on him as if the man were dismissed.

The sheriff hesitated, wishful to stay and hear whatever else might be said, but he finally climbed onto his horse and rode away at a slow walk.

Mac looked at Lois. "Mrs. Stringfellow, do you have that old stove working to where you might be able to boil up a pot of coffee?"

Lois Stringfellow took the hint and wordlessly turned to the trail that led to the tent and the old stove.

Mac said, "Boys, why don't you take a ride around, maybe scout through the bush a bit? It's too late to look for tracks, but you might find scarring or some unusual marks on the rocks or in the grass on the upper hills. The murderers had to get in and out of this place somehow. It's not likely they came right down the road."

Noah spoke up, looking at Bobby and Jeremiah. "You might want to take a look at the gully that runs off to the east there." He pointed out the direction. "It's farther up the hill and east of where I'm working."

He hesitated for a moment as if thinking. There were all kinds of implications to what he needed to say, and his first concern was protecting Casey. If he was aware of the sheriff's effort to pin suspicion on him and his family, he showed no sign of it. His biggest concern was the evidence that would point directly at the Clover ranch. That same evidence could also bounce back to point at the B-Bar and the Stringfellows.

Having these federal officers see the two dead Clover horses could open up two or three lines of inquiry. What were the animals doing on the Bechtel ranch? Who killed them? When? Was this the work of Clover, or Bechtel or, perhaps one of the Stringfellows? Or was it someone else altogether?

How would these deputies read the sign? He could easily see how he or his family could be implicated, but the deputies were sure to find the dead horses. The stink would lead them right to the location if nothing else did. It would be better if they heard it from him first.

He turned again to Mac. Bobby and Jeremiah were still listening.

"Dog came down to the tent some little while ago, stinking of death. Terrible smell. He was running around, all excited. I didn't know what else to do, so I waved him away and told him to git.

"I can't explain how a dog thinks, but that black and white mongrel took off a-runnin'. Run right up that low slope you see over there. Just kept on a-goin', barkin' 'n yappin' 'n lookin' back to see if I was followin'.

"I couldn't keep up, but he kept turnin' and waitin' for me, as if he wanted to show me something. Took me right up to that little gully I just told you about. Two dead horses lay near the bottom, as if they'd been slid over the side. Terrible smell. Might be some evidence there you'd wish to take note of."

After Bobby and Jeremiah had ridden off, Mac said, "Noah, why don't you show me around here a bit? You get your horse. I'd like to see your stock, your land layout, your borders, and whatever else you think might tell me something."

Once the two men were saddled and riding, Mac quietly said, "Noah, you're holding back something. The sheriff's gone back to town, and the boys are off up the hillside. It's just you and me. Talk to me."

After a short silence, Noah pulled his horse to a stop. They had ridden clear of the trees and the open grazing land lay before them, green and lush and well-watered by the frequent showers. A nice herd of white face cattle was lazily grazing.

Noah slumped in his saddle and turned to Mac. He was clearly uncomfortable with what he felt he had to say.

"Clover Ranch joins us along the east boundary. Herb Clover has always wanted this spread. Thinks of himself as a big man needin' a big ranch and a big herd.

"Randolph Bechtel, the original owner of the B-Bar, he put up with threats, cut fences, run-off cattle, and more threats, all done by Clover or his men. Came near to driving Randolph crazy. He feared what Clover might do next.

"Pa figures now, looking back, that us and a few of the other ranchers should have come up with some way to let Clover know he was over the line. We all knew what he was doing. Trouble is, that's not the way of ranching country. Man's expected to stand up fer himself. But Bechtel, he was a peaceful man. No match fer an aggressive rancher like Clover."

Mac asked, "What about the sheriff?"

"That's been a problem from the start. Dirk Burns ain't a bad man. He's just weak. Best friends with Herb Clover. Wouldn't do anything about the threats and such. Pa talked to him once about the situation. Sheriff said that if there was a problem, Bechtel should come himself. Bechtel never did, but what he did do was write up a will and added a document to it outlining what was to be done with the ranch if he was to die. Left the document with Pa. The will was with a lawyer in Santa Fe.

"When the old man did die, the ranch was taken over by young Bechtel, Casey by name. Him and his wife and their little boy. They were a while gettin' here. Took some time to get news down to Santa Fe, to that lawyer. Pa and us took care of the herd during that time.

"After the fire, Pa figured that lawyer had to get involved again. The document says to sell to whoever has the money but to never let the B-Bar fall into Clover hands. The lawyer apparently had instructions from Bechtel about what to do with the money."

Mac had carefully watched Noah as he spoke. If facial expressions could be trusted, Mac figured he was listening to an honest man.

"Clover given you any problem since you took over?"

"None at all. I figure he knows Pa and us boys won't put up with it."

Mac changed the direction of the talk just a bit.

"And you're saying the sheriff knew about the harassment but did nothing because of his friendship with Clover?"

"Can't figure no other reason why he didn't act. Of course, it's common for men on this frontier to take care of their own problems. The trouble with that, beyond Bechtel being a peaceful man, is there was one middle age man against Clover and all his crew. Without a shootin', there wasn't much Bechtel could do. It was really the sheriff's job."

21

Fremont County

MAC AND NOAH WERE SITTING ON THE grass, leaning against a couple of trees when Bobby and Jeremiah rode into the yard. They stepped to the ground and settled onto the grass as well. Lois brought the coffee pot and a couple of mugs. She had kept out of the conversation, busying herself at the tent and stove.

Mac just looked at his brothers, knowing they would speak when they were ready. Mac knew they might be holding back because of Noah Stringfellow.

Bobby glanced at Jeremiah and nodded just a bit. Jeremiah took the hint.

"Found the gully. You're certainly right about the stink. Impossible to miss that. Two horses, pretty much rotted down, so I expect the stink will soon be gone.

"Strange thing, though. One leg was pulled away from the rest of the pile. Exposed the brands on both animals. Clover. Those were Clover animals."

Looking hard at Noah, he asked, "You pull that leg out of the pile, Noah?"

"Never climbed down to them. Seein' and smellin' from the top was more than I wanted. I saw those brands, though. That's why I told you about them."

Jeremiah nodded his acceptance of that statement and turned to Bobby.

Bobby said, "Found something else, too. Big aspen grove up there. Do you know that grove, Noah?"

Noah answered, "I know it. Ain't been up that far in a good long while. No reason to go there. Nothin' I want up there, and I'm too busy to just be explorin' around. Why? What did you find that makes you mention it?"

Bobby, still studying hard on Noah Stringfellow, said, "Found a grave. Two graves, actually. Just the one hole, but two bodies. Again, it was the smell that caught our attention. You never smelled that grave, Noah? You nor your dog, neither one?"

"Never did. That's a bit of a climb from here. And like I said, there's nothin' up there I want nor need."

Jeremiah took over the telling. "Grave had been disturbed recently. We could see where it had been dug over and refilled. But the refilling was done hastily and carelessly, as if someone was in a rush to get shut of the place. Looks like maybe a coyote was scratching around too, exposing enough to allow the odor to make itself known.

"You seen any strangers over this way, Mr. Stringfellow?"

Noah had expected some suspicion to come his way. He was the one who finally benefitted from the death of both the Bechtel men, and he was the one who spent all his time here. He could see how the finger could easily point to him. He shook his head.

"We seldom see anyone here. Can't see nor hear the road. Anyone we see has to be right here on the B-Bar. We're pretty isolated by hills and bush."

Mac stood up and flipped the dregs of his coffee into the bush behind him. "Finish up that coffee, boys. I think we're about done here."

He spoke to Noah. "Noah, I'll be wanting to see that document you say Bechtel left with your Pa. Do you have it here?"

"Pa has it in his strongbox up to the home place."

Mac had expected that answer. "We'll need you to take us to the home place, Noah. We'll go now."

Noah cleared a stirrup so Lois could climb up behind him for the short ride up the trail. "I expect we're safe enough down there, but we aren't takin' chances until some of this mess is behind us. I don't like to leave Lois alone."

A short explanation by Noah had Zeb Stringfellow digging out the document. Mac asked for a sheet of paper, and with a pencil he found in a jacket pocket, he made a copy of the document. Zeb returned the original to the strongbox. The visit was kept short. Mac wanted to be back in the little town in time to talk more with the sheriff. He thought bringing out the lawman's relationship with Herb Clover might shed some light on the sheriff's actions. It did, but not much.

The next morning, after a night in what passed for a hotel, the three deputies rode into the Clover ranch yard. They followed the clanking of steel on steel and found Herb Clover in the blacksmith shop. He had taken off his shirt in the stifling heat.

Mac waited until Clover pushed the item he was working on back into the hot coals. Clover had seen the men ride up, but he didn't stop his work or acknowledge them. He jiggled the steel piece through the coals a couple of times and then pulled it out and onto the anvil. He picked up his hammer as if he was going to continue to ignore his visitors.

Mac said, "Put it down Mr. Clover. We have to talk."

Clover gave Mac a menacing look and stuck the hot iron with the hammer. Mac reached his hand toward the rancher, but Clover pulled his arm back as if to threaten Mac with the hammer. That was a mistake. In spite of his slimness and mostly gentle manner, Mac McTavish was widely known as one of the strongest men in the area.

Without seeming to hurry, Mac reached out and grasped Clover's upraised wrist. Clover tried to bring the hammer down, but Mac's grip was like a vice.

Mac said, "I expect you already know who we are, Mr. Clover. We're going to talk, make no mistake about that. It might just as well be now, and it might as well be peaceful. But just so you understand, if you threaten me again, hammer or no hammer, I'll break this arm. Now, drop the hammer and settle down."

Clover was still belligerent. "I got nothing to say, and I'm busy. Got a ranch to run."

"So have I, Mr. Clover. And a lot more ranch and a lot more work than this little show of yours.

But we're here to solve a murder and burning, and we're going to get 'er done. In fact, we won't stop until we have a guilty party either in prison or in a grave after a hanging. Your actions make me think you have a whole lot to hide. Now, do you want to talk, or do you want me to arrest you and haul you to Denver where the marshal can question you proper?"

"You got no cause to arrest me. You can't do it."

Mac forced a smile. He still held Clover's wrist even though the hammer now lay on the floor, and they still stood eye to eye. "Oh, but you're wrong. I can arrest anyone I have enough suspicion of, and right now you're on the top of my list. You might want to change your attitude."

Clover relaxed his tense muscles, but Mac held on until he was convinced the rancher was settling down. It took nearly a full minute. Finally, the four men were able to step out of the hot smithy and into the shade of a nearby wagon shed. Clover picked up his shirt on the way out.

Mac skipped the introductions, figuring the sheriff had been out for a visit with his friend. He would have told Clover who to expect a visit from. There was no other reasonable explanation for the poor greeting afforded them.

Mac started right in with questioning the belligerent man, hoping to shock him into saying something incriminating.

"Found two of your horses. Dead. Clover brand easily seen. Pushed into a gully above the B-Bar. How do you explain that, Mr. Clover?"

Clover fidgeted for a bit, looking for a way to put a bit of space between himself and the three deputies crowding him. Every time he moved either Bobby or Jeremiah or Mac inched closer.

"I have a lot of horses. Might not miss one or two until we bring them all in for winter feeding. Maybe you should ask Stringfellow. He's the one taken over that place. Could be he stole them."

Jeremiah laughed. "Now, Mr. Clover, that makes no sense at all. Why would a man with a pasture full of horses steal two of yours, then shoot them and dump them on his own ranch?"

Clover had nothing to say.

Bobby said, "Mr. Clover, I noticed when you had your shirt off that you have a bullet wound high up on your left arm. I'd say it's recent, no more than a month or two. Not fully healed yet. Looks like a nasty wound. Someone shoot you, Mr. Clover?"

Again, Clover had nothing to say.

Mac figured they were wasting their time, but he tried a different approach. "I understand you're real tight with the sheriff. He ride out here last night to tell you we would be coming to see you?"

Clover tried to hold his stare but finally swung his eyes to the ground.

"I need an answer to that question, Clover. I need it now, and I need it honest."

Almost smirking in his belligerence, Clover said, "Friend of mine. He might have come for a visit. Nothing wrong with that."

Mac was finished wasting time on the rancher, but he wasn't finished on the Clover Ranch.

"Mr. Clover, we'll be talking to your riders. Where will we find your foreman?"

"Don't have one. Waste of money. I manage my own crew."

"Ok, it's near lunchtime. I see a couple of men just corralled their horses. I want you to go to your house, and don't come back out until we're gone. And just to be sure you know the way, Bobby and Jeremiah will walk along with you."

It was an unhappy rancher who walked to the house between the two deputies. Mac went to the cookhouse to ask some questions of the cook. He introduced himself and accepted a cup of coffee.

"May I ask you a couple of questions?"

"Ask away, but I can't stop my work. Got a crew of locusts expected here any time. If I don't have grub ready, they're likely to hang me from the loft door."

Mac laughed, sipping his coffee. "Sounds like

my ranch. Nothing gets in the way of feeding time."

The cook stopped long enough to ask, "It true what was said? You really Mac from the Bar-M?"

"I am. I just took on this deputy thing because the marshal asked me for a favor. Now, what can you tell me? What's been going on around here?"

The cook said, "You got to understand, Mac. I ride for the brand just as much as the cowboys. The day I start slandering the ranch is the day I need to ride off."

"I understand that, and I appreciate it. I'm not asking for gossip or slander. I just need whatever will help me solve a burning and a brutal murder. Just tell me this: have you fed any men recently who were not on the regular payroll?"

"I can answer that because it's common knowledge around the ranch. Yes, five strangers rode in a number of weeks back. Had one dinner here in the cookhouse. Fed them after the regular hands were done. They hung around until late that evening, then saddled up and rode off. Never saw nor heard from them again."

"Get any names?"

The cook thought back. "There was a Sandy. One called Montana. That's an easy one to remember. Might have been a Sid. Can't think of any others."

Mac was satisfied with that. He decided to leave the riders out of the investigation.

"Thanks. This is just between the two of us—I say nothing, you say nothing. One further thing: do you have any idea who shot your boss or when it happened?"

The cook was clearly uncomfortable with the question, and he was slow to answer. "You're getting right close to my tolerance point there, Mac. I'll tell you this much. It happened when those others were here. Have no idea who done it." He turned to his cooking pots, putting his back to Mac.

Mac thumbed his hat a bit in respect for the aging man. "Thanks again. Take care. You ever find yourself riding our way, you drop in at the Bar-M. There'll be a welcome for you."

The cook acted as if he didn't hear. Mac smiled a bit to himself and walked out.

22

Bar-M Ranch

THE THREE DEPUTIES DIDN'T GO BACK to Clarence since they figured the sheriff had told all he knew or was willing to tell. As it was just coming on to the noon hour, they hoped to get a far piece down the road toward home before the sun was spent for the day.

Mac asked, "Either of you in real need of a noon meal? Personally, I'd rather make the miles."

It was agreed, and they kicked their horses into a mile-eating trot. At a small stream about three hours later, they stopped to rest and water the animals and took on a bit of grub from their saddlebags.

As they were standing around stretching their legs, Bobby fished in the pocket of his cowhide vest and held a small object out to Mac. "Found this in a pile of deer leavings up past that grave we talked about."

Mac took the object and turned it over in his hand. "Arrowhead. Not like any I've ever seen before. What's your thought?"

"That little piece of stone was wedged tight in a hip. The inside of the joint. We kind of figured the arrow must have gone right through the softer flesh and lodged tight. No shaft attached. It must have come loose when the shooter tried to pull the arrow back out. The thing is, there's no Indian activity up this way that I know of."

Without lifting his eyes from the arrowhead, Mac said, "C'mon, out with it. What's the rest of your thought?"

"I've been considering that feller we met on the ride up here. Had a bow fixed under the fender on his saddle. Was quite proud of bringing down a buck. Now, how many folks do you think are riding around the country with a bow and arrows who brought down a buck at just about the time we're talking about?"

Mac and Jeremiah were silent, studying their brother.

Mac finally spoke. "That's good thinking there, Bobby. Might be you learned a few things about lawing down there in Santa Fe. While Jeremiah was keeping the mayor's daughter from troubling you, I mean."

Bobby chuckled, but Jeremiah said, "That's about all I want to hear about that. And not one word back at the ranch, not even in fun."

With no more talk, they mounted up and headed for home.

They rode into the Bar-M ranch yard about midafternoon the next day after suffering the stifling heat of the rocky valley the trail wound through. Mac was impressed by the upper grass-lands, mountain meadows folks like Stringfellow found and settled. Except for the isolation, it was good ranching country.

On arrival at the Bar-M, they turned their horses over to Pepe and made their way to the house. They were ready for a good meal and a sleep in their own beds. Margo chased them out of the house until they had had baths and changed their clothes.

An hour later, clean and refreshed, Bobby walked into the house. Looking around and wondering at the quiet, he asked Margo, "Where are Matty and Greta?"

"They went to visit the folks for a couple of days. It's a bit crowded here, what with Jessie and her kids and all. You'll probably want to take a ride up there after dinner."

A few minutes later, Margo went through the same explanation for Jeremiah. He looked at Bobby and grinned. "I ain't all that hungry."

The two brothers were on their way north within a few minutes. Pepe had picked out a couple of rested horses for them to switch their saddles to.

After the family dinner was completed and the kitchen cleaned up, Mac and Margo climbed their little hill. Mac explained what had happened on the trip. Margo, happy there had been no gunplay, held his hand and asked, "What's next?"

"I have to go to Denver to talk to the marshal. I'll stay home one day to sort out anything that needs attention on the ranch, then I'll take the steam cars to save time. I shouldn't be gone but one or two days."

Margo asked, "What about the boys? Are they going with you?"

Mac explained, "No, they've suggested that they leave this situation with me for a few days while they ride out to look for rustlers. The thing up at the burned ranch is already over two months old, so nothing is going to change now. A bit of time isn't going harm the investigation. I'm just hoping the marshal will be able to point me in a helpful direction. I'm pretty much lost at this lawman thing."

ARRIVING AT the senior McTavish farm, Bobby leaped off his horse and swung Matty in a circle, hugging her tightly. Jeremiah and Greta both looked at the antics with longing in their hearts and said a casual "hello" before Jeremiah shook his father's hand and hugged his mother.

The senior McTavishes were showing their age a bit. It had been a long time since Hiram, tall, lithe, and strong as an oak branch, and Della, painfully lanky from hard work and short rations over too many years, had sold out in Missouri, loaded their "keeping goods" on a wagon with the younger kids, and headed out to find Mac, who was known as "Walker" to the family. The meeting had led to back-breaking hard work and thousands of miles on a wagon seat, walking, or on horseback, but the profits from driving wild longhorns to market had left them with a life of relative ease since arriving in Colorado. They stood arm in arm, enjoying the boys' antics and hoping they would find a good reason to settle down within easy visiting distance of the family.

23

Custer and Huerfano Counties

THE TWO BROTHERS RODE BACK TO THE ranch the next morning to meet with Mac and make their plans for the trip south. Another report of rustling had filtered to them, this time from an angry small-time rancher who had arrived at Ad's trading post after a two-day trip from his holdings south of the Bar-M.

Without mentioning his relationship with Mac or the brothers, Ad said, "So tell me about this. I've heard other mentions of lost cattle, and it all seems to be happening in the southwest corner of the counties. Are your losses in large numbers, or are they picking a few here and there?"

The rancher settled down a bit when he realized that Ad was really interested. "The numbers ain't much if it was a big rancher sufferin' the loss, but Minnie and me, we dried out down south. Lost most everything we'd worked for. Barely had enough set by to pick up a little piece of ground between two big ranches. We got no more cows than it takes to squeeze out a bare existence. Can't afford to lose even a single critter."

Ad thought the man's fury was spent just with the telling of it. Thinking of passing the information on to Mac, he was pleased when the man continued his story.

"We need us some law down there. The big ranches, they either don't know about their losses until roundup, or them that do know, they send out a few crew riders to find the lost animals. I don't have a crew. Far as that goes, I never heard of any ranchers finding their stoled cattle, either.

"When you see Minnie and me over there, you're seein' the whole of the Lazy A. That's all there is, and that's all there's like to ever be."

He repeated, "We need us some law."

Ad said, "It was my understanding that some federal deputies were working down that way."

"If there are, I ain't never seen them nor heard nothing about them."

When Jessie showed up at the store the next day, he sent the information to Mac.

Mac, Bobby, and Jeremiah were sitting in the cookhouse after the crew left for their day's work.

Mac started the conversation. "You're on your own down there. No way to get word back here if you need help. You happen to be anywhere near Luke's place or one of the bigger ranches, you can hire whatever men you need from their crews if the men can be spared from ranch work. I'll guarantee to make up their wage. The marshal might not like it, but he'll approve the pay anyway. You happen to be to the west, your best bet for help will be the sheep camp. There's always a few men just hanging around out there, and Manuel's always ready to ride. There's still some around who don't take to Mexes. Any arrests done, you do them yourself.

After a bit more back and forth and finalizing their plans, Mac said, "One more thing. I don't trust those deputies the marshal sent down there. I have some doubts about the marshal himself, but there's nothing I can pick out to make me feel that way. Just a feeling, is all. You watch yourselves, and don't trust anyone more than necessary."

Bobby and Jeremiah were saddling up when Mac strolled over to the corral again. "The women all right at the folks while you're gone, or are they planning on coming back here?"

Bobby answered, "Matilda's happy with the folks. She prefers it a bit quieter, although she likes the ranch too. Don't know about Greta. She keeps talking about returning to some big city. Maybe even going back to Los Angeles. This sweet-talking brother of mine can't seem to corral her."

Jeremiah tightened his cinch before he answered, "Can't figure a woman. I've asked that girl to marry up with me a dozen times. Yesterday I even offered to move back to California if that was what she really wanted."

Bobby looked up in surprise. "What did she say to that?" The brothers had never been separated, and the thought troubled him.

Again Jeremiah was slow to answer. He leaned his arms on the saddle and looked over the animal at Mac and Bobby. "Said she's decided we should go ahead and get married. Said too, that she's come to enjoy the ranch. Said to forget going to a big city."

He let the silence stew for a moment.

"How you gonna figure a deal like that? I'm a long way from understanding women."

Bobby laughed and congratulated his brother. Mac just shook his head. Even after all the years of marriage, he chose to avoid a discussion on the matter.

He said, "Ride careful, you two," and walked away.

24

Denver

CASEY BECHTEL, NOW CALLING HIMSELF RALEIGH Cater, chose to continue on horseback rather than take the rails to Denver. There were two reasons for this decision. The first was that he had no desire to be seen or known or remembered. The second was that he intended to avoid baths, haircuts, and clean clothes until the task he had assigned himself was completed. If he was to fit in where he planned to go, he didn't want to arrive in new clothing, after a shave, a bath, and a haircut.

He had found a couple of names in the letters and scribbled-on scraps of paper taken from the bodies up on the hill, and he got confirmation of those names when he examined the gunbelts taken from the dead men. Scratched into the leather on the inside of each belt was the name of its owner. That the names matched the letters and scribbles assured Casey of their validity.

With his first look at Denver, he pulled his horse to a stop. From his vantage point at the top of a small rise, he started to doubt himself, wondering how he could ever complete his mission. This was no cattle-country small town where the good-old-boy sheriff sat on a ladderback chair with his thumbs hooked into his red galluses.

Denver was an up-and-coming rail, cattle, and mining center. Raleigh had no idea how many thousands of folks lived in the city, but it was the most he had ever seen.

The task ahead of him seemed overwhelming. He had no idea where to find what he was looking for, but the only way to end any search was to start it, so he did.

He worked his way through the city center where the streets were lined with brick and stone hotels, retail stores, theaters, and a host of other businesses and filled sidewalk to sidewalk with traffic of every description. He rode up one street and down the next until he started to see rough saloons and low-cost hotels.

He put his horse up at a shamble of a livery stable. The filthy hostler didn't bat an eye at Casey's appearance. He did a double-take when

Casey lifted the bow and hung it over the saddle horn, but he asked no questions. If this was the part of town where a man had to be cautious of his questions, he had found the right place.

Swinging his saddlebags over his left shoulder and carrying a small carpetbag in his left hand, his carbine hanging from his right hand, he left the livery stable. He strolled along the boardwalk until he came to a hotel that looked a bit better than some. He would count it a victory if the bed had clean sheets.

He checked in and went to his room. He had nothing to do until the dark of evening hid the griminess of the district he had chosen for his search. Not trusting the door lock, he wiggled a straight-back chair under the knob, then stretched out on the bed and slept.

Casey awoke in the early evening. The loud hammering on a piano and the periodic shrieks of saloon girls rose from the first floor to assault his ears. He swung his feet to the floor, and again rehearsed his plan. 'Visit saloons and dance halls. Drink very sparingly. Ask a few careful questions. Listen well. Do nothing that would cause anyone to remember him. Find the men who murdered his wife and son.'

He had some names firmly fixed in his mind, names taken from the letters and the gun belts.

Hoby Stepchuck. Clarence Addy. As he thought about the names again, he wanted to add "murderer" to each one. The problem with that was that Casey wished to draw no attention to himself. Any show of emotion or anger was sure to cause someone to see him and take note.

He left the gun belts rolled up in the carpetbag, and his carbine lying on the bed. There was talk about the larger towns and cities shying away from folks carrying arms on the city streets, and most saloon owners reinforced that with rules of their own. Casey had no intention of inviting a confrontation over his gun.

He started the search three blocks north of his hotel. Entering a saloon, he stepped to the bar and ordered a beer. He had no taste for harder drinks, and little enough for beer, but he sipped it while he listened to the talk around him. He sized up the two bartenders, trying to decide which one might be the more talkative.

Just as he was about the take the last mouthful from the beer stein, the barman he hoped to talk to asked, "Fill 'er up?"

Casey smiled and gave a small shrug. "Naw, but thanks. Just the one to cut some of the trail dust. Not really much of a drinking man unless it's coffee. I do enjoy my coffee."

The barman wiped the bar as he put Casey's

mug into the tub of water behind him. "Don't touch the stuff myself. Seen too much over my years on this side of the mahogany."

Casey felt that he wouldn't get a better chance. "Met a man up this way about a year ago. Thought I might look him up if he's still around. Happen you ever heard of Hoby Stepchuck? About my size. Moves around some. Thought he might be back in Denver. I'd buy him a drink if we should happen to meet."

The barman wiped the wood longer than was necessary, and finally glanced up at Casey. "Never heard of him. And that's the truth, not just careful talk."

He continued to wipe until he'd thought out his warning. "You be careful, friend. You'll fool some with the beard and the clothes, but I make you for a man on the hunt. You're not really comfortable in this bedlam, and you don't fit in too well. You don't have the lingo, and you're clearly new to the game."

He was still wiping the bar. "Watched you come in. You didn't look around the room for your man. Came straight to the bar. Still haven't looked around. I wish you luck on your search, but you be careful. Strange things happen along these streets. You watch yourself."

After the man moved away to pull a beer for

another drinker, Casey dropped a coin on the bar and made his way to the sidewalk.

Three evenings of wandering through more saloons than Casey cared to remember got him exactly nowhere. Neither name brought a positive response.

With nothing particular to do with his daylight hours, Casey wandered over to the livery and put in an hour brushing and grooming the horse. The hostler ignored him the whole while. With every inch of the horse shining and his saddle wiped down, Casey stepped toward the big double doors. In the fine summer weather, the doors were tied back. He suspected that in winter they would be closed tight against the snow and wind. With the heat of summer enveloping the city, it was hard to believe that in a few months there would be winter storms cascading down from the Rockies just west of this mile-high city, but he knew it was so.

He was about to walk past the hostler when the man spoke for the first time. "Stayin' fer a bit, young feller?"

Casey turned to the man. "A couple more days, maybe longer. Do you need some more money to hold the stall?"

"Naw. Long's I've got yer saddle and gear, yer not goin' nowhere without ya pays up first."

Casey wondered why he hadn't spoken to the old man before this time. Liverymen saw it all. Of course, the men he was seeking might use a different livery, but it wouldn't hurt to ask. There were three chairs by the big door, and the hostler was settled into one. Casey took the one farthest away from the man.

Without preamble, Casey said, "I'm a stranger in these parts. Been here just the twice, once coming and once going. About a year ago, for a day or two. I was bound to look for gold. Saw nuggets big as yer fist in my sleep. Just had to pick them up and haul them to the bank. I was going to be the richest man on the diggings. Of course, I knew nothing at all about finding gold. Thinking back now, it seems dumb. I was acting dumb as a fence post."

"Find any color?" The old man had heard it all before. He wasn't really interested in Casey's story, but he didn't mind visiting from time to time. He'd been known to pass on a piece of gossip gained through his random visits. Picked up the odd coin from appreciative men.

Casey shrugged without looking at the liveryman. "I panned up a bushel or two of sand and near wore out a hammer banging it against some rocky outgrowths, but nothing. I'd make more money working as clean-up man here in this livery. Come summer's end, I rode back down the hill feeling foolish, realizing that every inch of that hillside I was working had been gone over a hundred times by men who knew more about mineral than I ever would."

The two men sat silently.

The hostler finally asked, "You headin' back up the hill?"

Casey looked at him and laughed a little. "Yep, but this time I'm lookin' fer work. Maybe working for a big mine or clerking in a supply store. Anything that pays wages enough to keep me fed and clothed, and sheltered from the weather."

"Seen ya doin' a lot of perambulatin' around." The old man left the question unasked.

Casey thought out his words carefully. "Me and that horse, we've been on the trail for more than three weeks. The bed in that fleabag hotel sure is a comforting thing, and the bed and the café meals and the rest for the horse are worth a bit of a delay in my travels, but I'll be pulling out in a day or two.

"Met a feller here last time I was through here. I was pretty down on my luck after a summer picking up nuggets that vanished as I touched them. I was heading back to Santa Fe. He bought me a couple of meals and gave me a gold twenty for my trip. I didn't take him for a rich man either. Maybe just a man who'd been there and done some things, understanding how it could be.

"I sure appreciated his attitude. Thought I might try to locate him, or one of the others he had hanging with him.

"Anyone robbing me right now would make himself poor wages, but I saved a bit from a ranch job down south. Thought I might return the favor if I could find the gent or one of his friends."

The hostler said, "What name are ye lookin' fer? Might could be I've heard of him. See near everyone at a livery, ya waits long enough."

Casey carefully said, "I never thought of that. I've asked around in a few saloons with no luck. The gent that staked me was Hoby Stepchuck. There were a couple more fellas, but the only other name I remember is Clarence Addy. You ever heard those names?"

The liveryman was silent for so long Casey though the conversation was ended with poor results. Finally, the old man said, "Never heard of ol' Hoby stakin' no one before. Ya must'a looked about whipped down ta a nub ta get his sympathy. That's a hard man, him and that whole crowd he runs with. Ain't seen Hoby for some time now. Couple of months, I'd say.

"Clarence ain't around neither. Him and Hoby

rode off back in the early spring, them and a couple or three of their friends. Hoby never would talk 'bout their reasons for ridin' out, but every few weeks, they'd come in ta have their horses shod. Old Buster back there does a shoein' job like no other. Good at it, he is.

"Ain't seen neither Hoby nor Clarence since they rode out."

Casey did his best to play it casual. "Well, perhaps I'll catch up to them if ever I find myself back in Denver."

He waited, hoping the old man's ear for gossip was stronger than his leanings toward secrecy. It took a while.

Finally, the silence was broken. "Ya might try down ta the Silver Arrow. Kind of a dump of a place. Buildin's near fallin' down. Spect it will one a these days, but those boys liked it fer some reason. Might'a been Rose 'er Maggie what attracted them. Sisters, they are. They own the joint. Serve up water-cut booze 'n sour beer. Do a couple of other things too, so's I'm told. Anyway, the boys like 'em.

"Ya might look around fer a feller named Sandy. Don't know any last names. This Sandy, big man, cruel eyes—he was tight with Hoby. Kinda run things, them two. Couple of others too—Sid 'n Montana. They sort of hung around and did what the other two told 'em ta do."

Casey kept the conversation going for a while, asking the old-timer about his mining and range experiences, but finally, the talk petered out. Casey stood and stretched. "Might just as well see what Bertha has on the stove for this evening. Can you join me over to the café, or do you have to stay here?"

"Na. You go ahead, young feller. I make out just fine on my little stove in the office here."

The liveryman gave Casey a hard look. "You're playin' a dangerous game there, youngster. Pays ta be extra careful. Couple folks 'v noticed your wanderings. Careful's the word."

25

Custer and Huerfano Counties

BOBBY AND JEREMIAH STOCKED UP WITH traveling supplies at Ad's. Again, the family had a laughter-filled lunch. On the way to the southwest ranching area, they figured they could spare the time for a quick visit with Margo's brother Bill, and then, after winding through miles of the Bar-M, cut south and west for a visit with their old friend Luke. In both places, they were greeted with handshakes from the men and hugs from the women. They stayed overnight with Luke and then headed west, up and over a small range of rough hills. The trail they followed led them into the Bar-M's sheep camp.

Bobby, always laughing and making friends, greeted the women working in the tent kitchen and teased the kids running every which way through the camp. Then he sighted a familiar rider on the other side of the camp area.

He shouted out "Hola, mi amigo Manuel. How is it possible that Imelda has not shot you yet?"

Many eyes turned to see who was shouting.

Manuel eased sidewise in his saddle and grinned at the sight of the two brothers. Reining his horse around, he trotted toward the men.

"Hola, mis amigos," he shouted over the din of the camp. He was grinning ear to ear. "But you are much mistaken, Bobby. Why should Imelda shoot me? Where would she find another even half so good? Am I not the best husband in the whole land? The strongest, the smartest, the most handsome, and the best lover, kind and patient, even when she is difficult to live with? All the women look at their husbands and wish they were Imelda."

Several women laughed and shook their heads. Imelda made her way out of the tent. She looked first at her husband and then at the brothers.

"Hola, Bobby. *Hola,* Jeremiah. Don't you believe what this lazy husband of mine says. I would trade him for a spotted pony if I could find some-one foolish enough to offer the deal."

Manuel had long thought that Imelda had spent too many years among the free-talking American women. She was copying their speech and mannerisms. He feared it was too late to change back to the obedient girl he had married so many years before. Secretly he liked the freedom the new Imelda showed to the world, but he would never own up to it.

Laughing even louder, Bobby slid off his horse and gave the woman a friendly hug, swinging her completely around in a circle. He set her feet back on the ground as Manuel was jumping from his horse. The two men greeted each other with a firm handshake.

Bobby said, "If I was not already a married man, I just might load Imelda on the back of my pony and run off with her."

Imelda screamed, "Bobby, you are a married man?"

"I am. You waited too long, Imelda. Now you will never get shut of this poor excuse for a husband."

"You must come and sit in the shade of the kitchen. I need to hear all about it."

Looking at this hard-working couple who had been family friends for so many years, and knowing the challenges working for the Bar-M had brought into their lives, Bobby thought they hadn't changed hardly at all. Manuel was still strong and lean, his eyes ever alert for trouble. Imelda had put on a bit of weight, but just enough to enhance her mature beauty.

The old friends talked their way through a good part of the morning. Jeremiah was impatient to get down to serious matters. After stuffing themselves on an excellent lunch, Jeremiah finally grabbed the opportunity to tell Manuel about their new job and their need for a couple of men to help in the search for rustlers.

Manuel grinned, thinking of the possibility of getting away from the sheep camp for a week or two.

"I have heard nothing of rustling or of federal deputies. Not many come to our camp. Is not good, this stealing of cattle. Next they will be stealing our sheep."

Manuel, a cattleman at heart, hid his grin, looking down at the table and shaking his head sadly as he said this.

Bobby laughed. "Ain't no rustler so low-down as to steal sheep, *amigo.*"

Manuel ignored the comment and came back with, "You will stay here tonight. We visit, we eat, we sleep. Tomorrow I ride with you. We have many good men here. I will pick two others. We find these stealers of cattle."

Remembering Mac's warning about ranchers who still distrusted Mexicans, Jeremiah said, "You will be welcome. The pay is small, but there will be something coming at the end of the ride.

You must let the two of us do the talking. And if there are arrests to be made, Bobby or I will see to it."

Manuel grinned at Jeremiah. "Sí, amigo, I understand. You and Bobby have the badges. All Manuel has is a gun. Or maybe two or three guns. It is good."

Jeremiah's shoulders slumped. He was hoping that taking these men with them would not turn out to be a mistake. He had watched Manuel and the others deal with threats on their trip west, with all their wagons, their remuda, and their thousands of cattle. Manuel could be a fierce and unforgiving fighter. He was older now, but it didn't seem like he had backed off any from his old attitudes. One change was evident, though. When they first met Manuel, he had been a brooding, angry young man, avoiding contact with all but fellow Mexicans, and seemingly seeking a fight every chance he got. He had backed down from his reclusive stand, at least.

As they were gearing up to leave the next morning, Manuel approached the brothers with two men riding beside him.

"It is a fine morning to ride. Diego and Rafael, they will ride with us. They are glad to be away from the sheep for a few days, and perhaps away from unhappy wives."

Manuel grinned when the men did not dispute his words.

By noon the next day, they had stopped at two ranches, asking about lost animals and making note of the names of the ranchers and the grass they claimed. None of them were fenced, so rustling would take little effort in these hill-surrounded grasslands.

Both ranches had lost cattle, and both had ridden out to search. Neither had had any success.

One man said, "Easy to lose cattle up in them hills. Hard to track. Nothing but rock and cactus in some places. Canyons and cut-backs just about everywhere you care to look, with enough small, hidden meadows to hold stolen animals on with little fear of being found out. Those meadows are nowhere big enough to ranch on, but a rustler could hold a few head in secret for quite some time."

At the third stop, they talked to a man named Buse Nordley. They sat their horses in a semi-circle, facing the man.

"Yes, I've lost cattle. Couple hundred, by a rough count. Won't really know until fall roundup, but more gone than this small ranch can afford. There's no doubt about that."

Jeremiah started asking for details, but the man stopped him.

"Why don't you boys step down and tie your animals off over there?"

He pointed at a small copse of trees with a tie rack built under the wide branches.

"It's comin' near dinner hour. I'll go tell the cook to throw a little more water in the soup. You fellers find some shade for yourselves. I'll be right back."

An hour of questions and answers left the deputies with a better understanding of the lay of the land in the southwest district but no real insight into where the rustlers were holding the cattle. Where they were finding a market was also a mystery.

Jeremiah changed the direction of the talk just a bit.

"There's been three other federal deputies working down this way for a while now. Have you seen anything of them?"

Rancher Nordley shook his head. "Never seen hide nor hair of any law, now or any time in the past. We're on our own down here. Big country, but not a lot of people. No real settlements, just a small trading post down on the border that's nowhere big enough to call a town. No elected sheriff or marshal. What lawin' gets done, we do ourselves."

Nordley seemed to have something else to say, so Bobby and Jeremiah waited.

Finally, the rancher seemed to settle his thoughts. Talking about another man on this frontier could lead to all kinds of misunderstanding and misery, so Nordley kept his speech mild and made no real accusations.

"Except for Oscar Gladsome over there at the Double G always pushing for more grass, we've had no real troubles the past three, four years."

Jeremiah dropped to his knees in the grass and spread out a military map the Denver deputy marshal had given Mac.

"Mr. Nordley, do you know the country well enough to sketch your holding on this map?"

Nordley dropped to his knees beside Jeremiah. He was a long time staring at the squiggly lines the military used to outline hills, mountains, and watercourses, dragging his finger along each one as he considered it. The other ranchers visited by the deputies had done the same, finally penciling in what they believed to be their holdings. The scale of the map was not helpful for drawing the limits of the ranches, but it was good enough to show the possible trails into the hills from each ranch.

Like many western families, the Nordley clan was anxious for outside news or just for a visit with new folks. Nordley invited them all onto the house's veranda after taking their dinner in the cookhouse, and Mrs. Nordley served coffee. Jeremiah's estimation of Nordley was raised several notches when the rancher included the Mexicans. Not all would consider them to be equals.

Manuel and his two chosen riding partners drank their coffee and ate the cake Mrs. Nordley served up. Manuel then got to his feet.

"We thank you most kindly, ma'am. Now I think my friends and I will see to the horses. They worked very hard today. We will clean them up and take them again to the water."

Buse Nordley stood and shook each man's hand. "It's good to have you with us. We'll see you at breakfast."

When the men were gone, Mrs. Nordley said, "Manuel speaks very good English. He seems like a gentleman."

Jeremiah pictured one particular fight the travelers had gotten mixed up in on the way West. Manual had been like a whirling dervish, shouting and shooting until the raiders galloped off for the hills, leaving three dead behind. There had been nothing at all gentlemanly about Manuel during those few frantic minutes.

"Manuel and his family came West with our family, and we've been together over fifteen years. His mother is our doctor. A *curandero* in the old Mexican style, but with some American teaching as well. Good woman to have around. Manuel and his wife now run the Bar-M sheep camp north of here. He'd rather fight than work, so we brought him along."

The deputies worked their way west after leaving the Nordley Ranch the next morning. It wasn't many miles before they started into higher elevation and rougher land. There was still enough grass to attract a rancher, but now it was scattered among the hills and small patches of forest. The cactus thinned as pines and brush took over.

Many miles later, one small holding was spotted off to the north perhaps two miles. They wouldn't have even noticed the place, tucked into the hills like it was, except Manuel had decided to ride north while he signaled his two riding partners to head south, looking for the tracks of driven cattle.

At Manuel's call, they turned their horses north to angle toward the ranch. When they were close enough to see the layout, they pulled to a stop.

Manuel grinned at the thought of seeing some action. "I think so this is your rustler headquarters. You see? The cabin is a shack, no more. No barn. No sign of cattle. No sign of a women. But many corrals. Why so many corrals?"

The five riders pulled closer together while they considered what they saw.

Bobby said, "Tight corner to lay claim to if a man was running cattle. Hills on three sides, and more rocks and cactus than grass. That might be a running stream behind the house. Hard to tell for sure. I'm figuring we need to ride in slowly, watching for trouble. Manuel may very well be correct."

As they nudged their horses into a slow walk, Jeremiah said, "The less said, the better. We'll tell them nothing about being deputies. We'll tell them we're just moseying around looking for opportunities.

At a gentle walk, they approached the isolated holding. They had each pulled their carbines, holding them butt-down on their right thighs, ready for trouble.

When they got within shouting distance, Bobby hollered, "Hello the house."

It took a minute, but finally, the door opened, and a man stepped onto the small, uncovered porch. He was in his stocking feet, and his shirt-tail hung loose. He leaned against a doorpost and sipped from a mug of coffee. The man said nothing, simply watching the five riders approach.

Pulling to a stop a safe distance from the house, Bobby said, "Saw your layout. Thought we might find some water for the horses."

The casual coffee drinker pointed to the side of the house with the mug. "Take all you want."

Four of the riders waded their horses across the little stream before turning them back toward the house. Only then did they allow the animals to drink. Manuel, always on the alert, kept his horse pointing toward the bush behind the house, where he could scan the hillsides and the scattered trees and shrubbery.

The man at the house seemed in no hurry to start a conversation.

Bobby took the lead. "Tight corner you have here for a ranch. Must suit you though, else you wouldn't be here."

"Man can do what he wants in a free country."

Bobby grinned at the man's belligerence. "I suppose you're right about that. Still, and all, a passing stranger might wonder. No cattle anywhere around, but enough corrals for a busy stockyard in the big city. No sign of work being done. Ya, a man could wonder. I'm wondering a little myself."

"Well, when you're done watering them horses, you can just take your wondering with you and get yourselves gone."

Bobby was enjoying the word games. He also knew the game could turn serious mighty quickly if his and Manuel's suspicions were anywhere near true.

Bobby pushed his hat back a bit on his head and smiled at the man. "Can't help wonder what would keep a man, or a group of men, for that matter, back in a lost corner of the world like this. This ain't no way a cattle ranch, yet there's all them corrals."

He paused as if thinking as he swung his eyes around the setup.

"Now you take us, for example. We're just five men wandering the country lookin' for a chance. An opportunity, you might say. Man never knows where his next break will show up. Could be over south of here, down to Las Vegas. Could be over east into the Panhandle. Could be west across these here mountains into Utah. Comin' place, Utah. Right smart number of folks piling in to take up that desert land. Or it could be right here. Right here in this little sheltered and hidden corner."

Bobby made a show of stretching in the saddle while he looked all around.

"Yep, might could be a man would find his main chance right here in this hollow in the hills."

He looked sternly at the man in the doorway. "What do you think there, stranger? Is our next opportunity found right here?"

The man in the doorway was joined by another man. This one had his boots on and his shirt tucked in. Hanging low on his right hip was a pearl-handled .44.

"You men have made a mistake, but it's not too late to back out. We're federal deputies, down here working out a rustler problem. We don't need to have the likes of you underfoot while we do it. Unless you're the rustlers?"

A man could've counted to four or five before the talker continued, "But no, I figure you're too lazy to be rustlers. Thieves maybe, you and them Mexes, but not rustlers. Best you make your way to someplace where there's something to steal. There's little enough on any of these ranches to attract the likes of you. I'll give you another couple of minutes to step off your horses and get a drink for yourselves. Fill your canteens. Then I don't ever want to see you again. That understood?"

The men took their drinks two at a time while the others watched the house carefully. Manuel was still watching the brush and rocks around the clearing.

Bobby took his reins in his hands after he remounted his horse and turned toward the house. "Not too sure how you're figuring to catch rustlers while you're settin' around the shack drinking coffee, but that's your problem. We'll be riding."

He kicked his horse into a trot. Looking at the two men as he passed the house, he smiled. *"Hasta la vista, hombre. Ride with care."*

The men swung wide, keeping the house in sight but themselves out of pistol range.

An hour later and five miles farther west, the deputies stepped down from their horses and lit a small fire to make coffee. Jeremiah had been stewing on an idea since the evening before, and as they rode away from the little shack, he shared his thoughts with Bobby.

Bobby grinned and said, "Now, that there is a great idea. Why don't you put it to Manuel right away?"

While they were waiting for the coffee to come to a boil, Jeremiah said, "Manuel, I'd like to ask something of you boys. How would you feel about sending Diego and Rafael back to the sheep camp? If they would pick up two or three more men and a wagon and team, we would be better prepared for our work. If there is some rope at the camp, they could bring that along too. They should get back as quickly as they can. We will hang around here somewhere so they can find us."

Manuel thought about that and then turned to Diego and Rafael, repeating the thought in Spanish. The men both spoke some English, but

Manuel thought it best to make it clear. The two men simply nodded. They finished their coffee, mounted up, and rode off without a word.

26

Denver

Casey, knowing it was time to drop his Raleigh disguise and seek the assistance of the law, was eating his noon meal in the small chili house across the road from the livery. He was tired of eating poorly, and tired of pretending to be broke. The ranch-sale money was safely stowed in a bank, and the money he had taken from the raider's bodies was tucked inside a roll of cloth and belted around his waist under his shirt. He still had most of the funds unearthed from the root cellar after the fire, too.

He was tired of the dirty clothes. He was tired of the smell, and the itch, of his own body. And he was tired of the scruffy beard.

He would be glad to see the last of the company he'd been keeping for the past week. After he finished this meal, he would clear out of his hotel, saddle up, and disappear. With this miserable disguise gone, no one would ever see Raleigh again.

When he showed up as Casey, he hoped the change in his appearance would isolate him from those who were watching Raleigh and tracking his activities.

He had not yet completed the bowl of chili when the chair opposite him was pulled out and a man he remembered seeing before sat down. A big man with a no-nonsense look on his face. Casey sat very still, slowly lowering his spoon. He said nothing.

"Mac McTavish, Mr. Cater. We meet again."

The two men sat silently staring at each other. Casey pushed the spoon back into the chili and glanced to the door as if he were looking for a way out.

Mac saw Casey's eyes shift.

"I'm alone, Mr. Cater. Or would you rather I call you Mr. Bechtel?"

Casey sagged back in his chair, feeling total defeat. Was this the end of his sleuthing? His attempt to find some kind of justice for Florence and the boy? Could it really be ending this way— in a low-class Denver chili joint? Was he to fail at this the way he had failed to protect his family?

He said nothing, but for Mac, Casey's silence and the sag in his facial expression was enough proof of his identity.

Mac leaned both elbows on the table. "Finish your chili, and we'll find somewhere to talk."

"I'm done. It ain't rightly fit to eat anyway."

Mac looked around the drab little café. Although he didn't have full knowledge of Casey's actions, he had to admire his disguise and his determination.

Casey, remembering that Mac was a federal deputy, said, "I'll meet wherever you say, but I can't be seen on the street with you. It's bad enough we're together in here. I can explain that later."

Mac nodded his understanding. "You wait here. I'm in the stable across the street. I'll get my horse and ride out alone, then wait for you three or four blocks west of here. That's a better part of town. We can go to my hotel room to talk."

Casey said, "I need a half-hour to clear out of the hotel down the street."

With no more discussion, Mac rose and walked out.

Casey insisted on a change to Mac's plan. Sitting their horses at the agreed meeting place, Casey said, "I'll meet with you and tell you everything, but first I need a bath and a change of clothes."

Mac led Casey to his hotel. "You go in alone. Get a room. They're used to men coming in off the trail, so they won't care about your clothes as long as you ask about hot water for a bath. When you're ready, come to room 214."

As a precaution, Mac said, "If you run, I'll find you."

"I won't run."

An hour later, Casey was bathed and clean-shaven. Putting on the clean pants and shirt he carried rolled up in the carpetbag, he started to feel fully human again. The worn and filthy clothing was dumped into a bin at the back of the hotel.

Casey knocked on Mac's door. With the beard gone, he probably could have escaped Mac's attention, but he'd made a promise.

Mac invited him into the hotel room, but Casey said, "No, it's better you come to my room. I have some things to show you."

Mac stared down at the gunbelts Casey unrolled on the bed. He picked one up and turned it over. "Hoby Stepchuck," he read out loud. He then looked at the other belt before fingering the pocket watches, the folding knives, the coins, and then the letters and scraps of paper. Lastly, he looked at Casey and, with a pointing finger, indicated the money. The unspoken question hung in the air.

"One hundred dollars each."

Mac nodded his acceptance of the number.

"You pull all this off the two bodies in that grave?"

"I did. Hardest thing I ever done, except for watching my wife and son die."

Mac allowed Casey a moment to collect his thoughts and emotions before asking, "Did you find the horses too?"

"I found them. I scrambled and slid, grasping shrubs for support, down into that little wash. Pulled the two animals apart to where I could see the brands. Clover. Those were Clover horses."

Casey momentarily had a grim look on his face as he remembered the incident.

"Hope to never experience anything like any of this again. The hurt and pain, the loss. The horror. The stink of burned flesh, and then the even worse stink of rotting flesh.

"One experience like that is enough for any man. I'll carry the memory all my life, I'm sure."

The two men took seats in the hotel room's chairs, with the little round table between them.

Casey had been holding back the question, "How did you find me? And why?"

Mac said, "I'm new at this lawman thing, but my two brothers have some experience. After a trip to Clarence, they tried to put the pieces together. Came up with a couple of missing parts.

"Other than that, some suspicion rose up just from common sense."

He hesitated for fear of adding to Casey's terrible pain. "We talked to Noah Stringfellow. He said he and his father pulled what bones were left unburned out of the debris of the house and buried them.

"This is difficult for you, Mr. Bechtel, I know. But the truth, according to Noah, is that there were only two skulls and no large bones, such as a man's leg bones would be.

"Then this little item turned up."

He lay the stone arrowhead on the table and said nothing.

Casey had to admire this amateur deputy.

"You found the buck."

"My brothers did, right after they found the disturbed grave. Dug this out of a front shoulder joint. Never saw an arrowhead like this one before. Looks like the work of a beginner. Then I remembered meeting a man with a bow tucked under his saddle fender. A man who said he had only recently learned the bow, and who was proud of bringing down a buck with it. The pieces just sort of fell into place.

"Of course, you might have headed back to Santa Fe or gone almost anywhere else, but you seemed to be heading this way. You mentioned the gold fields.

"I had to come to Denver with my report for the marshal. It was not any extra burden for me to look around once I was here. I went from livery to livery looking at saddles and finally found one with a bow draped over it." He left the rest unsaid.

Casey had nothing at all to say.

Mac got up and walked across the room, then back. He stood looking down at Casey.

"It's time you laid it all out for me, starting with why you didn't go to the local sheriff. Then you can explain why you didn't talk to the boys and me when we met on the trail. I told you who we were and that we were going to investigate a murder and burning.

"You could have helped us, and maybe we could have helped you. Finally, why didn't you go to the federal marshal's office here in Denver?"

Casey said, "I have nothing to keep secret now. I'll tell you the whole thing. To answer your first question, I'm assuming you met Sheriff Burns in Clarence?"

Casey waited until Mac answered, "We met him."

Casey nodded. "Could be he was a good enough cowboy, but he ain't much of a sheriff. Close friend with Clover, too. I saw the situation as hopeless. I figured that if people thought I was dead, I could move around freely once my beard grew out."

As if pleading for understanding, he continued. "Even at the time, I wasn't sure about my decisions. I was hurting pretty bad on top of losing my wife and son.

"I was shot twice and took considerable burns getting out of the cabin. Broken glass, and then thorn cuts to my feet.

"When I finally got up the trail to the Stringfellows', first by crawling or limping with the shovel as a crutch and then by riding my milk cow, I was near done in. I pulled out the next morning. I had already decided on what I was going to do, and I couldn't risk getting Stringfellow into any trouble. They were a help to me. Couldn't have gone on without that help."

He reached up and unwound the cloth he had taken to wearing around his head.

"You can see the scars on my scalp. My hair will never grow back in. It's sore to the touch and doesn't seem to be getting any better. I wear moccasins because my feet won't tolerate boots.

"I hurt something fierce even sitting my horse. Finally reached a sheep camp some days later. I'm not sure how many days. It's all kind of a blur of pain and hurt. Mostly I let my horse take the lead. He must have smelled the sheep camp and just walked in. I had to be helped off my horse.

"I don't remember much for the next two days. My memory says I was on a cot in the shade of a tent, but that may not be the whole of it. I remember a woman helping me eat.

"Lady there put salve on my burns. Seemed to help. Said it was from sheep's wool. Mexes. Good folks. Only name I remember is Manuel. Common enough name, but this man would be hard to forget.

"I'd learned their lingo living in Santa Fe. Turns out, those folks working the sheep spoke English almost as well as I do.

"You pretty much know from there. I told you about my Indian friend and all."

Mac repeated his original question. "Why didn't you talk to my brothers and me when we told you we were deputies?

"By that time, my plans were made. I was going to take those two names I found on the gunbelts and look for the three men who escaped the yard fight. I had no idea who I could trust, so I trusted no one. It's the same answer for the marshal up in Denver."

Mac was sympathetic, but not totally. The pioneer ranchers and farmers were mostly on their own. Law was dealt with by their own understanding and needs. Taking care of yourself was a big part of pioneer living. Local sheriffs were usually just men willing to stand for the betterment of the community. Being elected sheriff didn't mean the man knew anything about the law or investigations.

But Casey'd had an option. He could have trusted Mac. That might have saved a lot of time and trouble.

With no more preamble, Mac asked, "Did you shoot Clover?"

"Yes. I also shot two horses and two men. Killed them dead. That's them in the grave.

"Would've killed Clover and the other three raiders too, given the opportunity, but the cabin was burning down around me. I was already hurting pretty bad from the bullet wounds and the scorching. I had to get out."

Mac gave Casey a moment to get his thoughts sorted out.

"My wife and son were already dead. Shot right before my eyes. I was pretty busy trying to save myself, so there was no chance to check it all out, but those two bodies up on the hillside pretty much prove what happened."

"Clover was, for sure, there on the raid? No chance of a mistake?"

"No chance at all."

The two men spent the next hour talking and planning. Casey told Mac all he knew and all he had done. Mac continued to ask questions. They discussed ways of finding the three men the livery owner had named as friends of Stepchuck's.

That the three names matched those remembered by Clover's cook wrapped it together nicely in Mac's mind.

Casey said, "I'm strong for work, Mac. Never shied away from a good day's labor. But I'm not what you'd consider tough like some of those I saw in the saloons are tough.

"Fighting was never something I did much of. Those saloons and dance halls had me scared half to death. I didn't figure I could go after those three men myself, so I'd planned on cleaning up today and then seeing the marshal. Thought I had enough evidence to maybe get him to act. Seems interesting that you came along about that time."

Casey was curious about Mac's plans too. "So, Mac, I'm wondering why it's you here talking to me instead of the federal marshal? Seems like it's his job. I thought you were a temporary marshal for the southern counties."

Mac thought a bit and then said, "Let's just let that ride for a bit. Right now, I'd like it if you and I could work together without involving the marshal's office."

27

Bar-M Ranch

Margo strode to the cookhouse, hoping to find Taz. Breakfast was finished. He was usually at the barn or corrals at this hour, but she hadn't seen him there. She was covering for Mac while he was away, although there was really no need. The crew functioned well with Taz giving the daily direction.

Taz was a capable and loyal foreman, but sometimes he didn't notice the little things that Mac would notice.

Jerrod was following in his father's footsteps, and he had the same eye for details. The young man knew it wasn't his place to give orders or even suggestions. The time was not far off when he would be of an age to take some leadership of the Bar-M, but until that time came, he made his suggestions through one of his parents.

He had spotted a problem with a windmill the evening before, and Margo was intent on getting the information to Taz.

She walked into the cookhouse to find Taz drinking coffee with Jessie. Margo withheld her frustration. Jessie and Taz had been spending a lot of time together. She wasn't sure what it was all about, but she had some suspicions.

Margo quietly said, "Taz, were you aware of the broken windmill in the east pasture?"

Taz jumped to his feet.

"One of the crew told me this morning. I've detailed two men to take a wagon and some tools to fix it. I'll be riding out there a bit later to see how it went. The crew is all detailed off and working. I'm just answering a couple of questions Jessie had. Guess it's time to ride out myself."

He tipped his hat and left without saying anything more.

Jessie pushed her coffee mug aside and stood.

"Sorry, Margo. I didn't mean to get Taz crosswise in your eyes. His being here is totally my fault. It's still pretty early in the morning, so I didn't think another cup was going to set his day back any too much."

The two women walked outside together. As they were strolling toward the house, Margo said, "I know Taz is a good worker. The ranch always gets his best efforts. I'm not concerned about that. What I'm concerned about is Mac."

Jessie said, with a small laugh, "We've all been concerned about Mac, ever since he was too small to mount a horse by himself, back when he was still known as Walker. He's obviously capable of anything he puts his heart into, but he has no idea of layin' off for a few minutes. You know, just to enjoy the day. If I ever saw Mac lighten up a bit, I could die in peace."

Margo didn't answer as they continued on to the house, just indicated the rockers on the veranda. Taking one chair herself and waiting until Jessie sat down, Margo said. "What you say about Mac might very well be true, but it's not exactly what I was thinking about.

"I know Taz is not a time-waster. He would have been out of the cookhouse soon enough. Mac trusts Taz completely, and so do I. He's earned that trust time after time. That's not a concern."

"What is the concern, then?"

Margo picked her words carefully. The newly widowed Jessie had only recently arrived on the Bar-M after many years away. Margo wanted her to feel welcome.

"The concern, Jessie, is you. I know Mac has been wondering what your plans are. He's enjoying having you and the kids around. We all are, your folks, especially. You can't know how many times they talked about you over the years and wondered how you were doing.

"But it doesn't take a wizard to see that you and Taz are enjoying your times together. I know you have the kids, but you must still get lonely. The kids can't take the place of a husband, and you can't share your hopes and dreams with them. That's man-and-woman talk. Husband-and-wife talk.

"I don't know how much Taz has told you about himself, but I'm sure he's lonesome too."

Jessie gave Margo a quizzical look. "Do you care to explain that?"

"No. If Taz wants to tell you his story, it's best he does it when he's ready. Just understand that the man has not always been a ranch foreman or even a cowboy."

Jessie still didn't understand. "So, what is there to concern Mac? You haven't explained that very well."

"No, I guess I haven't. To get right to the issue, Mac is concerned about losing his foreman."

"What?

The two women looked at each and found nothing more to say on the subject.

Two days later Jessie and the kids were riding with Margo and her children, along with the cowboys who were in the habit of joining Mac's parents for church on Sunday mornings. Hiram had been a lay church leader and preacher ever since the elderly pastor in their little Missouri village retired, and Hiram had stepped in to fill the spot the old man had left vacant. He had done it ever since.

After settling in Colorado, Hiram and Della had built a brush arbor on their small farm.

Farmers and ranchers from some miles around gathered to sing, pray, and listen to Hiram preach the Word.

When the weather was favorable, lunches were laid out on the rough tables Hiram had built. The women always made sure there was extra food. Some of the single men, surviving week by week on biscuits and bachelor fixings, looked forward to the fried chicken or sliced beef laid out for sharing. Coffee boiled over the outside firepit.

It was their visiting time as well as their worship time.

Taz regularly joined the group traveling from the Bar-M.

Almost as if it was planned, Taz and Jessie

found themselves riding side by side. Jessie made a joke of it.

"I've been concerned that I might have gotten you into a tight spot, Taz."

"I'm not sure what you're referring to."

Jessie glanced at him, wondering if he really didn't know or if he was simply playing innocent.

"Well, Mac runs a pretty tight ship. Always has. I don't want him to be upset because you and I have the odd cup of coffee together."

Taz chuckled a bit. "Don't you be worrying about that. Neither Mac nor Margo is that closed-minded. They need to see that the work's getting done is all, but then, so do I. I'll know before anyone has to tell me when our visiting is becoming a problem."

Talking through a big smile, Jessie said, "Well, I'm glad you're coming to church with us. You can fight off any bears and such that might come along. I'm sure that will bring great relief to my protective brother."

It was a short ride to the grandparents' riverside property, but the riders were in no special rush. They always left the Bar-M with lots of time to spare, knowing the kids would want to run their horses and play games along the way.

For many years, Hiram and Della had operated a market garden in the fertile soil of their river flat. They had cut back on the workload a bit recently as time and years of work started to show up as aches and pains.

After the riders were on the way, Jessie turned to Taz.

"So, Taz, you've never told me where you're from or where you were raised."

Taz was a bit uncomfortable about spending so much time with Jessie and her kids, although deep down, he enjoyed it. He wasn't so much worried about the gossip around the ranch as he was about his own private feelings. Those feeling had been wrapped tightly inside himself years before, and letting them out might start something that would not be easily contained.

Despite all that, he found himself talking more freely to Jessie than anyone else he knew, but the time together also brought back a bitter-sweet time in his life. That made him even more uncomfortable talking about his past.

Taz considered all of that, his mind bouncing from one emotion to another as they rode on for another quarter mile. He had been alone in the crowd for enough years that the feelings had become natural, and yet he knew they weren't. There was no shame in his memories, only hurt and an anger that had mostly burned out over time.

After a minute of silence, he turned a bit in the saddle and glanced at Jessie. "I don't ever speak of this, Jessie."

He hesitated another moment, questioning his wisdom in sharing the story. Before he thought it all through again, he heard himself talking. It was as if one side of his mind was still questioning while the other side had already started the story.

"I was raised on an orchard in Oregon. Apples mostly, but a few other fruits as well. Pa kept cattle too. Said it was best to not pin all his hopes on just the one crop. A year the insects took the apples might be the year the calf crop would keep the family in funds. That was his thinking.

"Pa loved his fruit trees, and he was forever experimenting. Grafting one tree onto another and watching what happened gave him great happiness. Grafting is a slow process, and it takes years to gain results. Pa kept careful records, hoping one day to develop the perfect apple type for the part of Oregon we lived in.

"I worked with Pa, more with the cattle than the trees. Pa was forever teaching me, and I learned a bit.

"Time came that I was married. Bertha and me, we had two kids, a boy and a girl. We lived on the farm with the folks, with me caring for the cattle and pruning and grafting along with Pa between times. I hunted work on ranches or wherever I could find a payin' job for the winter months.

"One winter, the only job I could find was way over the mountains in eastern Oregon. Big ranch over there needed help feeding stock through the winter. While I was away, somehow smallpox got a foothold in our area. Took my entire family, except my two brothers and one sister who were living some miles away.

"The ranch where I was working was pretty isolated. Hardly ever saw any mail. I didn't even know what had happened to the family until two months later, then I couldn't get across the mountains for the snow built up. Time I rode up to the farm, it was all gone. Family buried in a churchyard close by and the house and barn put to fire by the neighbors along with other infected properties in the hopes of stopping the plague. All Pa's careful records had been burned up. There was nothing left to even call home except a few acres of land and some apple trees that needed care.

"I left the farm for my brothers to do as they wished with, rode past the cemetery to say goodbye, and haven't ever been back. I went to cowboying. Pa's careful teaching helped me to see my work as important. To Pa, any work done well was important. Helped me keep my head straight. Or mostly so, anyway.

"Still, I drank some, and I felt like I was ready to fight the whole world, given the opportunity.

"Mac pulled me out of a bad situation some little while back. Dragged me to the Bar-M and put me to work. Worked for the Bar-M for two years before he gave me this foreman's job. I owe your brother my life. Maybe my sanity too."

He took a long look at Jessie.

"Ain't never told that to anyone else. Ever. Mac and Margo know, but no one else."

Jessie was having trouble holding back her tears.

"Thank you for telling me. You can be sure I will never repeat the story."

They rode on for a couple more miles with the kids whooping and hollering, led by the twins. Jessie smiled at their antics, remembering how sad and silent they had been after their father died.

When the kids rode ahead, taking their noise with them, Jessie looked again at Taz. She laughed a little.

"I don't know whether to tell you this or not. Seems a bit more than a coincidence. The folks aren't able to keep up the vegetable farm anymore, and I can't stay on at the Bar-M the rest of my life. I have to decide pretty soon what the kids and I are going to do, and the folks are getting to the age where they'll need some help."

There was a pause as Jessie thought about the situation.

"The market garden has given the folks a good enough living, although they probably don't really need the money. But I'm not too interested in spending my life either hoeing or bent over pulling weeds. We've been talking about an apple orchard.

"Pa already has a half dozen trees that produce well, or so he says, and just a couple of miles upstream on the river flats, another farmer is already making a living with apples. Perhaps you'd agree to teach us what you know?"

Taz looked at Jessie and didn't say anything. Some of his thoughts frightened him.

After lunch, the family sat around the fire. Matilda and Greta were anxious to have any news from Mac or the boys.

"Haven't heard a word," was all Margo had to say.

28

Denver

MAC AND CASEY WERE PLANNING THEIR next steps in Denver. Their goal was to find and arrest the three men whose first names they knew. Once they were in custody and safely locked away, they could be questioned in detail. Hopefully one of them would say something that would help solve the crime.

Mac was a strong, determined man. He had used guns, both in the war and after, but no one would call him a gunman.

Casey had never shot at a man until the night of the fire. The two of them walking into a saloon in an attempt to arrest the three suspects was sure to turn into a disaster.

Mac said, "I'm thinking I should go in the morning and have a talk with the city police.

This whole thing is in their jurisdiction, and they might not appreciate me coming in here and acting on my own.

"If I explain our suspicions and describe the evidence, there might be a good chance of gaining their cooperation. Might be a possibility of keeping the whole thing peaceful, too."

Casey still didn't understand why they weren't talking to the Denver federal marshal, but he let it go, leaving the decision to Mac.

29

Huerfano County

MANY MILES TO THE SOUTH, DIEGO AND Rafael were leading a team and wagon, along with two additional riders, Matias and Joaquin. The wagon was being driven by Sergio, Manuel and Imelda's sixteen-year-old son. The good looking, curly-haired young man was excited to be off on his first real adventure and away from the hated sheep.

Sergio was not tall, but whatever he lacked in stature was made up by strength and quickness. His attitude and mannerisms copied his father's.

Diego had at first refused to bring the boy, but after much arguing between Sergio and his mother, Imelda simply shrugged and said, "You be careful."

Turning to Diego and Rafael, she told them,

"Take care of him. He thinks of himself as a man. I pray he will live long enough for that to become true."

All were armed and eager for a fight. The wagon was carrying a light load, just their bedrolls, food, a shovel, spare ammunition, and rope. A lot of rope. The men didn't understand what the rope was for, but Manuel had said to bring rope. Not the braided leather riatas that took so long to make, common fiber rope was what Manuel wanted. That Manuel had asked was enough. They were bringing rope.

The lightly-loaded wagon was an easy pull for the team. After a dinner stop and some time for the horses to graze and go to the stream for water, the men decided to ride through the night. They should make the rendezvous by noon the next day if they didn't get lost.

There would be no welcoming lights from neighboring ranches to show them the way. The ranches had been left behind to the east many miles past. They were in hill country, which was cut by crevasses and unexpected rocky ridges with cactus and shrubbery-laden hillsides. The wagon would follow close behind Diego, who was scouting the way.

After a long night of picking their way through the obstacles, they pulled the team to a stop at the hidden campsite, greeting the waiting deputies with quiet acknowledgments. The cook fire held a pot of venison stew, and the coffee was hot. `

Manuel was immediately on his feet. "Diego, what is the meaning of bringing Sergio on a trip such as this?"

There was still a need for quiet, so the words were forced through clenched teeth in a way that would terrify anyone but his old friend Diego.

Diego simply hunched his shoulders and responded, "First I said no, then the boy and his mother, they have many words. In the end, the mother said to be careful and to take care of her son. He is here because he wishes to be."

Manuel and Sergio fired hot words at each other until finally Rafael pulled Manuel away and told him to sit down. Bobby watched to see what followed, never having seen anyone put a hand on Manuel before and not pay a heavy price.

Rafael spoke firmly to Manuel. "Is it that you think Sergio is too young? Or maybe it is that you think your son is not *un hombre fuerte?* How old were you, Manuel, when you first lifted your hand to fight for your family?"

"I did what was necessary. That was long ago. Sergio is not to know war and fighting in a new land."

Rafael wouldn't let his friend off that easily.

"You and I, my friend, we were not yet fourteen years when we stood with our fathers to fight the *bandidos* who wished to take what we had."

Manuel looked at Sergio, who was the oldest of his four children, two boys, two girls. All had been born on or near the Bar-M. The two boys thought of themselves as cattlemen, so when the family first moved to the hills to care of the Bar-M sheep, Sergio was determined to stay with his grandmother in Mex Town, just a short ride from the Bar-M headquarters. He would work around the ranch, doing the jobs the ranch foreman sent his way. He would do anything to become a cowboy and a top hand. He made his hatred of the sheep clear to all who would listen.

That Sergio's parents had overruled the idea of living with his grandmother still caused sadness in his heart, and Manuel knew this. He often thought the boy might have been right. But on that matter, Imelda had shown her determination, and the children had all followed their parents to the sheep camp.

Perhaps now was the time for the boy to feel a bit more like a man. Still, Manuel would see that he stayed away from danger when they found the rustlers.

They let the team rest and graze that day. Diego and Rafael would rest also, as would Sergio.

Bobby and Manuel rode out to look for signs of driven cattle, taking care not to be seen. Jeremiah stayed in camp to watch over the sleepers and do some cooking. He was prepared to repel any hostility and to show his deputy badge if the need arose.

Jeremiah and Bobby knew that strong feelings against Mexicans were likely to pop up in almost any confrontation. Even ranches that hired Mexican riders weren't always as accepting as they appeared. It had been decided that one of the brothers would be with the Mexicans at all times. The men left in the camp would make an easy day of it.

Bobby and Manuel had seen no cattle tracks that indicated a driven herd. All the indications were that the animals were wandering and grazing, as cattle will do.

At the end of their day of scouting for tracks, the sky was lit by a band of yellowish-red light. The sun was making its way to the western horizon, and within minutes, it would drop behind the Sangre de Christos. Full dark would follow shortly after.

Turning to head back to camp, Bobby saw something move far to the north. He called Manuel with a wave of his hat, signaling him to remain quiet. Bobby then dismounted to show a smaller profile. He made his way to a copse of mixed bushes and pulled his horse into the maze. Manuel was beside him in just a few minutes.

Bobby was less worried about sound than movement. Speaking in a normal voice and nodding to the north, he said, "Movement over there. Maybe a mile, maybe a bit closer."

The two men cast their eyes around, seeking other movements. When they saw nothing, Bobby said, "I'm going to crawl up that little knoll over there to see if I can tell where they've gone. Maybe see what they're up to."

He slipped out of the copse and disappeared into the semi-darkness. Manuel couldn't see him and wasn't sure where he had gone.

Bobby returned a half-hour later. "Couldn't see much from that knoll so I crawled to the top of that higher one over yonder. I was just in time to see a couple of riders push the last of a small bunch into the forested hills. Must be a pass leading to more grass somewhere up there. I think we should head up that way. We could give the riders a welcome as they come back out. Maybe find out if it's a legitimate cattle operation or not."

Without any discussion, Manuel mounted up and led the way. They hugged the growth on the hills to hide their movements, and finally, with barely enough light left to see, Manuel lifted his hand and drew to a stop. Silently he pointed to the tracks, more than just a few. This passage was used regularly, judging by what they could see in the dim light. Bobby wondered how the searching ranchers had missed the trail.

Following the torn-up grass and turned-over rocks, the men were soon easing into a narrow passageway between two steep hills. They pulled up there, not knowing what was waiting for them farther along and not wanting to give away their presence.

After considering their situation and the distance back to their carefully hidden camp, Bobby said, "I think we should pull back into the bush a bit more and wait. If that's a legitimate ranch, the men will probably stay the night.

"If those were just the delivery crew for a rustling operation, there's a good chance they'll be coming back out by and by."

Bobby could still see enough of Manuel's face to catch the grin. "A rope makes no noise, my friend. If there are two, we catch them. If there are more than two, we let them go and follow."

Bobby chuckled quietly. "Do you think you can see where to throw a lariat in the dark, *amigo?*"

"We will get close, then we catch."

Bobby had always been drawn to this fighting man. On the way west, after leaving Texas, the two had ridden many miles together. Margo's brother Billy had ridden with them. He wished Billy was with them now.

A man who made friends easily and was casual at first glance, Billy later contradicted that impression by seeming to fear nothing.

Of course, Billy might rope and hog-tie a rustler and then preach him a sermon. Billy was determined that everyone should hear the Word at least once, or maybe twice, or more times yet. But Billy's ranch was a two-day ride from this trail through the hills.

Wishing wouldn't make him materialize.

Bobby and Manuel led their horses well back, one on each side of the trail. Holding the reins, they let the horses rest and graze on the sparse grass that fought for life among the rocks and cactus.

Less than a half-hour later, they heard a hoof dislodge a rock. The rock made a slight clunking noise against another rock, and then all was quiet again. The two watchers slid silently onto their horses and stepped them a bit closer to the trailside. They spoke softly to their animals, hoping to discourage them from whinnying a greeting to the oncoming horses.

A branch scraped rough cloth and there was a snapping sound when a rider pushed the branch away, breaking it in the process.

"Dang, it's dark in here." The voice was clear and close. Bobby and Manuel loosened their throwing ropes.

Manuel carefully rode his horse closer to the trail. The plodding of hooves said the riders were very close. Trying to count the horse's steps, Bobby thought there were only two riders.

Then they were right in front of them, just darker outlines against a backdrop of dark trees and desert hills. Two riders looking straight ahead, working their way through the night.

Bobby could hear the slight whirring of Manuel's lariat and then the plop as the braided leather struck one shoulder before sliding silently down, to encircle the man's arms and chest. Bobby's rope flew only a second later.

Bobby and Manuel both kicked their horses into action, dragging the rustlers backward from their saddles. "What the..." was all one roped man managed to say before he hit the ground with a cry of pain and a great exhalation of breath.

They dragged the rustlers fifty feet before leaping from their horses. Both horses knew to hold the rope tight, just as they would at a branding fire. Bobby and Manuel ran down their lariats until they reached the downed rustlers.

Bobby's man lay on his stomach. As he dropped his full weight onto the man, pressing his knees into the man's back, he heard another loud puff of escaped breath and then a gasp of pain. Even in the poor light, Bobby managed to reach the man's Colt. He removed it and shoved it into his own belt.

He then quickly pulled a short, thin rope from his pocket and tied the rustler's legs. Coaxing his horse to ease up, Bobby soon had enough slack in the catch rope to pull the man's arms back. He snugged them securely with another short rope, called a piggin' string on a roundup. He was partly out of breath, but he bent to the man's ear. "You even wiggle, and I'll shoot you dead."

Getting to his feet, Bobby coiled his lariat and hung it over the saddle horn.

Manuel's man landed on his back, giving him a better chance of fighting the rope and his captor. The rustler was reaching for his gun, with Manuel gripping his arm and holding it in place. They wrestled for a few seconds and then rolled over twice, becoming entangled in the lariat. Manuel had a death grip on the rustler's gun hand.

In the darkness, it took some time for Bobby to notice what was happening.

Waiting until the rustler was on the bottom, Bobby stepped hard on the side of the man's head.

"Just like I told your friend over there, you move again, and I'll shoot you dead."

All movement stopped, and Manuel soon had the man hogtied.

The disinterested horses were pulling grass from the side of the trail, the rustler's horses grazing right beside them as if nothing had happened.

Wanting a clear look at the downed men, Bobby pulled out a watertight metal tube of matches.

"Let's see what we have here."

He struck a match and held it up to Manuel's man.

"Never seen this one before."

He shielded the match from the breeze and stepped toward the other captive. Kneeling and taking the man by the hair, he turned his face up and held the match close.

"Well, lookie here! Why, we got us a deputy. Looks like a deputy and a rustler, all rolled into one tied-up thievin' ball. Now ain't that grand?"

As an afterthought, Bobby untied the neck scarves the men were wearing and gagged them.

"The less noise, the better," he said to no one in particular.

Bobby and Manuel stood side by side, studying their captives and catching their breath. Away from the confining, brush-clad hills, there was a bit more light. Through the nighttime gloom, the men on the ground were staring hatred and fear at their captors.

Bobby spoke to them.

"Men, if one of you wished to maybe have it go a bit easier on you when you get to standing before the judge, I'll take off your gag so's you can tell us a story."

The two turned their heads enough to look into each other's eyes. Turning back to Bobby, both shook their heads.

"Well, that's too bad. Not real smart. Make no mistake about it, fellas. You're going to prison. Either prison or Boot Hill, it's up to you. You fight us, it'll be Boot Hill.

"You know that if the ranchers had caught you instead of us, you'd already be dead. You might show some appreciation for our kind, gentle ways."

He grinned as he said it, but it was probably too dark for the captives to notice.

Continuing his intimidation of the rustlers, Bobby said, "Lonely country out here to spend the rest of eternity in, no one knowing or caring where your bones lie. Be better, I'm thinking, to not cause any trouble. Just accept that you're whupped.

"Now, let's get you on your feet and on your horses. We've got some riding to do. There's some fellers down here a ways just waitin' to play jailer with you."

They untied the men's legs long enough to get them mounted and then tied them again, draping a piece of rope under the horse's belly.

With lead ropes on the rustler's animals, they headed toward the camp.

Two hours later, the men were secured against a couple of small mesquites. With the ring of men facing them, they realized there was no chance of escape.

Bobby looked around the camp. "Men, we're riding out again. Be gone most of the night, maybe even into the morning. I expect the other deputy is back at that shack in the hollow of the hills. We'll just ride over there and get him. Diego, how would you like to ride with us?"

Fed and coffeed up, each man with a lariat and a pocket full of tie ropes, and with fresh horses saddled and ready for the distance, the three men rode out. They were determined to ride through the dark of the night, retracing their steps to the little isolated cabin.

Fearful of a horse stepping in a hole or stumbling over some obstruction, they kept their pace to a mile-eating trot. Manuel seemed to have the best night vision, as well as the best recall of the trail to the shack. He led out, with Bobby and Diego following. There was no talking. They wished to hear any noise before they were heard.

A three-hour ride had them sitting in the starlit semi-darkness looking at the darker outline of the rustler cabin.

Bobby whispered, "Well done, Manuel. Your memory was perfect. Now what? Do we wait until morning, or do we wake the shack up?"

Manuel took a long time to answer, but finally, he said, "The third man—he will be wondering where his compadres are. He might not be in the shack. If he is a careful man, he may be in the scrub or hidden in a corral. I think we will tie our horses here. We take the lariats, as before. We walk quietly. We stay together so we do not shoot each other. We will check the corrals first, then the bushes around the cabin. We make no noise. Only then do we call this man from his sleep."

They tied the animals, loosening the cinches just enough to allow the animals to graze and breath a bit easier. It was still a long ride back to the camp. The horses had work to do yet this night.

There was no water. That would have to come when it was safe to ride into the clearing and up to the little creek.

With his lariat draped over his left shoulder, and his carbine hanging from his right hand, Manuel led out. The other two men, also outfitted with ropes and weapons, followed him. They stayed close so they wouldn't get separated in the darkness.

The walk to the corrals took less than fifteen minutes. Manuel indicated that Bobby and Diego were to stay hidden in the brush surrounding the camp and stepped forward, moving silently. Bobby knelt on the rocky ground, watching intently, casting his eyes from the bush to the corrals and back again.

Diego knelt beside him, and Bobby leaned over to speak into his ear. "Watch the cabin."

Within twenty minutes, Manuel stepped out of the bush behind Bobby and put a hand on his shoulder. Bobby whirled and reached for his gun, and Diego rolled onto his side, ready to defend himself.

Before either man could say or do anything, Manuel whispered, "No man in corral. One horse."

Bobby blew out a held breath and lowered his weapon.

Diego's sudden smile showed a mouth full of shining teeth.

"You are very quiet, amigo. You are lucky Diego did not shoot his old friend."

Manuel said nothing, simply crouched and led the way around the corral. From there, they skirted the foot of the low hill, taking advantage of whatever darkness they could find. They heard nothing and made little sound themselves.

A full circuit of the shack left them at the front corner, but there was still no sign of another man. Manuel stepped to the side of the door and crouched low and tight against the wall, then reached up with the muzzle of his carbine and tapped on the door. There was no response, so he tapped louder. The men waited.

Finally, a sound came to them from inside. First, it was the rustling of rough canvas pants as they were being pulled on, followed by the clump of a dropped boot. A full minute later, it was the clicking of a carbine hammer being pulled back.

Manuel looked at Bobby, sending a silent message.

Bobby understood. He crouched beside Manuel and spoke. Not loudly, but enough to be heard inside.

"It would be best if you were to put that weapon down, deputy. Having it in your hands when you come out this door might just cost you your life. We captured your two friends, and they are all trussed up nice and quiet. Now we've come for you. There's no escape. We've checked the cabin, and this is the only way out. Come out quietly with empty hands."

"Who do you think you are? I'm a federal deputy marshal. I'm the law in this area. Best you sneak away and don't come back."

"That's what you told us when we were here a couple of days ago, but we liked the water here, so we came back anyway. Of course, we're also being paid to find and arrest the rustler gang that's been dragging animals off down this way. That would be you and your partners, mister. Deputies and rustlers both. That's a fine combination. Now, drop the weapon and come out.

"The next sound you hear from me will be exploding gunpowder. Then, if necessary, you'll feel the heat of the shack burning down around your ears. It doesn't have to be that way. But the choice is yours. Just don't wait too long."

Bobby and Manuel retreated behind the corner of the building.

The silence seemed to drag as three minutes went past, then suddenly the door was thrown open, banging against the interior wall. The darkness inside was total. The man made no noise before he burst out, firing down at where Manuel and Bobby had been crouched.

The fugitive leaped to the ground and started toward the corrals at a full run. He hadn't taken five steps when a bullet sprayed yard dirt at his feet.

The deputy turned in the darkness, searching

for the source of the shot. He raised his gun, ready to fire at the first man he saw.

"Don't do it," hollered Bobby. "You'll never make it."

The rustling deputy triggered three fast shots from his Colt in the general direction of the voice, but the lead sailed off harmlessly into the night.

Manuel's weapon spoke and a single shot put the man down, writhing in pain, his weapon forgotten.

Stepping close to the downed man holding his carbine in one hand like a pistol, Manuel stood, waiting to see if he would have to shoot again. He didn't. The rustler's head sagged to the ground, his Colt fell from his fingers, and he groaned, folding both arms across his stomach.

In the darkness, it took Bobby a minute or so to find the guns dropped by the deputy. He then quickly ran his hands over the man to look for additional weapons.

Diego carefully stepped onto the little porch, listening intently for more sounds from the cabin. Hearing nothing, he stepped inside and immediately took two careful steps to his left, keeping his back to the rough wall. There was still no sound. Fishing for a match, he held it in his left hand, extending the hand as far from his body as possible. He struck the match on the rough wooden wall. As the light flared, casting a dim glow into the room, he took a quick glance around the unkempt space. He appeared to be alone.

Diego stepped to the small table and lifted the globe on the lamp. As the room brightened, he took a more detailed look around, raising the three cots to be sure there was no one hiding under them.

Manuel and Bobby each took one arm of the downed rustler and dragged him into the shack where the weak lamplight could shine on him. They ignored his groans of pain.

The deputy lay on the floor, his arms wrapped tightly around his stomach, his teeth gritted in pain.

Bobby squatted beside the wounded man.

"I'm prepared to believe you've ignored a lot of good advice over your misspent life That's unfortunate. Might have made a difference. I always figure a body should heed good advice. Probably too late for you, buddy, but now I'm going to give you another piece of good advice. You know what I mean? So's you can face your Maker with this little go-around having been confessed and all. Crossed off the long list of trouble you've brought on yourself over the wasted years. Why don't you just go ahead and tell us all about it?"

The injured man looked hatred back at Bobby.

"We already got your partners, and we know where the cattle were headed. What we want to know is, who did you sell them to, and what tie-in do you have with that federal deputy marshal up in Denver? I think he's up to his neck in this thing. Probably in other counties, too. No honest lawman would deputize the likes of you three."

Bobby waited for a moment and then continued, "You're dyin' there, fella. Ain't no doubt about that. Might just as well get some things off your chest."

The deputy tightened his arms around his wound and thrashed his head side to side, tears of pain rolling down his cheeks. He pulled his knees up and groaned, then, with a deep sigh, his legs dropped back to the floor.

It was too late for more questions or for a confession.

The three men did a thorough search of the shack, taking whatever they thought might be of value to the court. There was very little anyone would want.

It wasn't until they searched the dead deputy that they found the money belt. Simply a wrapping of cloth from an old shirt, it was tied around the deputy's waist with the money tucked into the folded cloth. One side of the wrapping was soaked in blood.

Doing his best to avoid the blood, Bobby unrolled the makeshift belt and spread it on the floor. He thumbed through the stacks of bills. Swaying back onto his heels, Bobby looked at Manuel and Diego. "Whooey. That there is a lot of money. These boys have been making off with more than just a few animals."

The dead deputy was buried in a shallow grave behind the shack. There were enough loose rocks to tumble down and spread over the loose dirt to keep the scavengers away. No words were said over the grave.

Bobby shoved the bloody money belt and other evidence into the saddlebags.

Three hours later, the exhausted riders rode into camp, turning their horses over to Matias to be cared for.

Bobby and his riding partners went to their blankets, exhausted.

30

Denver

MAC AND CASEY WERE GOING THEIR
separate ways after breakfasting together in the
hotel dining room. Mac asked, "Do you have
plans for the day?"

"Thought I might try to find a bootmaker. See
if he can fit me up with something my battered
feet will tolerate. I'm actually pretty comfortable
in the moccasins, but I have to admit they kind of
make me stand out amongst folks. I'd prefer not
to be noticed, at least for now."

Mac's goal for the day was to try to gain the
support of the local police.

An hour later, after inquiring about the location of the Denver police station, he was sitting
in the office, waiting for a meeting with the chief.
When the secretary asked what the meeting was

about, Mac said, "Well, young lady, I think it best that I hold that information for the chief."

The young lady wasn't happy, but she didn't argue.

Seated on a wooden chair across the desk from McAdam Portier, the chief of police, Mac introduced himself, giving a shortened explanation of how he came to be a federal deputy. He laid out the crimes Mordecai Granger had deputized him to look into and solve, if possible. He made no mention of the rustling matter. That was many miles away, and of no importance to the man he was speaking to.

The other truth was that Mac had not been assigned to look into the rustling. He had taken that on himself, not feeling comfortable with the three belligerent deputies the deputy marshal had been traveling with when they'd arrived at the B-Bar.

The police chief grimaced at the description of the murders and burning. At this point, there was no need to mention that Casey had survived.

Mac then provided an update on his progress.

At the mention of the names Sandy, Sid, and Montana, Chief Portier shook his head and chuckled. It wasn't a happy sound.

"Known those three by reputation for years. Run together. Never do any work, but always seem to have money. Lots of rumors, but never any proof. These are bad actors if those rumors are anywhere near true."

When Mac added in the names Hoby Step-chuck and Clarence Addy, the chief stared hard at Mac, letting his breath squeeze out through pursed lips. He stood and walked to the window of his second-floor office, staring down at the traffic below.

He was a large man in body and taller than most. Mac figured the chief could have bent horseshoes in his younger years. He wondered how much his time at a desk had stolen from him. Regardless of his strength, standing at the window, the chief's shoulders sagged and he seemed to momentarily be without words.

He was clearly troubled by what Mac was asking.

"You've got the whole kit and kaboodle there, Mac. I suspect our overall crime rate would drop considerably if we could put those five away. What proof do you have on the gang?"

"The gang is down to three. Stepchuck and Addy are in a single grave up in the hills."

The chief said nothing, simply stared at Mac.

Mac bent and picked up the carpetbag he had carried into the office, laying it on the chief's desk. He opened the top and invited, "Take a look here."

McAdam stepped back to the desk and looked at the bag.

"What have you got?"

Without waiting for an answer, he reached into the opened top and pulled out a wrapped gun belt with the weapon still in the holster. He then pulled out the second belt.

"They're unloaded," Mac assured the chief.

As the guns and belts were being thoroughly examined, Mac carefully laid out the letters, money, and other small items taken from the bodies by Casey. He sat back down and waited.

When his examination of the evidence was completed, Chief Portier spelled out the obvious question.

"So, Mac, you're a temporary deputy looking into a serious crime, and you've done some good work here. But clearly, Mordecai Granger was expecting you to report back to him, so tell me exactly why it's you and not Mordecai who's sitting here asking for my help."

Mac had feared this moment. He had been hoping it wouldn't come, but he also knew there was little chance the police chief would let the matter pass, without at least a question. He studied the man as he tried to remember the words that had sounded believable when he'd rehearsed them in his mind earlier that morning.

"Chief Portier, I have to ask for your absolute confidence here. I understand the gravity of what I'm about to say, but the pure fact is that I don't completely trust Deputy Marshal Granger."

Chief Portier showed no sign of shock. He also showed no sign of agreement. Mac decided the man was a professional in all respects—and that he wouldn't want to play poker with him.

Mac continued, "When I say this, I'm not referring to this particular crime. I'm referring to a rustling matter we're also looking into, down toward Huerfano and Pueblo Counties and around there. We're trying to sort out some strange goings-on. Marshal Granger doesn't know we're doing that, so I need you to keep that quiet until we have it wrapped up."

McAdam Portier studied Mac intently, and when he spoke, he caught Mac totally by surprise.

"You're well known to me, Mac. At least your name is, and what you've accomplished on that semi-desert you ranch on. You and your Bar-M are much admired in ranching circles. I think that if you threw your hat into the race for governor, our current man might show considerable concern." He smiled as he said that part.

Mac grimaced at the thought of politics.

"This acting deputy position is about as political as I ever hope to get."

McAdam nodded his understanding. Mac suspected the man's earlier statement was leading somewhere, so he waited.

The chief carefully said, "Your request for confidence goes two ways, Mac. When I mention your Bar-M, you have to understand that I'd never heard of it or you until that fencing fiasco last year. Even with the distances separating us, news has a way of traveling. When your request for help from Mordecai was ignored, a lot of folks started wondering.

"The old-time cattlemen would have hunted down the fence cutters and those who were making threats and dealt with them on a permanent basis, but you didn't do that. You came to the law for help.

"With Denver being the hub of the cattle industry in the state, there are always ranchers, big and small, floating around town. Your situation was discussed in dining rooms and saloons, and some of those discussions found their way back to me. The issue of fencing the range has cattlemen taking strong positions on both sides.

"Many ranchers disagreed with you, liking the old ways, but some argued that the old ways had to be changed. That law and order had to take hold.

"On both sides of the argument, many wondered why we had a deputy federal marshal if he wouldn't act when a rancher needed help.

"Rumors started making the rounds, and the talk got serious enough that I put a couple of men on it. We kept it all hushed up. It's not my job to question federal authority, but I filed the evidence away in my mind. The evidence was mostly word of mouth, so I made no written record except for the notes my men brought back."

The silence dragged on as the two men locked eyes. Mac had little doubt about the chief taking up the arrest of the three fugitives. What seemed to be holding the deal back was the matter of not bringing Mordecai Granger into the picture. Mac very much wanted Sandy, Sid, and Montana to be safely locked up and questioned before Mordecai got involved. After that, it wouldn't matter as long as the rustling investigation was kept quiet.

31

Custer County

AFTER A HASTY BREAKFAST AND A SHORT time to stretch and visit the trees, Bobby and Jeremiah moved the two captured rustlers into the wagon box, tying them securely. To let them mount their horses would make it too easy for the men to escape or cause problems. As an added precaution, they gagged them to silence.

Sergio continued to drive the wagon.

The group made their way cautiously to the gap in the hills where the rustled cattle had been driven. Since they had been on horseback, they hadn't noticed the upward grade during the late evening ride the day before. The wagon team, however, was feeling the gain in altitude as they pulled the cumbersome conveyance over rocks and around larger obstructions.

They were working their way into higher country. Although still some way from the mountain peaks off to the west, the hills were nevertheless rugged and forest covered, offering a promise of what was to come for westward travelers.

The wagon was finally backed under a sheltering group of mountain pine, to give shade to both the men and the wagon team, then the team was staked out to graze on the sparse hillside. Sergio was to stay with the wagon, accompanied by Joaquin and Jeremiah.

Bobby was hoping to gain some indication of what they faced at the other end of the gap. The prisoners were given another opportunity to tell who the buyer was and where the animals were driven.

With the knowledge that the third member of the rustling team was dead and buried, the men were more willing to talk. With the first telling of the news, the two men didn't believe Bobby, but on seeing the blood-soaked money belt with its cache of large bills, they had no further argument.

Bobby hadn't known any of their names. It was too late for secrets. Their names would become known soon enough, so when Bobby asked, he got a quick enough answer.

"That was Galen Pickard y'all buried. I'm Blaze

Randolph. This here is Buzz Dover. The man that does the buyin', he goes by Punch. Don't know no other name.

"I doubt as how he's smart enough to be the top man, but he's the one takes the animals offen our hands and pays out the cash."

Jeremiah stepped into the conversation. "Any idea where they drive them to?"

"Don't know. Not exactly, I don't. Says he somehow broke a trail through most of the hills heading south. Just has to take to the flats for a few miles to get past the worst of the rocks. Less than a week of careful going gets him and his crew to New Mexico."

Jeremiah wasn't satisfied.

"Seems to me, selling brutes with a variety of brands coming down the trail from the north might not be an easy thing."

Blaze Randolph saw no point in holding back the little bit they knew. "They hold them in that little valley up that trail you caught us coming out of. Some good grass up there a ways. They burn a new brand as best as can be over the old brand and hold the animals until the burn heals up before heading out."

Idly Bobby said, "So they'll probably still be there, working on the ones you took to them yesterday."

Randolph nodded. "Them forty head, and a bunch brought in over the past couple of weeks. Maybe three hundred, all together."

Jeremiah knew there had been other animals stolen in the weeks and months before, but they were gone. They would likely never be seen again.

Bobby, Manuel, and the others checked their weapons, had a bite of cold breakfast leftovers, took a swallow from their canteens to wash the dried-out fare down, and rode for the gap.

The gap the rustlers had pushed the stolen cattle into was only wide enough for two riders to travel abreast. The slopes on either side were brush- and tree-covered.

With Bobby and Manuel taking the lead, they proceeded slowly, hoping to make a bare minimum of noise. According to the prisoners, the gap was less than a half-mile long. It then opened up onto a nice mountain valley.

It took a half-hour of careful going to put them at the mouth of the gap. Bobby lifted his hat, wiped his brow, and looked over the isolated valley. He and Manuel pushed their horses to the side under some trees. The other riders crowded up and sheltered on the other side of the trail.

The valley was just a few feet lower than the trail the men sat on. They saw smoke from a branding fire and three men working with ropes and branding irons, while one man was mounted. There was a crude shack nestled under the pines on the hillside. As they watched, a cow was untied and allowed to rise. She bellowed her unhappiness and trotted to join the other cattle.

The mounted rider coiled his lariat as he rode toward the gathered cattle and kneed the horse close to a big steer. The actions of the cutting horse were something to watch. The rider simply had to stay in the saddle. The horse did the rest.

As soon as the steer broke free of the animals, the rider threw his loop, catching the steer by his hind legs. He was dragged to the fire, sliding and fighting, and his angry bellow could easily be heard from where Bobby and the rest were hiding.

Bobby smiled at his partners.

"Now, ain't that a sight?"

The branding was being done almost at the other end of the valley. With the distance to cover, there was no chance of surprise if they simply rode down the slope and out into the open. Wishing to avoid a gunfight, Bobby asked, "What do you think?"

The men were silent for a minute. Finally, Manuel said, "They are four. We are five."

Before Manuel could say more, Bobby reminded them all, "We want to be five after we finish this, too."

Manuel could be recklessly brave at times, and he seemed to live a charmed life, but that could not be said of every brave man. To take a man home lying in the bottom of the wagon was no part of Bobby's plans.

Manuel remained quiet as he studied the tree-lined slopes on either side of the valley. Bobby and the other riders did the same. Few men had the same eyes for terrain as Manuel. The little group waited for him to speak.

A long five minutes went past before Manuel pointed.

"You see there, Bobby? Good cover most of the way. You and me, we walk. Horses too much noise. We stay in the trees. We walk close to those men. Maybe sneak through the cattle. Get closer. The man on the horse comes for a steer, we catch him."

He turned to Diego. "Diego, my friend. When you see us at the cattle, you come fast. You bring our horses. No shouting. Maybe the men do not see you at first."

Bobby added a warning. "We want these men alive if possible. Shoot if you must, but only to save your life."

With that, Bobby and Manuel dismounted and passed their reins to another rider. They checked their weapons and slipped soundlessly into the bush. They were lost from sight within one minute.

A full half-hour later, the waiting men saw Bobby and Manuel sneak out of the bush. The two men ran hunched over and disappeared into the gathering of cattle. There was a bit of shuffling and snorting from the captured longhorn-mix animals, but not enough to alarm the rustlers.

The rustlers turned another freshly branded steer loose while the rider coiled his rope. Casually he rode to the edge of the gather, seeking an unbranded animal. With his eyes on the cattle, he didn't see Manuel letting out his lariat.

Manuel was as close as he could get without being seen, but it was still a long throw, nearly the length of his finely braided *riata*. Manuel made three quick whirls of the loop over the backs of the cattle that surrounded him and let the rope fly. The way the loop touched on the rider's shoulder, Bobby was sure his friend had missed. But the braided leather *riata* was more supple than the iron-hard lariats. Bobby watched in wonder as the loop coiled like a snake and dropped neatly over the rider's shoulders and down to his chest, pinning his arms.

The startled rider, who Bobby figured must be Punch, the boss of the gang, frantically grabbed the leather, attempting to lift it. But Manuel ran to get free of the cattle, and then kept running, pulling the rider over backward but not off the saddle. The captured man grabbed for the horn and shouted for help.

The men at the fire looked up, staring in wonder long enough for Bobby to holler, "You're fair caught, boys. You can't get away. Drop your guns and lie on the ground."

He hollered this as he was running toward the roped rider. Coming alongside the screaming rider and the shuffling horse, Bobby whacked the man's hands with the swinging barrel of his carbine. When the man let go of the horn with a scream of rage, Bobby whacked him again, this time on the side of his head above his ear. The man stopped struggling and dropped to the ground.

The men working at the fire grabbed for their weapons, looking all around to see where the voice had come from. Turning at the sound of rapid hoofbeats, they saw three riders racing across the grasslands. They were nearly upon them. The rustlers glanced at each other and then over to where Bobby and Manuel were pointing carbines at them, then back at Diego. It was as if they saw death approaching. Casting their weapons aside, two of the men dropped the ground face-down.

The third man at the fire was determined to

run. Diego and his riding partners were running their horses at top speed across the meadow. As they neared the fire, Bobby's and Manuel's horses were turned loose. Two of the men dropped to the ground and held their carbines on the men lying there.

Diego followed the rustler who was trying to escape. Just before he reached the brush-covered hill, Diego ran his horse into him, tumbling the fellow end over end. He lay in a crumpled heap, one leg twisted awkwardly beneath him, obviously broken.

Diego dismounted, still pointing his Winchester at the hurting and screaming rustler. He bent and pulled the Colt from the injured man's belt holster.

"Not smart, you run. Now you have a broken leg. Not smart. Maybe we leave you here."

The injured man said nothing, biting down hard to keep from showing his pain.

32

Rustler's Mountain Valley

RAFAEL AND MATIAS WERE HOLDING guns on the two rustlers lying on the ground. The rider Bobby had laid low with the whack on the head was a long time coming around. He was still not moving. One of the other riders confirmed that the downed man was Punch, the leader of the gang.

All the weapons were gathered and held well out of reach of the outlaws. The rustler with the broken leg was known as Wally.

Bobby took a look at Wally and then walked over to the little shack. Knowing what had to be done but having no real idea how to do it, he ripped two narrow boards from the wall to use as splints.

Manuel and Diego had the injured man lying

on his back. His leg was still trapped awkwardly beneath him. When Bobby returned with the boards, and several short lengths of rope, Manuel and Diego tipped the man onto his side and held him firmly. Bobby sat, placed one foot against the man's back, and grasped the ankle of the broken leg.

Before he attempted to pull the leg straight, he hesitated, then spoke to the man.

"You got to understand something here, friend. I ain't never done anything like this before, so we're going to have to learn together, you and me. I expect it's going to hurt some. Now, you got you a choice. I can either shoot you and leave your bones for the coyotes, or you can let me do this, not fighting or resisting. This way there's a chance you can live a while longer. I expect you'll end up hung anyway, but if it was me, I'd hold to a chance of living a bit longer. A bullet is awful sudden."

Everyone was quiet while the man continued whimpering in pain. Bobby gave him a few seconds that seemed like minutes before he asked, "What'll it be, fella, a bullet, or my rough doctoring?"

Bobby was holding up a small round of firewood for Wally to bite on. He waved it before the man's eyes and waited. The man slowly lifted his hand, gripped the piece of wood, and placed it between his teeth.

"Do it," he gasped past clenched teeth.

Bobby thought through his moves, nodded at Manuel and Diego, and started pulling with slow, steady pressure. Spitting out the stick of wood, Wally screamed and thrashed his arms, flopping his head from side to side. Manuel and Diego laid all their weight on him, holding him firmly in place. Bobby figured the scream might have been heard in Santa Fe.

Bobby let up for a moment, knowing the leg was still a long way from straight. In spite of the rustling, he couldn't help feeling a touch of sympathy as Wally fought back the pain. Trying to escape five men had been an unwise move, and now he was paying the price.

Bobby made another slow, steady pull, twisting the leg somewhere close to the right position. Again, the scream of pain was startling, and some of the cattle shuffled nervously. Bobby let Wally rest for a full minute. Wally felt around until he found the stick, then pressed it between his teeth and held fast.

Bobby gave the leg a final pull, stretching the skin tight and hopefully, settling the shattered bone back into its intended location. The final pull on the leg resulted only in an anguished groan.

Bobby patted the injured man on the shoulder.

"Ya done just fine there Wally. If no infection gets into the break, you should live to see yourself hung soon enough. Now, lay still while I tie these boards on to keep this mess straight."

As exhausted as Bobby felt, he might have been the one with the broken leg. His hands were shaking, and he realized he had held his breath through most of the fixing. He struggled to his knees and then stood up. Eyeing the coffee pot sitting at the side of the branding fire, he hollered over at the other rustlers.

"Any coffee left in that there pot?"

"Some," said one of the men. "Was probably better a couple of hours ago, but you're welcome."

Bobby slowly walked to his grazing horse and dug his tin cup out of a saddle bag. He almost grabbed the hot handle of the pot but caught himself at the last moment. The rustlers had a filthy rag lying beside the fire, so Bobby picked it up and folded it into layers before using it to lift the pot. He took a sip of the scalding potion and shook his head. It was a rough brew even by cowboy standards, but he knew he would drink it.

After another minute to consider everything, Bobby said to his men, "I'm thinking we need to get these men mounted. Tie that sleeping beauty over his saddle and lift Wally on. He ain't never going to make it on his own. Don't you be undoing all my careful doctoring.

"Tie their feet under their mounts and their hands to the horns. We'll string a lead line from animal to animal, and I'll take these boys out while you fellas gather up everything here and start the cattle back to the gap. I'm going to go check out that shack, and I'll gather up anything of value. Then I'll take these fellas out to be held by Jeremiah and them."

A bare half-hour later, the rustlers were back through the gap and gathered in an unhappy group, all tied to trees with gun-bearing guards squatting on the sparse grass close by.

Bobby looked at Jeremiah, "How would you like to ride to that ranch we were at a few days ago? Buse Nordly's the man's name. I expect he's probably the closest rancher. Tell him we've got some cattle and ask him to send his riders hither and yon to tell his neighbors. Tell him we'd like it if they would come take these animals off our hands. I'll get a count. Get the real names of these rustlers too, if I can."

Jeremiah mounted up without a word and was soon lost in the hills and swales of the rocky upthrusts.

In another hour, the first of the cattle shambled out of the draw. Bobby said, "Joaquin, you and Sergio mount up and keep those cattle heading east. Go slow. It'll take a while for the herd to get through the gap. I'll stay and guard these here desperadoes." He grinned at the captives as he said it.

With the herd free of the gap, the riders dropped all the plunder from the cabin into the back of the wagon. They didn't bother bringing the bedrolls, but they did search them carefully before throwing them on the still-burning branding fire. Bobby gathered the plunder into a now-empty sugar sack and stowed it beneath the wagon seat. In a small metal box hidden under a built-in cot in the shack was another bundle of money. It was sure to be the funds to pay for this group of cattle, but they would have to wait for Punch to awake before confirming that.

They bunched the cattle again and moved out, pointed east. Sergio was enjoying the task, riding one of the rustler's horses. They gathered the unused horses and herded them beside the cattle. With the wagon bed barely large enough to hold all the trussed-up men, they left the spare horses saddled.

Manuel and Diego dropped back to join Bobby. Bobby had made a large pot of coffee which he poured for them. He added water and a bit more ground coffee, and waited for it to come to a boil. He then dug out what metal mugs he could find. When the coffee had boiled again, he gave a cupful to each of the restrained men.

"I'll happily watch you men hang, but I won't see you shorted on your coffee. I ain't anywhere near that mean."

With the coffee drunk and the fire extinguished, Bobby started untying the men's feet one at a time.

"All right, you desperadoes, into the wagon."

Manuel and Diego helped the injured Wally and then re-tied his hands behind his back. They left his legs free. He wasn't going anywhere on that poorly fixed leg. The rest of the men had both their hands and feet trussed up firmly again. The unconscious Punch was showing signs of waking up.

It was a heavy load. The team was going to earn a rest before they finished this pull.

Bobby smiled at Diego. "Hey, *compadre,* do you know how to drive a wagon?"

"*Sí, mi compadre,* I think I can do this." He sounded insulted.

Bobby and Manuel laughed. Diego was another moment figuring out that Bobby was teasing him. With his grin showing his teeth and his embarrassment at not understanding Bobby's challenge, he climbed to the seat and set the wagon in motion.

Bobby rode close to the side of the wagon. "Now listen, men. Manuel and I will be riding behind with our guns ready. If any of you cause trouble, you ain't ever going to see Denver. Understand?"

No one spoke, and Bobby took their silence as agreement.

Following far enough behind the herd to be free of the dust. The wagon rolled toward the Nordley Ranch.

The excited rancher and three of his men met the cavalcade about halfway along the trail. Jeremiah rode with them.

With the promise that Nordley would see that the animals were returned to their rightful owners, they turned the drive over to him. Some of the brands were so cleverly burned over that there would be some difficulty sorting it all out, but Bobby dragged a promise out of Nordley that it would all be done peacefully and fairly.

"I'll be back down this way by 'n by. I'll not be wanting to hear any stories that make y'all out to be less than honorable."

He told the rancher nothing of the impounded money. Whether this would be coming back to the ranchers was not up to Bobby or Jeremiah, so it was best left unmentioned.

Punch finally woke up. He had a fierce head-ache and was angry clear through. He shouted and made threats. Some of the talk bothered Sergio, who was again driving the team. He was seeing a whole new side of life that he had never suspected even existed.

A slow three days later, the group pulled into the sheep camp. The deputies and the Mexicans were welcomed with hugs and more food than was rightly good for a man.

The prisoners were fed and then re-tied.

After another uncomfortable night of sleeping on the ground, trussed up like lassoed calves, the prisoners were re-loaded. A fresh team was harnessed, and the group headed for the Bar-M. A couple of the men stayed at the sheep camp, knowing they were no longer needed, but Sergio refused to be left behind. The thought of being back on the Bar-M kept him smiling even as he took his place behind the team again.

It took two more days of travel for the slow caravan to arrive at the ranch.

After many happy greetings from the wom-en, Taz assigned a few riders to watch over the prisoners. One by one the men were untied and allowed to clean up in the crew's wash house. They were then given the freedom of the loft for the night, making their beds in the hay after a thorough search for matches. They ate sitting in a circle on the ground outside the cookhouse.

The next morning, with another fresh team, Bobby and Jeremiah pointed the wagon toward Denver.

33

Denver

CASEY FOUND HIS BOOT MAKER AND WAS soon stowing the moccasins in his carpetbag.

Mac went along with a group of Denver city police on the search for the three suspects, and they found them in the third saloon they examined. Mac had promised to stay out of the way, and he was happy to do so.

The arrests went so smoothly that Mac almost missed it. He had stepped to the side of the big room, looking for a place to observe the action from. By the time he found what he was looking for, Sandy, Sid, and Montana were in handcuffs and protesting their innocence.

One big policeman chuckled. "That's just what I told the chief not an hour ago. I said, "Why, those boys are probably right now out looking for good deeds to do. Maybe out invitin' folks to prayer meetin' and such. They're just the type, lovin' their neighbor and all that." The chuckle came close to outright laughter.

Several saloon patrons were clearly holding back their own laughter. It wouldn't be good to get on the wrong side of the three renegades if they were to find their way back into the saloon.

The men were loaded into a closed-in wagon and transported back to the police station, then separated into three different rooms. Within minutes, the chief, Mac, and two other policemen were seated around a table.

Chief Portier turned to Mac. "I'm going to ask you to let Donny do all the talking. He seems to have a talent for getting to the bottom of things. It's best if we don't interrupt him."

The man called Montana was brought in, still in handcuffs and still protesting his innocence.

Donny began the questioning, with the chief sitting back and the other policemen taking notes. Mac had never witnessed anything of that nature. He was fascinated by the process, yet hoped to never again be involved in any such thing.

They left the prisoner standing in front of the table with his arms cuffed behind his back.

The questioner started by saying, "My name

is Mr. Ramble. I'm going to be asking you a few questions. I need to hear answers that I can believe, or I'll be asking again. But first I need you to tell me if you're drunk or if you are capable of answering these questions."

"Never had but the one small drink."

"All right, sir. We will proceed. You appear to be in very serious trouble, sir. What you say here may set you free, or it may hang you. That, of course, will be up to a court to decide.

"First, sir, I need your correct name."

Montana hesitated, looking at the gathered men. "Don't know why I'm here or what you think I done. Ain't nothin' you can pin on me."

"Well, I'm very happy to hear that. But I will still want to ask you some questions, just to assure myself and these other men that what you say is the truth. Now, again, what is your correct name, the one your parents gave you?"

"Julian Creek. Prefer just Montana."

The questioning went on for several minutes, with Montana denying ever having heard the names Hoby Stepchuck or Clarence Addy. He denied being in the area of the Bechtel murders or knowing anyone in that part of the country.

The questioner asked, "How is it then, Mr. Creek, that the cook on the Clover ranch called all three of you by name? He said he fed you separate from the Clover crew. That you rode out after dark and he never saw you again. But that later that night, Mr. Clover arrived home with a rather serious gunshot wound. How do you explain that, Mr. Creek?"

Montana stood in stunned silence. Finally, he mumbled, "Cook made a mistake is all. Wasn't me up there."

After more questioning and more note-taking, he was thanked for his time. He was led away, and Sid was brought in.

Donny proceeded along the same lines, but Sid was clearly frightened. Mac figured the man was not too bright and guessed that he found his security in his association with the other renegades.

Sid reluctantly gave his full name and then, like Montana, denied knowing anything about the Bechtel murders or the firing of the cabin. He had no explanation for the cook's remembrance of their names.

Quietly Donny asked, "Do you know a couple of men named Hoby Stepchuck and Clarence Addy?"

Sid looked startled and swiveled his head toward the door as if there might still be time to run.

Donny quietly said, "Please look at me, Sid,

and answer the question. Montana has already been very helpful. I'm sure you don't want to be saying anything different from what your friend said, do you?"

Mac chuckled to himself. Donny hadn't exactly lied. He'd simply laid out a statement that could be taken whatever way the listener chose.

Donny waited for a moment while Sid chewed his lips and then pulled a desk drawer open. He pulled out the two wrapped gun belts, laying them flat on the table, then turned them over so the engraved names were visible.

"Now, Sid, please step up here and take a close look at these belts."

Sid took a couple of hesitant steps and glanced down.

"No, Sid, I mean take a close look. Tell us what you see."

Sid bent and studied the belts. "Looks like some writing scratched on there."

Donny smiled, "Yes, I would say you are correct on that, Sid. Whose names are those, Sid?"

The big man shuffled his feet and looked uncomfortable. He said nothing.

Donny asked, "Is it possible you can't read, Sid?"

"Folks had a small, hardscrabble place out-back of nowhere. Not much of a town. Not much of anything. No school. Pa didn't believe in it anyway."

Donny looked sympathetic. Mac wondered how the man managed all the different looks and voices.

"Well, I'm sorry you didn't learn to read and write, Sid. Perhaps you will have time in prison to do some studying. There should be a bit of time before you're hung."

Sid was startled. "I ain't done nothin' to go to no prison for, nor to be hung for."

Donny remained his quiet, thoughtful self.

"Well, you see, Sid, I don't exactly believe that. The names on those gunbelts are Hoby Stepchuck and Clarence Addy. It didn't take us long, asking around, to find out that you and Montana and Sandy were great friends with those two. Rode out together regularly. But, of course, they're both dead now, buried on a hill above and behind the Bechtel place.

"Burying them was a thoughtful thing to do. A kind thing to do. Some would have just left them to the coyotes and the crows. Did you help bury your friends, Sid?"

Sid was getting confused by all the talk, and he blurted, "The others was for just leavin' 'em, but ol' Hoby and me, we was pards."

The startled look on his face showed his realization of what he had admitted to.

With that break in the story, Donny soon had the rest. Sid was promised nothing, but when Donny offered to tell the court how he had helped the investigators, Sid laid it all out. The major piece of evidence came when Sid was asked where the one hundred dollars in each of the buried men's pockets had come from.

"Old Clover, him who wanted the ranch, he doled out a hundred to each of us. He didn't want to do it. Said that was a lot of money. Said it was crazy. That no one could just burn out a neighbor and shoot the folks. Maybe twenty years ago, he said, but not now. Him and his wife got into a terrible argument, her insisting Clover was a coward and pushing him to get it done. Finally, he showed the money and just walked away. We didn't see him again until it was time to ride."

The men seated around the table were startled into silence with that accusation against Mrs. Clover.

After an uncomfortable period of silence while Sid shuffled his feet and wordlessly worked his mouth, Mac said, "May I ask one question?"

Donny glanced his way and nodded.

Mac asked, "Sid, were any of you concerned about Federal Deputy Marshal Mordecai Granger investigating what was done on the Bechtel or Clover ranches?"

Sid halfway smiled.

"Him? Don't exactly know where he stands. Never done no investigations I ever known about. I heard tell he's up to his ears in some stuff."

Mac and Chief Portier glanced at each other in an unspoken message.

34

Denver

BOBBY AND JEREMIAH LED THE PRISONER wagon toward the outskirts of Denver. The trip from the Bar-M had been long and tedious.

They had kept their stops to a minimum. Even though the men in the wagon were prisoners and likely to hang, they still had needs that had to be attended to, and to let that many men out of the wagon one by one took a long time. To let more than one out at a time was to risk trouble, so they stopped twice each day and kept the wagon rolling into the evening when the team had to be rested.

Bobby brought up a loose horse and spoke to Punch. "Well, pard, I'd like it if you would mount this animal. We're nearly there, and I need for us to have a little talk as we go along. I'd like to get to know you a little better before they hang you."

The suggestion was met with shouted threats and profanity.

Bobby smiled at the man. "That there is a really poor attitude, Punch. It was much more peaceful, back there at the start, with you layin' on the wagon floor somewhere betwixt here and wherever it is you're going when your end finally comes."

Bobby drew his carbine and pushed his horse closer to the wagon. He lifted the weapon and held it over Punch, ready to swing for his head, but the rustler boss ducked and hollered, "Now, hold on. That ain't no way to treat a man. Untie me. I'll get on your horse."

Mounted and re-tied, with a lead rope holding the horse to Bobby's saddle horn, they moved a bit away from the wagon so they couldn't be heard by the others. Bobby rode close on one side, and Jeremiah was equally close on the other.

"So, Punch, I already have most of the story from those others, but I need you to tell me a story too." So far, he had nothing from the others, but Punch didn't need to know that.

"Don't know what yer talkin' about."

Jeremiah looked seriously at Punch. Feigning toughness that wasn't really a part of him, he said, "Punch, let me tell you why we let Bobby do most of the talking with you boys. It's because of his thoughtful and gentle nature. Me? Why, I'd have probably shot the lot of you back in the hills and left you to fertilize the grass.

"Now, you can answer Bobby's questions and tell him the story he wants to hear, or Bobby'll toss me that lead rope and you 'n me can find ourselves a bit of bush. Someplace where the stink of your rotting flesh won't keep the neighbors awake come nightfall."

Bobby started unwinding the lead rope from his saddle horn, smiling at Punch the whole while.

Punch swung his head from side to side, taking in his two captors one at a time. He couldn't decide if Jeremiah was serious. Finally, he chose to talk to Bobby. "What is it you want to know?"

The story wasn't long, but it confirmed what Mac and his two brothers had suspected all along.

They repeated the questioning with the two phony deputies, with much the same result.

Arriving in the more settled part of the big city, Jeremiah asked, "Where are we going to dump these boys while we search out Mac?"

After thinking about that for a minute or so, Bobby answered, "What would you think of asking the locals to hold them for us? Just a day or two till we sort some things out. Must be some barred-up rooms around here somewhere that'll hold this crowd."

Two hours later, after asking a couple of locals for directions, the wagon was backed up to the door of the city jail. The brick structure was solidly built, with bars on the windows, and cells that were considered breakout-proof. The federal deputy badges were enough to gain support from the locals.

Not knowing what else had happened with Mac's investigation, they asked for and received a promise of silence on the matter from the jailer.

Free of the burden of the prisoners, Bobby dug into the impounded money and doled out enough cash to cover wages. Manuel and the others left to find a hotel room and a bath, and to purchase a change of clothing. Manuel found a livery barn that could handle their horses. Sergio soon had the wagon shoved up to the side of the stable and the team in a large stall, being cared for by the hostler. All the saddle horses were stalled as well.

Bobby and Jeremiah were ready for a bath and a good night's sleep also, but the first order of business was to find Mac. Walking from hotel to hotel and inquiring gained results in the fourth place they entered. Mac wasn't in his room. While they waited for him, the two brothers took rooms and ordered baths. They dropped their saddlebags in their rooms and went shopping for new clothing.

They were eating their evening meal in the hotel dining room when Mac walked in. Casey was with him.

Bobby was reluctant to talk in front of Casey until Mac said, "He's already a part of this. Let's hear it."

They exchanged stories, with Bobby going first, aided by some details supplied by Jeremiah. The news disappointed Mac but didn't surprise him.

When they were done exchanging their information, the four men sat silently around the table.

Casey finally said, "I don't pretend to understand all that's going on but I'm thinking there's going to be a major dust-up before it's all sorted out. You are, after all, setting yourselves up to accuse a federal deputy marshal. That just can't be good."

Mac looked at Casey, "You're no doubt right about that. I'm asking myself how I ever got talked into this mess."

Bobby smiled at Mac. "Too late for that, big brother. You're in, and so are we. Don't know how it will all turn out, but I'm thinking we've done some pretty good investigating. Cut 'n dried before the lawyers get ahold of it. Even with whatever mischief that bunch comes up with, the court will have lots to go on."

Mac agreed, but added, "You know that Jeremiah and you have more riding to do, don't you? And you'll want to take Manuel and a couple of others with you. Better get that wagon greased up. It's seen a lot of miles, with more miles to come. Maybe throw a bed of hay in it this time. Make it a bit easier for a woman and kids."

None of them had ever contemplated arresting a woman, but the evidence clearly showed that Mrs. Clover was the driving force behind her husband's actions. They would have to bring the kids along. They weren't happy about that either.

When the wagon and outriders pulled out of Denver, heading for the Clover ranch, Sergio was still driving. Manuel, Diego, and Rafael were riding along.

Casey had stayed in Denver. Mac decided it would be best to keep his existence secret until they consulted with the court's lawyers.

The wagon wheels were greased, and the bed held a foot of hay. Their bedrolls, food, and other supplies were stowed beneath a newly-purchased tarpaulin, and the Denver city police supplied the deputies with several sets of handcuffs.

Sergio held the team to a trot, and the miles rolled away behind the almost empty wagon.

The posse stayed over at the Bar-M for one night. They could spare no more time than that.

While they were there, they convinced Jessie to accompany them. The men were uncomfortable with the arrest of Mrs. Clover. Having a woman along might make the whole thing go more easily and give the prisoner some confidence in the treatment she could expect.

Pepe caught up the well-rested sheep-camp team and switched them for the hard-worked Bar-M team.

Three days later, they were camped on the outskirts of the Clover Ranch. They had avoided the village and the other ranches.

There was still an hour of darkness left before the sun would light the day when the deputies quietly rode into the ranch yard. Bobby rode directly to the house, along with Jessie.

Jeremiah headed for the bunkhouse. Sergio would hold the wagon back until he was called. There was just no way to keep the noise of a wagon from penetrating the still morning. If the men hoped to approach the ranch in silence, a rattling wagon would not be helpful.

As soon as a light showed in the bunkhouse, Jeremiah lifted the latch and walked in. The man who had lit the lamp was standing in the center of the room. Three others were in various stages of rising from their night's rest. There was enough light to see that only four beds were slept in.

"Federal Deputy Jeremiah McTavish here, men. I need all of you to stay in the bunkhouse. You may get dressed if you wish. You're in no danger. I just need you to stay quiet and allow us to do our duty. And please, don't anyone do anything foolish. It would only get you arrested, and maybe dead, if you were to touch a weapon."

Every eye was on him. No one spoke.

Jeremiah nodded toward Manuel.

"This here is Manuel. He's a properly sworn deputy, and he's a friend of mine. He's going to be staying with you for a while."

A hardened sleepy-looking rider was shocked. "A Mex? You ride with a Mex?"

Jeremiah pointed a withering look at the man.

"I have, and I do. For many years now. You'll cover some ground and shake some trees before you find a better man. But the thing is, he don't hold to no foolishness. Neither do I, for that matter, so you just sit tight while we go about our business and you'll have no trouble at all. Now, I wonder if there's one of you can put some breakfast together. Your cook is going for a ride with us."

After a half-minute of silence, one man stood and started stomping into his boots.

"I'll do it. Not as good as cookie does it, but it'll be better than going hungry."

Jeremiah and the new cook walked out together. Jeremiah signaled Rafael to come with him.

Entering the cookhouse, where the still sleepy cook was just getting his fires started, Jeremiah called, "Cookie. Come out here."

"Get out of here. No one's allowed in my kitchen till coffee's ready. Y'all know that. Get out."

Jeremiah said, "Federal deputies here, Cookie. I'm not looking for coffee. I'm looking for you. Come out here where I can see you."

The disheveled and startled man poked his head around the corner. "Ain't never seen you before. How would I know who you are, or even that you're a lawman?

"Take my word for it and get yourself out here. I just want to see that you're alone, then you can go back to your cooking."

The cook stepped out holding a stick of firewood in one hand. The other hand held a splitting hatchet. He looked from Jeremiah to the cowboy who had offered to do some cooking and then back at Jeremiah. He said nothing.

Jeremiah said, "Lay down the hatchet and step out here."

The cook did as he was told. Jeremiah lifted his Colt and cautiously peered around the corner into the kitchen.

"Ain't nobody there," said the cook.

Jeremiah still took a careful look around and then spoke to the two men.

"You can go back to making breakfast, cookie. I was planning on holding you right now, turning breakfast over to this man, but the thought of food sounds appealing. You'll cook for seven of us first. Probably for the family, too. After we leave, the crew can do what they have to do to get food on the table for themselves."

The two men glared at Jeremiah and then at each other, then the cook looked the cowboy up and down. Finally, he said, "You go wash yourself, then get in there and set some dishes out. And stay out of my way."

Jeremiah stepped outside, and with a shrill whistle, called Sergio in with his wagon. The young man stepped to the ground and walked to stand beside the team. Diego joined him. Rafael was in the cookhouse, keeping an eye on the happenings there.

When the first lamp light showed in the kitchen of the big house, Jeremiah banged on the door with the butt end of his carbine.

"Federal deputies here, Mr. Clover. You're under arrest. Come out now."

A sudden stillness fell over the house and the ranch yard. The kitchen lamp was blown out. Semi-darkness and silence descended on the scene, although the sun was beginning to lighten its world.

Suddenly the door opened. Clover ran out, his Colt scattering lead before him, seeking a target. Bobby and Jessie ducked to the side of the door, and Clover ran past them. He spotted the wagon and took aim at the two men standing there. Diego caught Clover's movements through the gloom and grabbed Sergio, hugging him and pulling him to the ground.

Before completing the fall, Diego suddenly jerked and moaned. Lying under Diego, Sergio could feel his friend shuddering in pain. He pushed the larger man off and squirmed to a crouch, seeking questionable shelter behind the horses. From there, he hollered for help.

Jeremiah dove to the ground when the shooting started. At Sergio's shout, he leaped to his feet and ran to the wagon.

The shooting stopped when Bobby took a few quick steps, caught up to the fleeing Clover, and laid him low with the butt of the carbine. Looking at the fallen man, his hat askew and his hair soaked with blood from the split scalp, Bobby thought, *This is becoming a habit.*

Jeremiah turned Diego onto his back. Diego groaned with the pain of movement. "Easy, *mi amigo.*"

Jeremiah opened the downed man's vest and shirt, searching for the wound. Diego wore no long johns, which were common with cowboys. His bare torso was becoming covered with blood, but Jeremiah could see that the wound was far to the left side. It was not too far from a complete miss.

Jeremiah spoke to Sergio. "Run to the cookhouse. Bring clean cloths, and tell them we need hot water."

Sergio was back in less than a minute. He knelt beside his suffering friend and passed a cloth to Jeremiah. Jeremiah pressed the cloth to the wound and spoke to Sergio.

"We have to roll him over. Do you think you can hold this cloth firmly in place while I tip him up to see where the bullet entered?"

Sergio was pretty shaken. At first, he was squeamish about getting blood on his hands, but once he started the task, he didn't pull back. Jeremiah rolled Diego onto his side. Again, the wounded man groaned.

"Maybe it would be best to leave me lying, mi amigo. The pain is very much."

Jeremiah continued lifting and rolling as Diego groaned.

"We have to stop all the bleeding, Diego. Stopping it on one side is not enough. But at least the bullet went right through. Hang tough, my friend. We'll have you wrapped in just a few minutes, and we'll get you to help as soon as possible."

Deciding that Clover was in no condition to move very far, Bobby pulled the man's hands behind his back and snapped a pair of handcuffs on. He left him lying unconscious and ran back to the house. Together, he and Jessie stepped through the open door, both holding their weapons ready but pointed at the floor.

Looking all around for movement, they saw no one, but they heard a child crying somewhere at the other end of the house. It was a certainty that the family awakened with the gunshots. They had to assume that Mrs. Clover was hunkered down somewhere with her children.

Jessie decided a female voice might ease the situation.

"Mrs. Clover. I'm here with a group of federal marshals. Your husband has been arrested, and we need you to come out. You are in no danger. No one here is going to hurt you. Please come out."

Mrs. Clover spoke from where they heard the crying child.

"What do you want? You have no reason to trouble me or mine. Be gone with ya."

Jessie tried again.

"We can't do that, Mrs. Clover. You have to come out. Bring the children with you. I guarantee that the men here will cause you no trouble. Two of them are my brothers, and both are sworn federal deputies. They're gentlemen, Mrs. Clover. You can depend on that. But they have a job to do, and they're determined to do it with no one getting hurt if that's possible. Please come out."

It took the full of three minutes with the sounds of much shuffling and movement, plus more childish crying, but finally, Mrs. Clover emerged. Her three children were dragging themselves along behind her. The youngest was hanging on to her dress. It appeared obvious that the shuffling and noise from the back room had been Mrs. Clover getting the kids up and dressed. They were disheveled and sleepy-eyed.

As Mrs. Clover stepped into the kitchen, Jessie said, "Thank you, Mrs. Clover. It's easier if we all work together."

Mrs. Clover let out a frantic scream when Bobby quickly snapped a set of handcuffs onto her wrists and said, "You're under arrest. Please don't do anything foolish."

"What do you think you're doing? I've done nothing to get arrested over. Let me loose."

Jessie assured her, "It's just a precaution, ma'am. We will be taking you and Mr. Clover to Denver to stand trial. Again, you have my guarantee that you will be treated with respect and safety until that time."

Bobby said, "All right, all of you, let's go to the cookhouse and see if we can find some breakfast. We're going to make some miles today. You'll want a good feed."

Loading the still-unconscious Clover into the wagon reminded Bobby of the situation with Punch a week or so before.

"Easier to just shoot them," he said quietly to himself. "Less trouble."

With the breakfast dealt with and the crew turned loose, their weapons left in the bunkhouse, the Clover family was hustled into the wagon. Jessie had worked with Mrs. Clover to gather clothing for the kids and whatever food was on hand to add to the depleted food stock on the wagon.

Diego was carefully loaded, and the kids were instructed to keep away from him. Jessie tied her horse to the back of the wagon and sat beside Diego.

The cook was mounted on a Clover ranch horse. Jeremiah warned him, "Even look like you're going to head for the bush, and I'll handcuff you to your saddle horn and tie your horse to the wagon."

The cook appeared to take the warning to heart.

A big ranch team was brought from the corral. It would be used to spell the Bar-M team, since the brothers intended that this would be a quick trip with long hours in the saddle.

Bobby and Jeremiah hung back as the wagon and the other riders were leaving the ranch yard. Bobby had something to say, and something to ask, of the crew.

"Men, you're being left in charge of this ranch. Clover trusted you, and we're going to trust you. I wouldn't want anything to happen that would disappoint me. I don't know how this is going to end.

"The Clovers are being charged with murder and with burning down the Bechtel cabin. I don't really expect they'll be back, but if y'all will stay and look after the place for a couple of weeks, I'll do my best to get some news down to you. Get you some pay, too. Somehow. I'll figure that out after we rid ourselves of the prisoners."

He waited for a moment for questions. When none came, he said, "Any of you want to tell me anything about the murders and burning?"

Into the silence, Bobby finished, "Didn't think so."

He kicked his horse into motion, and he and Jeremiah were soon riding beside the wagon.

"Kick 'er up a bit there, Sergio. We got a wounded man that needs help, and miles to go."

35

Denver

MAC WENT TO SEE DENVER POLICE CHIEF McAdam Portier again.

"I need your advice. You already know that I'm not a trained peace officer. Nor am I in for the long term, but I've taken my charge from Mordecai Granger seriously. My two brothers and I dug into the murder and burning issue and the rustling issue. In both cases, we found things that disturbed and surprised us.

"We've found solid evidence on the rustling matter that gives me great doubt about how to proceed. You and I discussed it briefly, but we were only speculating at that time. Now I have concrete proof. Three of the men we arrested for rustling pointed their fingers directly at Mordecai Granger as the top man in the scheme. The men were interviewed separately, and they all said the same thing.

"This has nothing to do with the murders at this point. We've found nothing there that would pull Granger into that terrible situation. The rancher and his wife haven't been interviewed yet, so we don't know what will eventually turn up. The boys are riding for the ranch now. They'll bring the suspects back in a week or so.

"For now, it's only the rustling. Deputy Marshal Granger made it clear to me from the beginning that his three chosen district deputies would care for that matter. I was to have oversight of the southern counties but, really, he only wanted me to work on the murders and burning.

"It was only after we gathered all the evidence we could find at the murder site that we decided my brothers would take a ride south. They had nothing to do in Denver that would help the case, which left them with time on their hands. A ride to the south seemed like a logical next step, so I agreed.

"They returned a small herd of cattle to the ranchers and hauled in that bunch you were kind enough to place under guard. Brought back a surprising stash of money too, taken from the rustlers. Once those boys decided there was no way out, they spilled the whole thing. The story is extremely troubling."

Chief Portier took a full minute to study Mac, then again, he stood and went to stare at the traffic below his second-story window. Mac figured it was probably a habit for a man who preferred action to desk work.

Without turning around, the chief said, "You have no choice, and mercy help you if you're wrong."

"If it turns out that I'm wrong I'll go back to the Bar-M and probably never leave it again. But if I'm right, I'm sure the senior marshal's office has to be informed. We will need a replacement deputy marshal out here, and someone to take control of the whole thing."

Chief Portier was silent for another half-minute. Finally, he spoke. "I agree with what you say. Here's what I'll do for you. I'll send a wire under my name, which will leave you out of it for now. I figure no one back East even knows about your hiring, but they know me. I'll send the wire this afternoon."

Mac hadn't thought of asking that of the chief, but thinking about it, he could see that the man was correct.

"I appreciate that, Chief. I'll owe you one."

The chief took the seat at his desk again, still studying Mac. "You know what you have to do now, don't you?"

Mac had known both fear and determination, sometimes in equal amounts, for most of his life. He had never found any benefit in delay.

He took a deep breath and got to his feet. "I'll need the loan of another of your cells."

"Yes. You need more than that. You need me and some of my men. We'll all go together. The federal office is only a couple of blocks away. We'll hope to do this peacefully."

Mac looked like he was mentally trying to confirm a decision. When he was sure, he said, "One other thing. I'm telling you this so you won't think I'm holding back on you, and so that someone else in the chain of responsibility will know. Casey Bechtel, the small rancher whose cabin was burned and who was supposed to have died with his wife and son, is alive. He somehow managed to escape the flames and survive. He was shot twice and pretty badly burned, but he got away. He's here in Denver.

"After looking at the evidence on the Bechtel Ranch, I had some suspicions. It took a bit of doing, but I tracked him down here in town."

The police chief pursed his lips as he absorbed this information. Mac gave him all the time he needed to think it through. When he spoke, he had a couple of questions.

"Why didn't he come forward, and why is he in Denver?"

"He had no faith in the local sheriff. The sheriff and Clover are the best of friends. Casey was sure it would all get swept under a rock and forgotten for lack of evidence, so he decided to let people think he had died in the fire. That way, he could move around without being known. He grew his beard out and wore old clothing, hoping to be seen as just another aimless wanderer. He went down to Santa Fe, where he's originally from, using the time to heal from the fire and gather his thoughts.

"He came back determined to kill Clover and fire his ranch, but when it came down to it, he couldn't pull the trigger. He changed his mind and went searching for evidence. It was him who found the dead horses and the dead men. It's him who found those gunbelts and the other items you have locked up. He actually did good work.

"With the help of a livery owner, he got the names of the three remaining murderers, too— the ones you arrested and have as guests of the city."

Chief Portier was a long time absorbing it all. Shaking his head, he said, "I'll want to meet him sometime. The replacement marshal will want to see him as well."

The two men studied each other for a while before McAdam Portier said, "Let's go arrest a lawman. Then I'll send that message."

36

The Trail to the Bar-M

SERGIO TROTTED THE TEAM AS LONG as he thought they could keep up the pace and whenever the two-track passage winding southwards was open. The trail was rough at best, with many dips and hollows. There were rocks everywhere, many of them embedded into the trail. It was impossible to provide a comfortable ride for the injured Diego or for Mrs. Clover and the kids.

Clover woke up with a serious headache and a terror-filled mind. He was wild with anger at being arrested and feared where the matter was going. To face a judge or a battery of lawyers was beyond his imagination. He seemed more concerned about his own arrest than that of his wife.

When Clover began shouting and threatening, Bobby rode up to the wagon.

"Clover, you get one chance only. I hear another sound comin' out of yer yap, I'll either bat you again with my carbine stock or tie the dirtiest rag I can find fer a gag to keep you quiet."

Bobby rode away, figuring the man would either sort it out or pay the price.

After four hours of steady travel, Sergio pulled up beside a small trickle of water and tucked the wagon into some sparse shade. Everyone but Bobby dismounted or stepped off the wagon to get a drink or attend to personal matters. Bobby posted himself at the edge of the clearing. He figured there was no one thinking of escape in this rock-strewn, unsettled land, but he remained mounted and watchful just the same.

Jeremiah led his horse to the stream, then turned him loose to graze on whatever he could find. He walked out to where Bobby sat his animal.

"Go on in, brother. Get yourself a drink. Ain't no one dumb enough to run in this wilderness. I'll watch just the same."

With everyone enjoying the shade and water, the cook broke out some leftover breakfast to share around. The kids were fed as much as they wanted before the adults cleaned up the balance.

At the end of an hour, they were back on the trail, fighting rocks and rough riding again.

In the late evening of the second day, they pulled into Mex Town and eased Diego off the wagon. With Mama providing guidance, the injured man was carried into the house and laid on a small cot.

Anxious to see to the injured Diego, Mama took only a minute to greet Manuel and then Sergio. As a mother and grandmother, she took great pride in her two men. She gave Sergio a hug, held him at arm's length to look at him, and beamed. *"Hombre joven y fino.* Look at you."

With that, she gave him another hug and turned to Diego. Hers were the only medical skills available for many miles around.

They left Diego with Mama and moved on to the Bar-M, which was just an hour's trot down the trail. After one night at the ranch and three more on the road, the weary travelers pulled into Denver.

37

Denver

CHIEF PORTIER ACCOMPANIED MAC ON the short walk to the federal office. The two police patrolmen followed close behind, driving an enclosed wagon.

Mac found himself counting steps, something he couldn't remember ever doing before. He almost felt like a condemned man counting his steps to the gallows.

Mac was going to arrest his boss, the federal deputy marshal for the territory. Had anything like that ever been done before? He couldn't imagine that it had. Neither Mac nor the chief spoke during the short walk.

Mac's mind was racing, sorting out questions. When and where does a man go wrong? Every man faces difficulties and hardships, but most stay true to their path. Only a small percentage of struggling men cross to what they hope will be an easier path. Was the marshal greedy at heart, or did the possibility of easy wealth push him beyond his self-control and better judgment?

These and many other questions had Mac wishing he had never gotten involved in the first place, but once started on a path, Mac knew no way except to complete the task. He would see an end to the matter before him and then return to the ranch. He couldn't imagine anything that would drag him away from his beloved Bar-M ever again.

The consequences of being wrong about the marshal were impossible to calculate, but he couldn't be wrong. The sworn evidence was overwhelming. Still…

When Mac and Chief Portier arrived at the office door, Mac entered first. Then Chief Portier entered, followed by the two patrolmen, who were to wait in the front office. The wagon team was tied off directly in front of the office door.

A young man known to Chief Portier as Kenny sat at the desk in the outer office. He looked up from his work when they entered. "Good morning, Chief Portier. What can I do for you?"

The chief answered, "Just sit still. Say and do nothing."

Kenny was a bit startled by the chief's tone of voice.

The chief took a step toward the inner door and then, as if a new thought had entered his mind, turned around. He stepped back to confront the young man.

"Do you have a weapon on you or in your desk, Kenny?"

Kenny looked startled at the question and swallowed loudly as he studied the questioner.

"Deputy Granger wants me to have a pistol. It's for my own protection. You know, supposing some hard case were to decide to seek revenge or something like that."

"Where is it?"

Kenny pulled the top drawer of the desk open.

"Right here."

The chief leaned over the desk, putting his hand on Kenny's arm.

"Don't touch it, Kenny."

With that, Chief Portier reached into the drawer and lifted the loaded Colt out.

"Is this the only one, Kenny? Don't lie to me."

The seriously shaken young man stammered and swallowed loudly again.

"Yes."

"That's fine, Kenny. Now, why don't you go for a walk? Not too far. We'll want you back shortly."

The thoroughly frightened Kenny rose from his chair and stepped out of the building.

With that, the chief moved to the door of the inner office and turned the knob. Without waiting for an invitation, he swung the door wide and walked in, followed closely by Mac. Marshal Mordecai Granger was sitting behind his big desk with a thick paper file in his hand. He looked up sharply at the intrusion.

"McAdam! What brings you here this morning? And Mr. McTavish!"

The marshal's eyes swung from one visitor to the other and back again. Slowly he rose to his feet. He looked anxious, and perhaps a bit frightened.

"What's going on, men? Is there trouble of some kind?"

Mac knew it was his turn. Chief Portier had done his part. He also knew there would be another weapon in the desk, and perhaps one under the marshal's coat. He didn't know how to confiscate them without causing more trouble than it was worth. Thoughts were flying through his mind a mile a minute.

The next step had to be done sharply and quickly, and he was the one who had to take that step. Mac was trembling inside. Somehow, for just the fraction of a second, his mind was filled with the terror he had felt before each charge he and his fellow infantrymen made during the war. An infantry charge comes down to one of two possibilities: you will survive, or you will not.

Mac didn't sense that his life was at risk with the marshal, but his peace of mind and maybe a portion of his way of life definitely were.

Mac said, "Deputy Granger, you're under arrest. Please put your hands behind you. I'd just as soon keep this peaceful."

The two men stared at each other for a second or two, which felt like an eternity. Even though he knew he was going to bluff, Mordecai Granger could feel it all coming to an end. All the planning, all the recruiting of men, all the tactics, all the money salted away, and the large sums he yet hoped to salt away. It was ended. He knew it. He felt it.

In spite of all that, he said, "Arrest? You can't arrest me. I've done nothing to be arrested for. Anyway, you work for me. You take orders from me, and I demand that you explain yourself."

Mac hoped the tremble in his belly wouldn't transfer itself to his voice.

"Actually, sir, I *don't* work for you. I work for the country. I work for my fellow ranchers and cattlemen. I, and the men working with me, have done a thorough investigation. Several men are in the City jail. One man is dead and buried, and there have been injuries. Cattle have been returned to their owners. Large sums of cash have been impounded and are here in Denver in safe-keeping.

"My investigations have pointed the finger of guilt directly at you, so put your hands behind your back. Don't move or reach for a weapon."

Granger was startled into immobility. During the short lull, while the deputy marshal soaked in this information, Mac took one of his wrists and pulled it behind Granger's back. Stepping behind the deputy, he snapped the handcuffs onto that wrist and reached for the other arm. Granger suddenly realized what was happening and jerked his hand, but was unable to escape Mac's grip.

He swung his free arm around, twisting and turning, reaching for Mac, hoping to pull himself loose. Mac turned with him, holding his wrist firmly.

The marshal thrashed and writhed, shouting and cursing and trying to free himself. The office chair was kicked over, and several items from the top of the desk went flying onto the floor.

Trying to make himself heard over the shouted oaths and threats coming from Granger's mouth, Mac said, "You're only making things worse, sir."

Mac held firmly to the marshal's wrist, fighting

the man until they were up against the back wall, where the marshal was soon overpowered by the work-hardened rancher. Mac grabbed Granger by the shoulder and turned him to the wall. With his own shoulder tucked into the deputy's back, he managed to grab the free arm and twist it until it was behind the prisoner, and he snapped the handcuff in place.

Mac flipped the marshal's coat back, looking for a weapon, and found a small revolver tucked neatly into a shoulder holster. Lifting the weapon to safety, he asked, "Is this the only weapon you carry?"

The deputy marshal didn't answer, so Mac ran his hands around the man's waist and down to his boot tops. He found nothing but a small folding pocket knife, which he pulled out and passed to Chief Portier.

Stepping away but not relaxing his grip on Granger's wrist, Mac said, "Sir, I regret this. I never once suspected, although I wondered why you deputized those three you brought to the Bar-M. There had to be better men than that around.

"We've done our investigations and made several arrests. Those we arrested all told the same story, and the evidence is clear. You are under arrest for cattle-rustling.

"I'm no lawyer, but there's no shortage of them around. They'll have to figure out if there's anything else. Now, Chief Portier has kindly offered a private cell for you, where you'll be held away from the other prisoners. I'd appreciate if you'd walk to the wagon out front, and we'll give you a ride. If you don't make a foolish scene, there'll be no need for anyone to even notice. I'm thinking that would be best for everyone."

The defeated and thunderstruck prisoner was led out and seated between the two patrolmen, and they had the team moving before anyone on the street noticed what was happening. Deputy Granger would be in his new temporary home within minutes.

Kenny watched the action from a short distance away. Mac waved for the young man to approach.

"Kenny, I want you to lock up the office and give me the key. Then you are to go home, and you are to speak to no one. Do you understand me?"

Kenny's nodding head was all the assurance Mac was likely to get. The young man walked into the office, picked up his jacket from the back of a chair, blew out the lamp on his desk, and locked the door. He dropped the key into Mac's hand and walked off.

With the arrest behind him, Chief Portier sent the wire to the federal marshals' head office. Using the fewest words possible, it simply stated, Need Senior Deputy Marshal Denver soonest."

It was signed, McAdam Portier, Denver Police Chief.

The chief and Mac then visited the federal judge's office. After waiting almost an hour for the man to complete some other matters, the case was laid before him.

Judge Tate Thomas listened carefully, shaking his head from time to time as he heard the evidence against the marshal. When Mac finished talking, the room fell to a hush.

With a great sigh, Judge Thomas heaved his corpulent body out of his chair and paced the floor behind the desk. He stood still long enough to light a fat cigar. Mac was wishing he could open a window, but he said nothing. He and Chief Portier sat in silence.

The judge finally turned to Mac.

"You're absolutely positive?"

"There is no doubt at all unless all those involved contrived to tell the same lie. They were questioned separately, and their stories were identical.

Again, silence overtook the room while Judge Thomas resumed his pacing.

After an uncomfortably long time, the judge turned to the Denver police chief.

"Portier, you're a man of some wisdom in matters of the law. You have had many years of experience. I've never known you to make rash decisions, and now you're sitting in my office supporting Mr. McTavish. Can I assume that your own investigation supports these findings?"

Chief Portier answered, "You can. And further, I would suggest that a thorough examination of the marshal's records and associations would be in order. And his bank account. This is a big state, and there are a lot of cattle on the range. It's logical to assume that what Granger had in place in the south might also be in place in other districts. We can't let that go without taking a look at it."

The judge hung his head, his gray beard spreading over his suit jacket. Cigar ashes fell to the carpet unnoticed. Without looking up, he shook his head.

"What a mess. What a mess."

As if a new thought had occurred to the judge he said, "I'll have to get a wire off to the federal marshals' office."

McAdam said, "I sent one about an hour ago. With a supporting message from you, I think the senior people will act promptly."

"All right, leave it with me. I'll let you know what's happening."

Addressing Mac, the judge said, "You've done good work here, Mr. McTavish, you and those working with you. Please extend my thanks to the others. Will you be staying in Denver for a while?"

"No. I need to get back to the ranch, but if I'm needed, just send a wire to Pueblo. I'll arrange for someone there to bring it out to the Bar-M.

"There are a couple of other things to deal with that are beyond my authority. First, the associate deputies I hired need to be paid. Next, the money found with the rustlers is currently in the chief's safe. Perhaps it needs a better home. Someone will have to decide what's to be done with it, too. Does it go back to the ranchers?

"And then, the Clover Ranch is running without supervision or payment for the ranch hands. None of these can be let slide. The Clover kids also need to be cared for."

The judge jotted the questions down as Mac was speaking. Looking down at the paper, he answered, "If you can stay over one more day, Mr. McTavish, I'll sort out those matters by tomorrow morning. I'll have to consult with our federal attorneys. Please come to this office around mid-morning tomorrow."

Mac and the chief went to the hotel dining room for lunch. Both were emotionally exhausted. They weren't sure of the next legal steps. All they knew was that the judge had told Mac to be prepared to return in about one month, he and his deputies and Casey.

38

On the Bar-M

SERGIO RATTLED THE WAGON BACK down the road toward the Bar-M as quickly as the team and the two-track road conditions would allow.

The riders had the urge to pick up the pace, but the speed of travel was set by the wagon team.

Casey trailed along with the rest of the riders. Everyone was anxious to get home. They had been on the trail longer than what was at first planned. Of course, there were benefits. When the judge authorized Mac to use the confiscated money to pay the men and cover expenses, Sergio had been given a full wage equal to the others. It was the first cash money he had ever earned. The coins were burning a hole in his pocket, but when he suggested they stop for a small bit of shopping, no one even bothered to answer. He had a new hat in mind, and perhaps a small bag of hard candy.

Manuel assured his young son that they could stop at Ad's and pick up a few things. At the mention of Ad's, Sergio simply nodded at his father. Sergio secretly hoped to be allowed to stay and work on the Bar-M, but he said nothing of this, waiting for the right time.

Making conversation to break up the monotony of the long trip, Bobby asked Jeremiah, "So, what's the plan with you and Greta?"

"Don't know as we have one yet. Last we talked, she said not to worry about it. The ladies are apparently were going to get their heads together and plan my future. I can only hope they come up with a good one." He said it all through a lopsided grin and then hunched his shoulders.

Bobby couldn't think of a single sensible reply, so he said nothing at all.

On reaching the Bar-M, the riders divided, the Mexicans planning a full day at Mex Town, where they would visit, see to Diego's health, and renew acquaintances.

Casey was heading back to his old ranch home. He wished to visit the Stringfellow family.

Sergio was staying at the Bar-M. He had approached Mac, telling him of his desire to be a cowboy and his willingness to do anything at all that would lead him in that direction. Mac had called Manuel over so the three could talk privately.

"Manuel, I would do nothing that might bring a problem between us, nor would I do anything in secret with Sergio. You must be a part of this talk. Sergio has asked that he remain on the Bar-M. He wishes to be a cattleman. I have not answered him yet."

Father and son studied each other for a moment before Manuel spoke. Finally, looking back at Mac, he said, "This, his mother and I have known. He was very young when he first had this thought. Well, he is still young, but perhaps not too young. If he stays, what would be his work?"

The way Sergio's eyes lit up almost made Mac laugh out loud. It was as if the young man sensed hope that he had never felt before.

Mac looked directly at the boy who wished to prove he was a man.

"Sergio, if you want to learn cattle and ranch work, you must be willing to start with small jobs. My own children were taught this way. Jerrod is a bit older than you and has been here all his life, doing whatever he was asked to do. Still, he had not been given a full rider's responsibilities yet.

"You must be willing to help Pepe with the stables and with the horses. You will sometimes work with the cook, learning about food, but also cleaning tables and peeling potatoes. You will sometimes drive a wagon with supplies to the line shacks. You will sometimes help the fencing crew. With each job, you will see what is needed. In the end, you will become a cowman if you watch and learn.

"If you will do this, I will pay you. You will earn less than the cowboys, but still, you will be paid."

Mac and Manuel watched for a reaction from Sergio.

With a face-splitting smile, he gave his response.

"I will do what I am told, and I will learn. I am hoping you do not tell me to work with the sheep."

With a chuckle, Mac said, "No, we will keep the sheep up in the hills."

Sergio and Manuel studied each other for a moment. Finally, the father stuck out his hand like he would for any man. He put the childish hugs behind them, although Sergio might have given his father a hug if the way was opened for that. It was not.

39

On the Bar-M

THE FAMILY GATHERED TOGETHER TO hear the wedding plans. Jeremiah felt like a spectator rather than one of the two people at the center of the event. So far in the deliberations, the ladies had done all the talking. Jeremiah looked at Bobby and Mac, hoping for some expression of sympathy. Neither would look directly at him.

Bobby's wife Matilda was sitting next to him. She had little to say either. She finally leaned over and whispered to Jeremiah, "If you'd have done this yourself back in California, you wouldn't be suffering through this now."

Jeremiah whispered back, "I tried."

The whispers drew a questioning look from Greta, the soon-to-be bride.

A plan to stage the event under the brush arbor Hiram had built for church gatherings was finally agreed upon. To help in some small way, Jessie said she would ride to Pueblo, where she would see the Rev. Grover Brocklehurst. With the agreement of the good reverend, the festivities would be set for Saturday, three weeks from then.

Assuming his presence was no longer required, Mac got to his feet and reached for his hat. No one stopped him when he stepped to the door, so Bobby and Jeremiah followed him out.

Walking across the yard, Jeremiah laughed.

"Don't hardly seem right that my opinions played no part in all of that."

Bobby chuckled in agreement. Mac was already thinking of his next challenges on the Bar-M.

As the three men were saddling horses, Mac asked, "Either of you wanderers thought of building a house? Or where it might be best to live? Or where the money to build it will come from?"

Bobby grinned and asked, "You see how it is, Jeremiah? Big brothers so busy growing old he somehow thinks he's the only responsible one in the family."

Jeremiah answered, "I hadn't noticed that, but now that you mention it, I think you might be right."

The two men laughed before Bobby took up the thought again. "The thing is, big brother, both Jeremiah and I have most of the money from the cattle drives still tucked away in Denver banks. Split between three banks, on account of we don't trust any of them. I think we can afford a nice piece of land and a shack, at least. Maybe a jacal if the women don't put up too much of a fuss. That way we could keep some of that money for important things like horses and fancy saddles."

Mac looked at them over the saddle he had just finished tightening in place.

"I'm surprised, but I'm proud of you too. For saving that money, I mean. I'm somehow doubting the women will be wanting to set up housekeeping in a jacal, but if they do, where do you propose to put your stick-and-mud houses?"

Bobby, serious now, answered, "There's a bit of land still available up near the folks. I saw a piece close to the river with a nice growth of trees on it and a wet-season stream. I'm thinking being a bit closer to the folks would be good for them in their declining years. Being closer to town would be better for the women, too. It would only be a few hours ride to the rails. We could get the women to Denver to see the lights once in a while."

Jeremiah asked Mac, "What's next for you and the Bar-M?"

"We have a batch of about three hundred

feeders ready for shipping. When we stopped in Pueblo, I ordered some rail cars. They'll be here in a couple of days. The boys are putting the drive together this morning. They'll get on the road tomorrow morning early."

Jeremiah said, "Sure different with the rails close by. Still, there was something about the long drives. Built up a lot of memories on those."

"Yes," answered Mac. "There was something, all right. There was dust and storms and stampedes and sleeping on the ground for weeks at a time. There were injuries and sometimes deaths. There were bandits wanting to steal, and Indians wanting to get paid to cross their land, and at the end of the trail, we were at the mercy of the buyers. I can understand why you would have fond memories of all that."

Bobby had to have the last word. "But you got to admit, we saw some country."

Mac changed the subject. "I won't be going on this short drive to the rails. Taz and the men can handle that. I have to go back up to Fremont County to pay the Clover cowboys, and I need to give them some instructions from the judge.

"Got to square a thing or two with that sheriff, too. I figure to be gone five or six days. I'd like it if you two would side me on the trip. I'm not expecting any trouble, but I'd hate to be alone if something should come up."

40

Fremont County

The rider pushed his horse to the limit, bringing a wire out from Pueblo. Because Mac was on the trail to the Clover Ranch, Jerrod led the rider to his mother since Margo handled ranch matters when Mac was unavailable. She took the telegram, opened the envelope, read the short message, heaved a great sigh, and dropped her hand to her side, clutching the paper and wrinkling it in the process.

Jerrod and the delivery rider waited silently while Margo stared off toward the hills. Finally, the rider spoke.

"So, do you have a return message?"

Margo studied him for a moment before saying, "Yes. Wait here, and I'll write it out."

Pepe outfitted the rider with a fresh mount, and the young man was soon on his way.

When the rider was gone, Jerrod walked back up to the house. Margo was sitting on the porch with Jessie. The twins and the younger kids were at the dining room table, busy with schoolwork that their mothers would check carefully before they gained their freedom for the afternoon.

Jerrod stood at the bottom of the steps and waited for his aunt to finish what she was saying.

When his mother lifted her eyes to him, Jerrod asked, "What was in the wire, Ma? You looked upset."

"I am upset. I'll be so glad to see the end of this deputy business. Your father is needed back in Denver. There was a jailbreak. Apparently, some of the rustlers were still free. They must have come from another part of the state. They overpowered the jailer, and that crooked marshal and several of the rustlers escaped.

"If the marshal ever had a chance of declaring his innocence, that's gone. He's a fugitive now. It's a bad business all the way around. I wish your father and uncles weren't involved."

Jerrod stood still for a few moments, thinking that through. Finally, knowing there was nothing he could do, he turned and walked back to the corral where his horse was tied.

Taz wouldn't return from the drive for another three or four days, and Jerrod was filling in for him while he was gone. Even with some riders pushing a herd to Pueblo, there was still a lot going on around the Bar-M.

Jerrod called Sergio. When the Bar-M's newest hand emerged from the stable, Jerrod said, "Saddle up. I'll show you the feeding grounds. I need to take a look at the hay meadows, too."

Margo watched from the porch as the two young men rode away. Jessie couldn't help noticing the pride in the mother's eyes as her eldest son went to his work, teaching the younger man along the way.

Mac, Bobby, and Jeremiah pulled up in front of the sheriff's office in Clarence. They dismounted, tied their horses, and stretched some of the kinks out of their backs. From the office window, Sheriff Dirk Burnes had watched them ride in.

Stepping out of the office door, he said, "Afternoon, men. What brings you to Clarence?"

Bobby, always the aggressive one, said, "That's a strange question coming from a lawman, considering all that's been going on around this berg."

The sheriff looked lost, as if was wondering what might happen next.

Mac was tired, and their horses were near exhaustion. He and the brothers had ridden for two long, grueling days with little food and less sleep to get there. He was in no mood for word games.

"Sheriff, we're going to take our horses to the livery stable for water and grain, then we're going to go to that poor excuse for a café across the street and get whatever they might have available for food. After that, we're going to ride out to the Clover Ranch.

"You're coming with us. Get your horse saddled, and be ready in a half-hour."

The sheriff was all set to be belligerent.

"I got no reason to go to the Clover. It's late in the day, and. I'm going home. And in case you didn't notice, I don't answer to you."

In three fast steps, Jeremiah had his two big fists scrunching up the sheriff's shirt front. He slammed the startled man hard against the wall, lifting his heels off the sidewalk. The sheriff's head snapped back, and his hat flew sideways and then dropped to the sidewalk. He closed his eyes in pain when the back of his head connected with the wall.

"We didn't come here for arguments. We have business on the Clover. Legal business. And it involves you. You can come on top of your horse or dragged behind it. It makes no never mind to me. But you're coming. Make no mistake about that."

The three McTavish brothers picked up the reins and walked their horses the short distance to the livery.

As they sat in the window of the café eating their dinners, they watched the unhappy sheriff lead his horse from the stable to the rail in front of the jail. He would not be happy, but he would be ready.

Arriving at the Clover, Mac called the riders to the cook shack. The crew numbered only four, and they each found a place to sit. While Mac stood, waiting for them to get settled, he looked around the cookhouse. He was pleasantly surprised that it was being kept clean and in good order.

When they were all present Mac said, "I have news, men. I have your pay, too. We'll deal with one thing at a time, then we'll count out your wages.

"First, both Clover and his wife have been arrested for murder. The lawyers may find other things to charge them with for the burning. There's no telling what all they'll be dealing with before this is over. They're in jail in Denver waiting for the judge to set a court date, but the evidence against them is very strong. I don't expect you'll ever see them down this way again, but for now, they still own this ranch. Your jobs are secure until the court says otherwise.

"You're saddled with a position of trust. I hope you're all up to it. We wouldn't want to find out that a bunch of cattle was run off or the family treasures somehow walked away."

Mac paused, waiting for anyone to speak if they had something to say. When no one took up the offer, he continued.

"You will be paid on time.

"I was going to leave the funds for next month's pay with the sheriff, but I've changed my mind. We brought him out here this evening thinking to put a longer-term plan into place, but that isn't going to happen. Not with the sheriff, anyway. I thought it through on the ride from town. There's a few questions about your sheriff that I can't seem to get my head around."

Mac fixed the sheriff with a hostile eye.

"You're free to return home, sheriff, but understand this. I'm instructing these men to get word to me if they ever see you anywhere near the Clover. *Comprende?* I don't know if you were involved in what went on before, but I've come to not trust you."

Without a word of response, the sheriff walked out the door. Every eye turned his way as he left, and no one seemed unhappy to see him go.

When the door closed again, Mac said, "I'm thinking of asking the senior Stringfellow to handle your pay. He has no conflict of interest that I know of, and he seems to be a decent sort of man. He might be of help to you, too, if you have problems on the ranch. Do any of you object?"

Still the men were silent.

Mac changed the subject for a moment.

"How is it going with the grub? You all appear to be healthy and I saw no new graves riding in, so I suspect you're somehow taking care of yourselves."

Each man had something to say to that, but none of it needed a response from Mac.

One man threw a bread crust at the rider who had been doing the cooking. He followed that up with, "Known camp cooks to be called 'belly–robbers,' but that's too kind for ol' Buntine here."

They all laughed, and Mac again changed the subject.

"I'll leave some money for grub, too. You're being trusted to buy kitchen supplies with it, not booze. If you buy booze, do it with your own money.

"You won't be able to charge any more at the general store. We'll be riding into town tomorrow to square up the account. I'll want them to close it off."

With the matters at the Clover ranch dealt with, Mac and his brothers asked to be shown the shortest route to the old Bechtel place. An hour's ride covered the distance separating the two ranches.

Noah watched them as they rounded the hills into the ranch yard. They were met with handshakes, and the invitation to get down and rest a bit.

By now, the whole country would know that Casey survived the fire. Mac asked, "Did Casey showing up alive cause any difficulty in town or on the other ranches?"

"None that I know of. Some were pretty surprised, but I think the other ranchers were happy to get that news. The most upset was the sheriff. Him and Clover were pretty close. Don't know what all was going on there, but I got the feeling that he'd have been happier if Casey had just stayed dead."

Lois walked out of the trees where the tent was pitched and offered to put the coffee on.

Mac said, "Thanks, Lois, but we'd like to get up the trail to the home place before darkness hides it."

Zeb Stringfellow welcomed them, putting up their horses and convincing them to stay the night.

Sitting on the veranda after supper, Mac waited for a quiet moment before saying, "Zeb, I'm going to ask you to do something on behalf of the court in Denver. All of Clover's holdings have been taken in by the court but it will be a couple of months before the whole thing is wrapped up. In the meantime, the court has released funds to keep the ranch going.

"I've just given the Clover hands their wages and enough money to buy what they need for the kitchen, and I've promised them their wages at the end of each month. I have the funds with me. I'd like to leave that money in your trust if you'd agree to hold it. You could ride down at the end of the month, pay the hands, and again give them money for supplies."

Zeb considered that for quite a while before putting his questions into words.

"What about the sheriff? He's the law in the area. Might make more sense to pass that responsibility on to him."

Mac was quick to answer.

"That was my first thought too, but his actions and a couple of things he said got me to wondering. The fact is, I don't trust him."

Zeb chuckled. "You're a wise man, Mac."

During the evening meal and the visiting on the veranda, Casey and Julia Stringfellow seemed to be in their own quiet world.

Earlier, Casey had introduced the family members Mac and his brothers hadn't met on their first visit.

He gave the women special credit for their

kindness after the fire, emphasizing the gentleness of Julia as she swabbed his burns with ointment and wrapped them with clean cloths.

The family looked on silently but knowingly.

The following morning, the three brothers rode back to Clarence. Mac walked into the general store, while Bobby and Jeremiah took chairs against the front wall.

When Mac pulled out the leather wallet he kept his money in and offered to pay off the Clover account, the storekeeper looked greatly relieved.

"Wasn't sure how that was going to work out. Thought I might have to eat that one."

Mac counted out the payment and then advised that the account must be closed.

"I'll not be doing this again. You charge any more to the ranch, it won't get paid."

With that matter settled, Mac walked over to the sheriff's office. The door was locked. The old-timer who had been holding down a chair during Mac's first visit was seated in the same place as if he'd never moved.

"He ain't here anymore, young fella. Rode into town near dark last night, loaded up some truck from the office, plunked the door key onto the mayor's desk, and rode out. Never spoke word one."

The old man cackled and shook his head.

"Not one single person in town bothered askin' where he was a-headin' fer. Mostly glad to see his horse's tail a-swayin' up the road."

Mac nodded, thought for a moment, and walked back across the road.

"Let's go home, boys. We're done here."

41

Bar-M Ranch

MARGO PASSED THE CRUMPLED TELE-gram to Mac and waited in silence while he read it. He had just arrived back from the latest trip to the Clover Ranch.

Mac slowly sank into his usual veranda chair and looked up at Margo.

"Escaped? How could that even be done? The jail is a brick building with iron bars everywhere. Someone must have opened the doors.

"And it's been over a week. He's either captured again or gone. He could be almost anywhere at all by this time, him and his accomplices. If they caught a train, they could be in California or New York by this time. There's just no telling. Even on horseback, they could be in Wyoming or Texas or Utah. It's doubtful they're sitting in a saloon in Denver waiting for some lawman to pick them up."

Margo had nothing to say.

Jessie brought out some coffee and fresh rolls direct from the oven. She went back for a plate of cold sliced beef and cheese.

Knowing it was a good time to be somewhere else, she walked to the stable, where several of the cousins were supposed to be helping Pepe. In truth, they were probably playing in the loft. Pepe would smile and keep their secret.

It was so good to hear her kids laughing again. She wouldn't have had the heart to break up their play. Losing their father had nearly torn their young hearts apart, and playing with their cousins was becoming a big part of pushing that memory into the past.

Margo's parents kept Ad's Trading Post and Smithy open to serve the ranchers from the more westerly parts of the county who preferred to avoid the longer ride into Pueblo. The store was gradually changing from the one-stop general store it had been for fifteen years. Now, with Pueblo offering every imaginable convenience and more stores than any one town really requires, most ranchers, enjoying the broad selection available, were heading that way to fill their needs.

The trading post was holding a bit less stock each year.

In truth, Ad didn't mind having his business slow down. As he considered all the torn-off calendar pages of his memory, he couldn't escape the truth. There were more years behind him than there were in front.

He and Amelia were the grandparents of a sixteen-year-old young man, along with several other kids, and they had ample resources set by for their old age. It was time to slow down.

Ad was especially weary of the blacksmithing. He remembered when he could work all day shoeing horses and forming iron on the big anvil and still feel good at sundown. Now, each time he took care of a difficult horse, he seriously thought of shutting down the smithy entirely.

Margo still purchased as much as she could from her parents' store, but every few weeks someone on the Bar-M dressed out a team and drove to Pueblo in a rattling buckboard, carrying a shopping list. The large ranch crew created a constant demand for supplies.

With Mac's call back to Denver, Margo decided to.go along, turning the wagon trip with her husband into a shopping trip in Pueblo. The opportunity didn't often present itself. Jessie stayed behind to care for the younger kids. Jerrod accompanied his parents and drove the wagon home with his mother.

Mac caught the train to Denver.

From the station, Mac hired a livery coach for the ride to the federal marshals' office. A senior marshal, Corky Hambley, had been sent out to replace Mordecai Granger.

Marshal Hambley was slight of build and not more than six inches over five feet tall. There had been instances in the past where men had misjudged the marshal, taking his smallness to be weakness. In every case, that had proven to be a mistake. He was not big or strong enough to take down most men with his fists, but with a gun or a lariat or a blacksnake, he was a force to respect.

Mac and Marshal Hambley shook hands. "It's good to meet you, Mac. I've been hearing glowing reports of your work."

"Most of that work was done by my brothers and the Mexican men they hired and deputized. And by Casey Bechtel."

"I understand, Mac. It's often the case that the difficult work is done by the line riders while the man with the title takes the credit. It's a mark of your character that you pass the credit along.

"But that's not really why I called you back to Denver. You know about the jailbreak. Just exactly how that happened is still a bit of a mystery. I was on the train from the East when it took place, so I have no first-hand knowledge. I can say that McAdam Portier is both embarrassed and livid. He stomped around some and raised a lot of dust, but none of that answered any questions, nor did it recapture the escapees."

Mac was quick to defend the police chief. "I worked closely with Chief Portier during the set-up and the arrest. He's a good man, and I have full confidence in him. Is it possible there was some-one on the inside that Deputy Marshal Granger was able to recruit into his band of rustlers?

"Ex-Deputy Marshal Granger." Corky Hamb-ley was quick to correct him.

Mac smiled at the swift reply. Clearly, the new deputy was a bit touchy about the reputation of the marshals' service.

"Yes, of course, I understand he would be removed from the marshals' service, but that doesn't answer the question. He seems to have or-ganized an impressive band of rustlers. Whether he was involved in other crimes, I have no idea, but it doesn't stretch the imagination too much to think he might have recruited someone inside the jail.

"However, I'll leave that to you and McAdam to sort out. My interest lies in the southern district.

"I haven't seen a name list, but it's my understanding the rustlers we arrested have escaped, along with Granger and some others. Did the murderers from the Bechtel ranch escape as well?"

The new Marshal seemed to heave a sigh of relief.

"No, I'm pleased to answer. They were housed in a different building. McAdam tells me that wasn't a planned thing, only a matter of running out of jail cells, but it worked out to our benefit. That's by far the more serious crime, although we don't take rustling casually. As far as we know, none of the rustlers have been violent. There's been no shooting reported.

"And we still have one. The gent with the broken leg tried to escape with the others. A City policeman found him lying on the sidewalk with his leg re-broken. The doctor put him back together, but my understanding is that he won't be going to any local dances for a while yet."

Mac nodded at this information. "It could be that if he'd spill what he knows, there may yet be a chance of grabbing up the others."

Deputy Hambley answered, "Could be, but I don't somehow think he was very far up the food chain. He might not know any more than he's already confessed to. But on the other matter, things are moving ahead.

"The lawyers are rapidly putting together the case on the murders and burning. Hopefully, we'll see those boys standing before a judge before long.

"The other good news is that that Herb Clover and his wife are still securely tucked away."

Mac nodded his approval of this before asking, "What's been done to try to find the escaped men?"

"That's a problem. Chief Portier's jurisdiction doesn't extend beyond the city of Denver, and with Granger out of office and on the loose, the district office wasn't any help. Kenny, who worked in the front office, has disappeared. Granger left no information on sub-deputies or others he may have called on to form a posse in the past.

"I was still on the train. Even if I had been here, I would have been starting from nothing, so I wouldn't have been able to get it done either.

"Chief Portier wired the Cheyenne office and asked for their help. They sent a few men out to scour the northern part of the territory, but they were almost a week getting to it. And then, I'm told, that land up there off to the west where they were most likely to go if they were horseback is mostly vertical, with steep tree-covered hills and deep valleys. Thousands of square miles, and almost no people. Hopeless, without a major mistake by Granger or one of his men.

"I'm afraid our wayward deputy is gone, him and his rustling pards. All of them."

Mac, still focusing mostly on the murders and burning, said, "Well, we stopped the rustling for a while, anyway. Returned some cattle and impounded some money."

42

Denver

MAC PUT THE RUSTLING MATTER OUT of his mind. He and the others had done their part—they had broken up the rustling ring and dragged the men to jail in Denver. Others would have to sort out what happened after that. He wasn't about to waste any time on a search. The wilderness around Denver was immense. In and around the gold hunting hills was a spider web of trails, with abandoned claims and cabins. Any one of them could be used as a hidey-hole.

Or, if they were looking for distance, the rail lines would take the fleeing criminals anywhere they wished to go.

There was little chance of finding them, but he figured the rustlers would make a mistake somewhere down the line. Someone would grab them at that time.

But Mac had serious questions about the Clover matter. Some of it just didn't make sense. Even on the wild frontier, a person could not simply murder his neighbor and take his land and cattle. And Colorado could no longer be considered a wild frontier. Denver was a booming city, and Pueblo, the closest center to the Bar-M and the Clover ranches, was no longer a small trading post but a busy town with all the modern conveniences.

Mac mentioned his concerns to Deputy Marshal Hambley.

Hambley suggested he talk to the court lawyer. "Harry Devon is one of the lawyers the court assigned to the case. Talk to him. He may have more information."

Harry Devon and Mac shook hands and then sat down in Devon's office. Devon smiled, "Quite a mess you brought us, Mac. Don't know that I've ever seen the like."

Mac didn't feel much like returning the smile. "Well, none of this was by my choice. When I was asked to take on a deputy position, it was my understanding that it was a temporary post. I'm hoping that's still true. I failed to find any enjoyment in any of this, but that doesn't mean that my brothers and I didn't put some effort in.

"We're all happy to see it coming to an end,

but I still have questions that bother me. Most of Clover's actions make no sense. Just no sense at all. I think I'd like to talk to him. Can you arrange that?"

Devon stood and said, "Let's go for a walk."

A short half-hour later, they were shown to a private room in a small jailhouse. With handcuffs and shackles firmly in place, Clover shuffled in. The jailer reluctantly left him alone with Mac and the lawyer. Mac assured the man that all would be well.

"Pull a chair up outside the door if that would make you feel more secure. The window is barred, and I see just the one door. There'll be no trouble."

The three men settled into chairs. Clover folded his arms across his knees, hunched his shoulders, and focused his eyes on the floor. Mac thought he had never seen a more dejected look on a man's face.

Harry Devon asked the first question. "Have you hired a lawyer, Mr. Clover?"

"Don't know no lawyers. No point anyway. Just a waste of money. Y'all already know what happened. Ain't no matter anymore. There's nothing left. Nothing at all that can be saved out of this mess. My life is over.

"We had a good ranch. Doing well enough.

Stupid. It's all stupid. Can't fix it. Not sure I care anymore."

The court lawyer responded, "This might not be the best time to be thinking about money. I advise you to get a lawyer. I can contact one for you if you wish."

The response from the shackled man was to hunch his shoulders even tighter. "Only if it will help my kids."

"I'll send one over to see you."

Mac looked sternly at the prisoner. "You're charged with murder, Mr. Clover. Maybe other charges too. If you're found guilty, you already know you'll be hung.

"But there's a couple of things I don't understand. I'd like your help in figuring them out."

With that statement, Clover raised his head to look Mac in the eye. "I'll not be talking about that nor anything else, 'cause it don't matter no more. But I'd like it if you could tell me about the kids. Then I want to hear about what's happening on the ranch."

Mac looked at the lawyer. "This is Mr. Harry Devon. He's a court lawyer. He might know about the kids. I do not."

Clover swung his head to look at the lawyer but said nothing, waiting.

Devon cleared his throat. "I actually know

little about them either. Someone else is dealing with that matter. But I can at least tell you that they're well cared for in a private home. They were not put into an orphanage or anything like that. If you'd like, I'll see if I can arrange a visit."

Clover gave a sad smile. "I'd like that very much, but I couldn't let the kids see me in shackles. If you could arrange a visit in this office or somewhere close by, I'll give you my word of honor that I'll do nothing to make you regret your efforts."

The lawyer seemed to be looking right through Clover, as if to see if there was duplicity there or if he could be trusted in this promise.

"I'll see what I can do, but I know nothing of the ranch."

Mac took over the conversation. "I went to the ranch a week ago. Your men are working, and the place looks cared for. The cookhouse was clean and orderly. As far as I know, the ranch house hasn't been touched. The crew was paid, and will be paid again at the end of the month. The men are aware of the situation, and have agreed to hang on until the trial decision is made. The court has put up the funds to cover ranch costs until the trial. After that, there will be some decisions to make."

Clover simply nodded his head. "Thanks for doing that."

The room fell to silence as if each man was waiting for the other to speak.

Mac and the lawyer looked at each other. Given Clover's refusal to talk about the crime, there seemed little point in continuing the meeting. The two men stood, and Mac opened the door and called the jailer. They were soon back on the street and walking back to the office.

43

Bar-M

THE COURT DATE WAS FINALLY SET. There was just one week to go before the big trial would begin. Mac had no involvement in that, so he caught the train and was back at the Bar-M that evening—just in time to get dragged into the wedding planning. Margo insisted that he accompany her to his folks' farm the next morning. Everyone was gathering since there was much to discuss.

"I don't recall that we went through this much nonsense before our wedding. Don't recall that we invited anyone else's input either. Why not leave Jeremiah and his girl to themselves?"

Margo didn't think this expression of doubt worthy of comment. In any case, there were memories of the circumstances that had led to their wedding that were best left to the haze of the past.

If pushed, Mac would have to admit the truth; he saw no purpose in having someone else's wedding taking him from his work. Margo didn't wish to discuss that either. As it was, Mac had pushed the trip to his folks' farm into late morning. The work of the Bar-M always came before what he considered to be foolishness.

When Mac pulled the one-horse buggy to a stop in the farmyard, Jeremiah and Greta were deep in wedding talk. They were sitting alone beneath the shade of the brush arbor. Glancing around, Jeremiah waved at the new arrivals before he turned back to Greta.

Della called everyone in for lunch. The family had been gathering at the parents' small farm regularly since all the kids came home. All the kids, that is, except Nancy and her family.

Hiram and Della seemed to have more lightness in their steps with the family gathered.

The lunchtime turned into a festival of ideas, as everyone had their say on how the wedding should proceed. Each idea seemed to be more ridiculous than the last.

Bobby suggested that a brass band should be hired from the city. Jessie wondered if it would be a good idea to have a big wedding complete with a dance. They could invite folks from miles around. As the proposals began to pile up, everyone broke out into laughter.

Jeremiah and Greta glanced at each other, knowing everything was being done and said in jest.

Bobby brought it back to reality with the thought that the two could just ride into Pueblo and get married without telling anyone.

Della didn't seem even a little bit amused by the suggestion. Wagging her finger at her son, she said, "Don't you dare, young man."

Greta finally had her say. "I'm from the big city. It's taken me a long time to start to adapt to this country way of life, but I've learned to love it. I'm still not sure where we'll build this *jacal* Jeremiah keeps talking about, but I'm looking forward to settling down. And I can't think of anywhere I'd rather be married than right here under that brush arbor, with Dad standing beside the preacher as we say our vows."

Calling Jeremiah's father "Dad" was a major step toward fitting into the family.

Two days before the trial was to begin, the three McTavish brothers boarded the train for Denver. With all the traveling back and forth on the rails, Mac had arranged for the livery to maintain a half-dozen Bar-M horses and some tack. There would be no more waiting for someone to pick them up.

Back in Denver, the brothers finally found time to spend an evening with Nancy and Jonathon and their kids. Although it was a pleasant evening of remembrances and reminiscing, there was a momentary chill in the room when Mac reminded his sister how long it had been since she'd visited the folks.

"They're enjoying having Jessie home, but that doesn't take the place of seeing you, Nancy. You and the family."

Nancy had never managed to fit comfortably into farm or ranch life. Although she and Jonathon had worked incredibly hard and done their part on the westward trek, once they'd arrived in Colorado, they had settled in Denver.

She and Jonathon had totally adapted to life in the big city. With their share of the earnings from the original cattle drives and with Jonathon's banking job, the family had established themselves in a well-to-do part of town. They missed the family, but the thought of an extended vacation at either the Bar-M or her parents' small farm filled Nancy with dread.

The conversation and the evening ended with Nancy saying, "Tell the folks I promise we'll make the trip this summer. We'll take the train to Pueblo if someone will pick us up."

Mac just nodded at this promise, and then, with the excuse of a big day to come, the men took their leave.

44

Denver—Court

THE COURT WAS CALLED TO ORDER IN the recently completed Federal Building. Judge Matthew P. Grimes presided.

With most of the suspects having escaped and disappeared into the wilds, the rustling matter was laid over for a later time. It was the judge's desire to deal with the more serious matter of the murders and burning first.

A jury was selected, and the court was called to order.

The opening formalities dealt with, the government lawyer, Harry Devon, stepped forward. "Mr. Casey Bechtel. Would you please take the witness stand?"

With his hand on the Bible, Casey swore to tell the truth and took his seat.

"Mr. Bechtel. We are concerned with the events that took place on the night of the fire. Please tell the court about those events."

Casey shuffled a bit in his chair, turned to look up at the judge, glanced uncomfortably around the packed courtroom, and then cleared his throat.

Lawyer Devon spoke quietly. "We all understand, Mr. Bechtel, that this is difficult for you, and that a courtroom can be an intimidating place. Please, take your time and speak clearly. Start from the beginning, from your first waking moment."

Casey called up all the self-assurance he could muster and started the story, and a hush fell upon the crowd. In halting words, he described the flickering light on the window. The light that woke him. He described the first shots that broke the window and hammered into the pine log behind the bed. He told how Florence fell and hit her head on the wooden bed frame, of how she had held firmly to their baby.

He went on to describe his mad scramble to reach the carbine above the cabin door and how he eased the door open, hoping to defend himself and his family.

When he told of the fire torches crashing through the windows, several gasps were heard from the listeners.

Every person in the courtroom understood the hazards of fire in wooden frontier homes. Fire was an unhappily common disaster of the era. When Casey talked about the rapid spread of the flames, the heads of the listeners could be seen nodding.

With a hesitant, quiet voice and trembling lips, Casey described Florence screaming in terror and stumbling in the dark to escape the flame-engulfed bedroom.

The courtroom remained silent until Casey said, "Never in my lifetime will I be able to forget the sound of those shots taking the lives of my loved ones. Three of them."

He said it very slowly, not striving for effect but struggling for inner calmness that would allow him to finish this awful tale.

Every eye turned to the two defendants when Casey told how he saw Herb Clover sitting on his horse beside the corral. He admitted to shooting Clover and to seeing him drop his rifle, clutch his arm, and kick his horse into retreat.

Herb Clover dropped his chin to his chest and his eyes to the table top. Mrs. Clover sat upright, glaring hatred at Casey.

More gasps were heard with the description of Casey's mad leap through the window after having been shot.

He told of huddling in the trees and eating raw eggs, of riding the cow up the trail and receiving help from the Stringfellow family. But after the shooting of Florence and the baby, the rest of the story was almost anticlimactic.

Lawyer Devon stood. "Your honor, there is more to tell, but perhaps the witness and the court would benefit from a short break."

Judge Grimes said, "I absolutely agree. Fifteen minutes."

When the court was called back, Harry Devon addressed Casey again. "Mr. Bechtel. You have admitted to shooting Herb Clover that dreadful night. Was anyone else shot?"

"Yes. I shot and killed two horses the raiders galloped through the yard. I shot and killed two of the raiders, as well."

"What did you do after you left the Stringfellow ranch?"

Casey told about his time in New Mexico and of his learning to use a bow and arrow.

"What was your intent with that, Mr. Bechtel?"

"I wanted revenge. All I could think of was revenge. To kill Herb Clover and burn out his ranch."

"And yet, there sits Herb Clover. What happened Mr. Bechtel?"

"I couldn't do it. I had him in my sights and the fire arrows ready to burn the hay and barn, but I just couldn't pull the trigger."

45

Denver – Court

THE REST OF THE STORY WAS TOLD SIMply and graphically by Mac, with his brothers each taking the stand to confirm what was said. Bobby and Jeremiah described finding the dead horses and the grave holding two dead raiders.

Harry Devon asked, "Were you the first to find the horses and the grave?"

"No. we could tell the grave had been opened and re-closed, but we didn't know who had done it. At that time, we all thought Casey Bechtel was dead. We didn't find out differently until later."

Denver Police Chief McAdam Portier took the stand and described the finding and capture of Sandy, Sid, and Montana.

"It's my understanding that they will be facing the court sometime soon."

There was much more talk, but the defense lawyers had nothing to say. The evidence was overwhelming.

After the lunch break, Harry Devon called Herb Clover to testify.

"Mr. Clover, your lawyer will have the opportunity to address the charges against you, but for now the evidence would appear to be irrefutable. In fact, you indicated as much when you and I had a meeting just a few days ago.

"But I am left with a couple of questions. Perhaps you can tell the court, Mr. Clover, how you ever hoped to get away with murder and the burning of a ranch, and how that series of crimes would benefit you or your ranch holdings? Perhaps you can also tell us if you considered the impact this would have on your wife and children."

The bitterness of Clover's reply shocked lawyer Devon and everyone else in the courtroom.

"My wife. Yes, let's consider my wife."

He spat the words out with venom.

"I'd like to have never laid eyes on her. I hope to never lay eyes on her again. If she were to disappear in the dark of night and never be seen again, that would be the answer to years of desperate prayers.

"Only one thing of value came from knowing her, and that was my kids. They're good kids. I just hope when they get older, they don't some-how take after their mother or her family.

"Everything else in our marriage was ugly and cruel. Every day I live, I hate her more."

There was not a sound heard in the shocked courtroom. Mac, studying Mrs. Clover, thought he had never seen such a look of loathing. Even during the war, experiencing the terrible deprav-ities man can inflict, he had never seen its match.

Harry Devon said, "Mr. Clover, we have the testimony of one of the surviving raiders that you didn't want to undertake this crime. That it was Mrs. Clover who insisted."

Mrs. Clover was having trouble controlling herself. Her lawyer placed his hand on her arm, but she brushed it off.

Clover was quick to answer. "We fought something terrible, the wife and me. I told her plain that we couldn't get away with it, and that anyway, no piece of land is worth that cost. The evil woman wouldn't back off. Said she'd made it plain to her brother that there was to be no killing. The men were to just scare the Bechtels off and burn the ranch. That we would be able to claim the layout as being abandoned."

Mrs. Clover leaped to her feet. Her lawyer tried to pull her back down, gripping on her arm. "No. Don't…"

"You sniveling coward. You never done one single thing in your whole life that I didn't have to figure out for you. All you had to do was…"

Three court guards grabbed her. "Take her out of here," shouted the judge.

She was dragged from the courtroom, screaming in rage.

When the court had settled down a bit, the judge said, "Let's get on with it. We'll deal with Mrs. Clover in due course. I want to see the end of this sordid matter."

Harry Devon stepped back toward the witness stand. "Mr. Clover, you said earlier that the brother who did the arranging for you had been told there was to be no killing. What about that?"

"That was all just words to keep me from screaming even louder than I already was about the stupid idea. Of course, those renegades planned no such thing. They set out to murder the Bechtels right from the start. Thought it was great sport.

"The murders weren't none of my doing, though. I agreed to the burning, but never murder."

The lawyer looked at Clover in wonder. No matter what part each spouse played, there was no getting around the fact that a terrible crime had been planned and carried out.

And now there was a new name brought into the riddle.

The lawyer took up the questioning. "Brother? A brother, you said? This is the first I've heard about a brother. Who is this brother?"

As far as Herb Clover was concerned, his life was over. He was holding nothing back. He just wanted it all to end.

"I thought y'all knew. The wife was a Granger. Her brother is Mordecai Granger, the deputy marshal."

A stunned silence filled the courtroom. They had recently identified Granger as a rustler, but even as seriously as rustling was seen by ranchers, most would say it was a far step from rustling to outright murder.

It took several moments for the courtroom to settle down again. The judge allowed the time without interruption.

When all was quiet again, Devon nodded at Herb Clover. "Proceed, Mr. Clover."

"There's another brother, Heck by name. Heck, he's never been up to no good. Keeps himself low. Never makes any noise around town so's you might notice him. Never uses his last name. Always has money to spend, though.

"Rides around a lot. Used to visit us every now and then. It's him that carried messages between the wife and Denver. It's him and Mordecai that arranged for those renegades. Evil. The whole family is evil, every last one of them."

The room fell to silence, and Harry Devon struggled to find words to frame the necessary questions.

After a silence that dragged on for thirty seconds, he asked, "What made Mr. Granger think he could get away with sending a deputy up to investigate the killing and not have the truth be found?"

Without lifting his head, Clover mumbled, as if he wished to protect Mac's feelings.

"He said he would wait until enough time had passed for the evidence to be washed out by the rain or blown away by the wind. He said in this big land, it was common for news to travel slowly. He would just wait, and then he would deputize an amateur with no law experience. There would be no chance at all of an amateur sorting it all out.

"And he said the local sheriff didn't amount to nothing at all, so any investigating he did would get nowhere. Eventually, it would all fade out and be forgotten.

"He must have been pretty surprised when Mr. McTavish took his assignment so seriously."

Harry Devon tried one more time for new information.

"Mr. Clover, is there anything at all that you can tell us that might help sort this whole thing out more clearly?"

Clover didn't even look up. "No. let's just get this thing over with."

46

Denver

BY THE TIME HERB CLOVER STEPPED down from the witness chair, the afternoon was far gone.

Judge Grimes said, "That's enough for today. We'll reconvene here at nine tomorrow morning."

With a bang of his gavel, he stood and disappeared through a door beside the judge's stand.

McAdam Portier and several of his deputies, along with a half dozen court guards, escorted the two prisoners to the front door. They were handcuffed, but their legs were not shackled. The street was jammed with horses, wagons, pedestrians, and on-lookers. Directly in front of the door sat an enclosed prison wagon. Two city policemen held down the driver's seat, both carrying weapons.

Chief Portier, directing the activities of the guards, stepped toward the wagon drivers. Shouting over the noises of the street, he said, "As soon as you hear that back door close, you get these animals moving."

Both men nodded and the driver held the reins tightly, ready to move.

The chief gave an arm signal. The front doors of the courthouse opened, and the prisoners were led out.

Timed almost to the second, with their steel shoes clattering off the hard city street, a dozen riders forced their horses through the crowd. Two of the riders were leading saddled and ready animals behind them.

The riders swarmed around the prison wagon and the prisoners. A shot rang out, and the wagon driver slumped sideways against his partner. Another shot clipped one of the guards holding Mrs. Clover. The guards and City police pulled their weapons, looking for the source of the shots. The street turned to bedlam almost immediately, with screaming people running in all directions.

A gruff voice shouted, "Maddy, grab this horse."

Mrs. Clover broke free and leaped into the saddle, her handcuffed fingers grasping the horn. Clover was barely an eye-blink behind her climbing aboard the second riderless animal. But now the guards had their targets. Shots were coming fast and at close range from the mounted rescuers, and with the guards and city police returning fire, the street became a shooting gallery, with several men already down.

Chief Portier was startled to see Mordecai Granger urging his sister to mount an animal and ride. The chief and the ex-marshal's deputy saw each other at about the same time. Granger took aim at the chief, but his horse refused to settle. His shot was lost in the melee.

McAdam Portier's shot was also spoiled by the prancing horse, but it wasn't a clear miss. Granger dropped his weapon to the street, grabbed his shoulder, and slumped over the saddle horn. He kicked his horse toward an opening in the traffic, slapped Maddy Clover's animal on the rump, and shot through an opening in the milling animals.

Where the shot came from was unknown. The first anyone saw of the situation, Maddy Clover was slumping sideways in the saddle, her eyes closed in pain and her shirt front soaking red. Her lax fingers slipped from the horn, and her sideways slump became a free-fall. She hit the road and lay still.

Clover, himself was already down, was curled up in pain with blood pouring from his thigh.

Three guards lay in the street, and six rescuers were down and dead.

Mordecai Granger and what was left of his rescuing party were gone. With the still-milling crowd blocking the view of their escape and Granger's knowledge of city streets, they were out of sight before anyone even knew they had fled. As before, chasing the former deputy would be futile. In any case, none of the guards or city police had mounts handy.

47

Bar-M

MAC CLIMBED THE LOW RISE BEHIND the ranch house in the pre-dawn darkness. A mating pair of ducks had taken the rushes growing on the far side of the pond for their summer nesting ground, and he enjoyed watching their early-morning antics as the sun rose over the eastern flatlands to announce the new day.

The yard dog followed Mac up the dark trail. The black and white mongrel sat on his haunches and watched in silence as Mac prayed and worshiped.

When the sun broke the eastern horizon, Mac sat down to read. The Bible his father had given him on his twelfth birthday was ragged and worn, but it was the book Mac carried up the hill every morning.

Margo joined her husband after she judged he'd had the necessary alone time. They had things to talk about this morning. To help with the discussion, she wrapped a jar of hot coffee in a heavy towel. Pouring a mug for each of them, she settled against the back of the small bench and said, "So tell me."

Mac took a deep breath and let it out slowly as if ridding himself of a wearisome burden.

"The important thing to know is that it's over. The good side is that a few men are in jail. The unhappy side is that several are dead. A few found their just reward in their deaths, but there's lawmen dead too. That's a steep price to pay for keeping the peace.

"Herb Clover had his charges reduced a bit. He'll spend his life in prison. I suppose that beats hanging, but it's still not a bargain.

"The three renegades who did the awful deeds on the Bechtel ranch will be hung. They found no mercy in the court.

"The ex-marshal and the few men who survived the raid on the courthouse are gone. Where they'll show up next is anyone's guess.

"The court and the marshals' service both gave special thanks to Bobby and Jeremiah. To the Mexicans they hired, too. Each one received a letter of thanks with their pay.

"The Clover kids will be going to one of Herb Clover's brothers, and the ranch will be sold. There will be money enough from the sale to provide for the kids."

Margo got right to the point she was most interested in. "What about you? Where do you stand in all this?"

Mac smiled for the first time. "I'm done. I resigned, and there was no argument. I have to think the boys and I did a bit toward bringing justice, but I'm happy it's over. I'm not cut out for that life. I belong right here on the Bar-M with you and the kids, and with the land and cattle we've worked hard to care for."

They each re-filled their coffee mugs and sat quietly drinking.

Mac said, "There's another thing. I came near to forgetting. Casey Bechtel has been appointed deputy marshal for the southern counties. He'll take up his position in Pueblo. Bobby and Jeremiah are officially his sub-deputies. Either of the boys could have had the deputy position, but neither wanted it."

Margo wasn't easily moved, but the fire and shooting horror on the Bechtel ranch had gripped her heart when she'd first heard about it.

"I'm happy for Casey, I suppose, but still, his wife and child are dead. Nothing much worse in this world than that."

Mac chuckled. "You're right, of course, but I'm thinking Casey's been making a lot of trips to the Stringfellow ranch. Might be he won't be alone much longer. He'll never forget his first family, but perhaps there's the hope of something new."

Margo gathered up the mugs and the jar. "I suppose you can sit here all day, but I have work to do."

Mac rose to his feet and started down the trail. The dog barked for the first time that morning, wagging its tail in happiness as it followed its master. Margo's comment about work was not worth disputing.

48

Hiram and Della's farm

THE BRUSH ARBOR WAS PACKED WITH people. Chairs, benches, straw bales had all been forced into service. Still, many folks were standing, lining the sides and back of the small space. Many of those attending were friends from Mex Town and the sheep ranch.

The outdoor ovens were heated, and the big sheet-iron grills were hot and ready. Between the Mexican ladies and the farm and ranch ladies, there would be no shortage of food for the celebration.

At almost the last-minute Nancy and her family had decided they couldn't miss the wedding. With their arrival, the family was together for the first time in many years. Della's joy was complete.

All the kids were sitting on the ground in front of the first row of chairs. All, that is, except Jerrod and his cousin Moss. The two had become inseparable since Jessie's arrival on the Bar-M. As the oldest, they had taken positions with those standing along the side. Near them was Sergio, relieved from his work for this one afternoon.

Jessie was sitting with Taz, who had asked for the day off. Mac had some misgivings about the growing relationship, but he pushed them out of his mind. They would have to make their own way. Jessie had never been much at following the rules anyway. She had always been one to step out without asking for opinions. If she found herself alone, she didn't worry much about it. Judging by the protective stance Taz was taking, Mac figured Jessie wouldn't be alone when she looked around.

With the bride and groom standing solemnly in front of Hiram and the Rev. Grover Brocklehurst, with Bobby and Matilda standing on either side, Bobby leaned toward his brother and whispered so that everyone in the front of the gathering could hear.

"There's still time to get out of this. I've got a saddled horse behind the shed."

Greta started to laugh. Bobby straightened back up when his father gave him a stern look.

Sitting his horse, unseen by anyone at the wedding, a rider parted an overhanging branch on a small rise a half-mile away. Mordecai Granger was alone. He had parted company with all but his brother Heck, who was waiting farther west with the pack horses.

Heck Granger thought it was a foolish move to ride anywhere near the Bar-M, but Mordecai was determined. He couldn't have explained why he had that need. His hatred for the Bar-M and everyone associated with it was burned deep into his soul. He just had to take one more look, then the two Granger brothers were off for California. But he thought they just might be back someday.

A Look at: Terry of the Double C

"MR. STOCKER SAID IF I COULD MAKE MY way here by this evening there would be a job waiting. I'm here."

On his first full day of work on the Lazy-S, Terry was led to the horse stable by Big Mike. "I spect you know what a shovel is, and that over there is a wheelbarrow. Spect you know that too. Your job, for now, is to keep this barn clean and the horses fed, watered and groomed. You ever been around horses before?"

Terry nodded, but Mike wasn't looking his way, so he simply followed the nod with "some."

Terry needed two things that summer. One was to put away a few dollars towards the cost of college, the other was a rest from his chaotic home life. If the path to his future started in the stable, he would make the best of it.

Cattle, cowboys, a brush with a cougar, and, of course, a beautiful rancher's daughter, all lead the young and inexperienced Terry on an adventurous path into adulthood, all in the shadow of the magnificent snow topped Rockies.

AVAILABLE NOW ON AMAZON FROM REG QUIST AND CKN CHRISTIAN PUBLISHING

About the Author

REG QUIST'S pioneer heritage includes sod shacks, prairie fires, home births, and children's graves under the prairie sod, all working together in the lives of people creating their own space in a new land.

Out of that early generation came farmers, ranchers, business men and women, builders, military graves in faraway lands, Sunday Schools that grew to become churches, plus story tellers, musicians, and much more.

Hard work and self-reliance were the hallmark of those previous great generations, attributes that were absorbed by the following generation.

Quist's career choice took him into the construction world. From heavy industrial work, to construction camps in the remote northern bush, the author emulated his grandfathers, who were both builders, as well as pioneer farmers and ranchers.

Quist's heart was never far from the land. The family photo albums testify to how often he found himself sitting on a horse, both as a child and into later life, when he and his wife owned their own small farm, complete with kids and horses.

Respect for the pioneers, working alongside skilled, tough workmen, and learning from them, marrying his high school sweetheart and welcoming children into the world, purchasing land for the family to grow on, and riding horses with the kids, all melded together to influence Quist's life and writing. Over, and under, and wrapped around his life is Quist's Christian heritage. This too, shows itself in his writing.

Quist's writing career was late in pushing itself forward, remaining a hobby while family and career took precedence. Only in early retirement, was there time for more serious writing.

Quist's writing interests lie in many genres including children's work, short lifestyle stories, cowboy poetry, western novels, plus Christian articles and novels.

Woven through every story is the thought that, even though he was not there himself in that pioneer time, he knew some that were. They are remembered with great respect.

Find more great titles by Reg Quist and Christian Kindle News at http://christiankindlenews. com/our-authors/reg-quist/